THE RAID

Also by Randy Lee Eickhoff

A Hand to Execute
The Gombeen Man
Exiled

THE
RAID

Randy Lee
Eickhoff

A TOM DOHERTY ASSOCIATES BOOK

NEW YORK

THE RAID

Copyright © 1997 by Randy Lee Eickhoff

A Forge Book
Published by Tom Doherty Associates, Inc.
175 Fifth Avenue
New York, NY 10010

Forge® is a registered trademark of Tom Doherty Associates, Inc.

Design by Brian Mulligan

Library of Congress Cataloging-in-Publication Data

Eickhoff, Randy Lee.
    The raid / Randy Lee Eickhoff.—1st ed.
        p.   cm.
    "A Tom Doherty Associates book."
    ISBN 0-312-86238-5 (hardcover : acid-free paper)
    1. Heroes—Ulster (Northern Ireland and Ireland)—Fiction.
2. Tales—Ulster (Northern Ireland and Ireland)   3. Cuchulain
(Legendary character)—Fiction.   4. Epic literature, Irish—
Adaptations.   I. Táin bó Cúailnge.   II. Title.
PS3555.I23R3   1997
813'.54—dc20
                                                            96-44308
                                                            CIP

First Edition: March 1997

Printed in the United States of America

0 9 8 7 6 5 4 3 2

for Jack Braden
and the sons and daughters
of
The Wild Geese

To
Michael Carey
for his wit and wisdom,
generous help,
and friendship.
go raibh maith agat

For we inhabit a wood
unknown but to our Muse,
our houses of hazel and ash
as old as the white stag

Contents

A Note on the Translation   9

A Pronunciation Guide   11

Introduction   19

Chapter One: The Bed Argument   32

Chapter Two: The Rising of the Connachtmen   42

Chapter Three: The Connachtmen Discover Cúchulainn   54

Chapter Four: The Telling of the Youth of Cúchulainn   73

Chapter Five: Death Stalks the Connachtmen   99

Chapter Six: From Finnabair to Conalille   109

Chapter Seven: The Duel   126

Chapter Eight: The Bull and the Mórrígan   142

Chapter Nine: The Bloodbath   164

Chapter Ten: Cúchulainn's Battle With Fergus   181

Chapter Eleven: The Battle Between Ferdiad
and Cúchulainn   194

Chapter Twelve: The Curse Lifts From the Red Branch   229

Chapter Thirteen: The Armies Move Forward   246

Chapter Fourteen: The Last Battle   255

Glossary of Names and Terms   269

A Note on the Translation

Sed ego qui scripsi hanc historiam aut uerius fabulam quibusdam
fidem in hac historia aut fabula non accommodo. Quaedam enim
ibi sunt praestigia demonum, quaedam autem figmenta poetica,
quaedam similia uero, quaedam non, quaedam ad delectationem
stultorum.

—from the *Book of Leinster*

This version of the *Táin* is not a literal translation. The various re-
censions alone prohibit that, but more important, the character of
the original is lost in direct translation. What is poetic and lyric in
Gaelic becomes turgid and stolid in English. Whereas several feminine rhymes are possible in the Gaelic, in English a consecutive
feminine rhyme scheme is almost impossible to accomplish with
any great success in a work like the *Táin* without sacrificing con-
notation. Consequently, I have deliberately altered the poetic elements from the original to clarify aesthetic vagaries.

Celtic bards or poets apparently altered their stories from prose
narrative to lend an air of mystery or otherworldliness to their

recitations. Although the mysticism of the original construction can be appreciated in the original Gaelic, direct translation into English only obfuscates the allusions even more. Consequently, I have tried to give a poetic interpretation of the allusion in addition to a translation.

I have added some images to clarify instances in which the direct use of idioms in English makes no sense at all to the modern reader. Additionally, I have added some epic similes to clarify intonations and connotations that the ancient listeners would have automatically accepted and understood.

Lastly, I have included a glossary of names and terms to assist the reader who is unfamiliar with their use.

—R.L.E.

A
Pronunciation
Guide

THE FOLLOWING PRONUNCIATION GUIDE is not to be regarded as being chiseled in stone; it is to be a guide only. It is impossible, however, to give the exact pronunciation of all words as stresses and accents vary widely throughout the country. The reader needs to be aware that Irish today is much different from the Irish of yesteryear. Once, a traveler in Ireland could make his way from the south to the north and encounter little difficulty understanding the various dialects along the way. Today, however, the traveler with Irish will find himself struggling to understand speakers in various sections of Ireland. The language is broken down into various dialects such as Ulster Irish and Munster Irish. The following is a composite of the main dialects based on the so-called "standard" or official form.

Consonants at the beginning of a word are usually pronounced the same in Irish as in English, i.e., "c" becomes "k." Consonants in the middle of words change.

"b" becomes "v."

"c" becomes "g" or "k" as in "car." When it is followed by "i" or "e" it becomes "key."

"ch" carries a guttural sound as in German, i.e., "Bach."

"d" becomes "th" as in "then" but when used with "i" or "e" it sounds like "j" as in "juice." When "d" is used with a broad vowel ("a," "o," or "u") it sounds like the English "d" as in "door." "dh" when used with a broad vowel sounds like the "g" in "gift."

"g" is a soft guttural as "gh" or "kuh."

"m" is usually pronounced as "v" except in a few cases when it appears as the last letter (i.e., "Fedelm").

"t" appears as "d" but when followed or preceded by one of "e" or "i" it is usually pronounced like the "ch" in "chip." When "t" is followed by "a," "o," or "u" it is pronounced like "tea."

"s" is "sh" if followed or preceded by "e" or "i."

"th" is aspirated as in "this."

The digraph "ao" can be pronounced either "ee" or "ay."

The consonants "l," "n," and "r" seem to change constantly. "l" with a slender vowel sounds like "uhl," while at the beginning of a word it sounds like "lie." "n" usually sounds like the English "n" except when it is doubled ("nn"), which has a very slight nasal sound. When it is followed by "e" or "i" it acquires a "y" sound. When "nn" appears at the end of a word it sounds like "ng" as in "bing." "r" and "rr" are very similar to that found in English but sometimes it sounds like "ir" when it appears in the second syllable.

Short vowels are pronounced the same as in Latin while long vowels are marked with an accent and are pronounced as ah, a, e, oh, oo. The accent does not appear on capital letters as a rule although there are a few exceptions.

"ai" becomes "ah" if it appears in the first syllable such as "Ailill" and "i" if in the second or third as in "Cúchulainn." If the word ends in a final "e" with "ai" in the second or third syllable, the final "e" is pronounced.

"iu" is usually pronounced as "oo."

"ui" becomes "i" with the "u" slightly rounded.

"ei" is pronounced like "e."

NAMES

Aife: EE-fe (an exception)

Ailill: AHL-il

Aithech: AH-thax

Amargin: AV-ar-ghin

Anu: AH-NOO

Badb: bive

Bricriu: BRICK-roo

Buan: BOO-an

Buinne: BWIN-neh

Cailleach: KA-lox

Cathbad: KAFF-ah

Celtchar Mac Uthidir: KELT-har mak OO-he-der

Conall Cernach: KO-nul KAR-nox

Conchobar: KON-chov-or or KON-nor

Connacht: KON-NAXt

Cormac Connlongas: KOR-mac kon-LIN-gus

Crunniuc Mac Agnomain: KROON-yuk mak AH-hyo-vin

Cúchulainn: koo-HOOL-in

Culann: KOO-lun

Cúroi: koo-REE

Cúscraid Menn Macha: KOO-skri MEN MAX-ah

Dáire Mac Fiachna: DAH-ruh mak FEE-an

Deichtine: DEkh-tin-e

Deirdre: DER-drah

Dubthach: DUV-thakh

Emer: AY-ver

Eogan Mac Durthact: O-wen mak DOOR-haht

Eochaid: OCH-i

Etarcomol: ED-ar-KO-vol

Fachtna Fathach: FAH-nah fach

Fedelm: FEDh-elm

Fedlimid: FEDh-lim-ith

Ferdiad: fer-DI-ad

Fergus Mac Roich: FUR-gus mak RO-eh

Fiacha Mac Firaba: FEE-ya-hoo mak FEER-ahv

Findchoem: FIN-gem

Finnabair: FIN-AH-ver

Findbennach: FIN-ven-nah

Fraech: FRAY-x

Gae Bolga: guy BOOL-guh

Galeóin: GAL-owe-in

Laeg Mac Riangabra: LOYth mak RE-yan-gahvra

Laegaire: LOYh-i-ree or leer-ee

Leborcham: LE-vor-sham

Lugaid: LOOkh-ith

Lugh: LOOH

Mac Roth: mok-ROTH

Macha: MAha

Maeve: MAY-v

Maine: MA-nee

Maine Athramail: MA-ne Ath-ra-vil

Manannán: man-NAH-un

Mórrígan: MO-ree-han

Naoise: NOY-she

Nemain: NEV-in

Ogham: OH-um

Scáthach: SKAW-thash

Sétanta: SHAY-dan-duh

Sualdam: SOO-ul-dav

Tuatha Dé Danann: tu-AH-THA day dan-UN

Uisliu: ISH-loo

PLACES

Aí: EE

Áth Gabla: awth GAV-la

Benn Etair: ben AYD-er

Breslech Mór: BRES-la mor

Brug: brooh

Cain Bile: kahn BEL-eh

Colptha: KOLP-thuh

Conaille: KON-il-ee

Craeb Ruad: KRAYV ROO-uh

Cruachaín Aí: KROO-uh-shan EE

Cuailnge: KOO-ling-ee

Cuib: quiv

Cúil Sibrille: kil SIV-rel

Dub: doov

Dún Sobairche: DOON SOV-ir-she

Emain Macha: AV-in MA-sha

Femen: FEV-in

Fid Dúin: fee doon

Focherd: FOW-hart

Fúal Medba: fwal MA-the

Granaird: GRAN-ard

Int Ildathach: int IL-da-thah

Iraird Cuillen: IR-ard QUILL-in

Lethan: LETH-on

Lough: lock

Lugmod: LOO-th

Maeve Sleachtadh: MAV SLA-tah

Mag: maguh

Midi: MIth-i

Midluachair: MIDH-LOO-a-hir or MIth-LOO-a-shir

Murtheimne: MUR-thev-nee

Sídhe: Sheeth

Sinann: SHIN-un

Síuir: SHOO-ur

Sliab: SHLEE-av

Sliab Cuilinn: SHLEE-av KWIL-en

Sliab Fuait: SHLEE-av FOO-id

Sliab Mondairn: SHLEE-av MON-dirn

Táin: toyn

Tethba: TETH-va

The hounds of Culann are riding
Tonight over Lissadell Bay,
Ossian, Mac Cumhaill, Cú Chulainn
From Ben Bulben toward Knocknarea.

Clouds of soldiers follow
Miles high and miles wide,
All with their swords out gleaming
To beat back the fathomless tide.

For centuries the curse of Ulster
Has kept their hands sullied and red.
No child of theirs will know slumber
Till he lie in his watery bed.

The heroes of Ireland are riding
From Emain Macha and Cruachan Aí
With one great shout they fall
Forever into the sea.

—Mícheál O'Ciardhi
"Deirdre's Curse Upon Ulster"

THE RAID

INTRODUCTION

THE *TÁIN BÓ CUAILNGE,* the national epic of Ireland from the Ulster Cycle, is not the entire story of its central hero, Cúchulainn. In fact, we join the *Táin* after the groundwork has already been established by other stories. For the majority of the Irish in the seventh and eighth centuries, these stories were so familiar that simple reference to the main characters was enough to provide background for the listeners. This, however, is not true today, for few people are aware of the "Ulster Curse" as it may be and what precipitated it, the birth of Cúchulainn, or the general cultural background that gives meaning to the story.

Although some regard the *Táin* as a myth, seeing Cúchulainn and others as euhemerized deities, we cannot assume that the leading characters are anything more than part of a *seanchaí*'s art. We cannot find any extant historical evidence that substantiates the existence of Cúchulainn although his king, Conchobar, does appear in records as the ruler of ancient Ulster sometime around 30 B.C. At the time, Ulster was a difficult land to travel in what with dense fog and heavy undergrowth, almost surrounded by river, bog, and mountains. Perhaps one mighty warrior could have held the few passes and fords from an army, but it really doesn't matter. It is the *idea* of Cúchulainn that is the important part of the *Táin*. His legend is a symbol of Ireland—one man standing alone against terrible oppression. Over the years since Oliver Cromwell took his army from the southern end of Ireland to the northern end in the seventeenth century, killing, raping and destroying, leaving burnt grass in his path, Ireland has been fighting against England. When one considers the legend of Cúchulainn, one can understand why the early rebels chose *Sinn Féin*—"Ourselves alone"—as their motto. Small wonder that a statue of Cúchulainn alone stands in the Dublin Post Office where the Irish rebellion began in earnest.

Those who would like to further their studies of the *Táin* may wish to consult other translations, most notable of which are Joseph Dunn's *The Ancient Irish Epic Tale Táin Bó Cúalnge*, London, 1914; Winifred Faraday's *The Cattle-Raid of Cualnge*, London, 1904; Cecile O'Rahilly's *Táin Bó Cúalnge* from the *Book of Leinster*, Dublin, 1967 (for the scholar, a most valuable translation); Thomas Kinsella's *The Táin*, Oxford, 1969; and Lady Augusta Gregory's *Cuchulain of Muirthemne*, London, 1902. I caution the reader, however, in the case of the latter, for this is a culling of Cúchulainn stories that Lady Gregory made from a series of stories that she translated in a Victorian manner. By this, I mean, that Lady Gregory deliberately left out the sensual aspects that permeate the ancient Irish writings. In a letter to some friends, Lady Gregory confessed that "I [deliberately] left out a good deal I thought [the reader] would not care about." The modern reader, however, does not share the reticence of the Victorian reader and for that purpose, this is a far more complete translation of "The Raid" than the one that is included in Lady Gregory's work. The original work shows ancient life in all its raw sensuality. Attention is drawn, for example, to Fergus's loss of his sword while committing adultery with Maeve (who finds him somewhat lacking in sexuality), which results in much phallic joking at his expense throughout the rest of the *Táin*.

One point must be emphasized here in regard to Maeve. Although many like to see Maeve as Ailill's queen, the ancient tribes had no queens. Some women, however, were granted queenlike powers by their husbands. Maeve may be powerful, but her power is only as strong as her husband, Ailill, wishes it to be. She was not called "queen of Connacht" during her own time as Ireland did not have ruling queens then. Maeve did, however, defy the tradition by acting as a sort of warlord. This is probably why she is often referred to as a queen for her behavior was certainly "queenlike," and it is thus that I use the term "queen" in reference to Maeve in the following story.

Likewise, mention needs to be made here about the role of kings. The title of king was not an inherited title but rather an elected title according to old Brehon Law, which is superseded only by the Code of Hammurabi as the oldest codified system. Those who stood for the office of king had to belong to the senior line, or branch, of the dominant warrior clan. Therefore, when Conchobar is referred to as king of the Red Branch, it is because he is the clan ruler of the leading clan of the Ulaid or "wool-gatherers."

Much of early Irish literature has been lost for it did not exist in a written form but was handed down over the centuries through the oral tradition: from singer to singer, *seanchaí* to *seanchaí*. Certain sections of the central story were undoubtedly altered by the singers or storytellers of the various provinces, who focused upon what was important to their particular people or clan. These snippets underwent constant alteration until the central story all but disappeared. In certain cases, as we can tell from a careful study of the Ulster Cycle, some stories undoubtedly disappeared for great gaps exist between some of the stories, gaps that logic tells us probably were once filled by stories or minor episodes that provided a transition from one tale to the next.

Eventually, in the seventh century, these stories were written down by medieval monks in illuminated manuscripts, on parchment in some cases, then later transcribed into more formal units. Basically, the ancient Irish stories can be subdivided into four groups: those pertaining to the Tuatha Dé Danann, the Ulster Cycle, the Fenian Cycle, and what we may call a Post-Fenian Cycle.

The Tuatha Dé Danann refers to the various tribes who supposedly traced their lineage from the goddess Anu or Danu, a mother goddess associated with fertility celebrations. According to legend, the Tuatha came from four cities in the northern islands of Greece—Failias, Goirias, Findias, and Muirias—bringing with them their knowledge of the Druidic arts (a possible reference to the Eleusinian Mysteries), and defeated the Fir Bolg for control of Ireland. They were discovered by the Fomorians ("sea-comers" or "those who live under the sea") and the ensuing battle suggests a battle between darkness (the Fomorians) and light (Tuatha Dé Danann), a common theme in stories from ancient cultures. The Tuatha are the ones who are commonly referred to as the gods of Ireland. According to legend, they came to Ireland from Greece, bringing with them the Lia Fail, a stone which utters a shriek at the inauguration of the rightful king; the invincible spear of Lugh; the deadly sword of Nuada; and the ever-plentiful cauldron of the Dagda, the "Good God" or "Father God" of Ireland. This story can be found in the account of the third invasion in the *Book of Invasions (Lebor Gabala)*.

The Ulster Cycle concerns itself with the exploits of the Red Branch knights led by their king, Conchobar. These stories are probably the best known and form a nucleus from which one could show a relationship with the *Mabinogion* (especially with five of the tales added by Lady Charlotte Guest from *The Red Book of Herest*). Most assuredly, we find similarities in heroic elements between the *Táin* and *Beowulf* which could suggest a transient myth, but nothing more closely related than the beheading game found in *Fled Bricrend (Feast of Bricriu)* and *Sir Gawain and the Green Knight. Fled Bricrend* was composed, it is believed, sometime around the eighth century while *Sir Gawain and the Green Knight* appears to have been composed in the late fourteenth century. In Sir Gawain, we find similar knightly attributes to those in Cúchulainn although Cúchulainn appears to be a much ruder form of a knightly warrior than Sir Gawain. This could suggest that the cruder knightly elements in Cúchulainn were refined when transferred to Gawain, when definitive chivalric rules or rules of etiquette became more important to the people than the rules of warriors.

Cúchulainn's personage apparently was developed from Lugh, the Gaelic sun god, the god of genius and light. Perhaps Cúchulainn's patronage is one of the reasons that his body is transformed by the *riastradh,* a seizure ("warp-spasm") that causes him to shake uncontrollably from head to foot and revolve within his skin. His features become blood-red, one eye growing almost Cyclopian in size while the other becomes tiny, his mouth stretching into a grotesque form and issuing sparks, his heart booming in his chest like a *bodhrán,* and a nimbus or "warrior-light" rising from his brow. It is this "warrior-light" which I have elected to translate as a "hero-halo" that reminds one of the glorious light that emanates from Lugh's own forehead. This emission of light suggests an attempt to bring light into the darkness of the ancient Celtic world, but the usage of light in reference to Cúchulainn is also seen in Gawain. Gawain's name is derived from the Welsh sun god Gwalchmei and means "bright-haired." Consequently, we have this common reference between Cúchulainn and Gawain in regard to divinity or a mystical divinity in the reference to a divine light. Both heroes become warriors of the light or protectors of the light. A remarkable similarity.

The Fenian Cycle refers to stories of Finn Mac Cumaill and his son Oisín along with other heroes of the Fiana, a group of heroes *(laochs)* locked together by passing a series of tests that formed them into a *curaid,* the "comitatus," if you like, of *Beowulf.*

The Post-Fenian Cycle consists of a group of stories from roughly the third century B.C. until the eighth century A.D.

The *Táin* has many similarities with other epics: the hero hearing a call to adventure and obeying it, being forced to undergo a series of tests before he is suddenly given illumination (knowledge), and undergoing yet another series of tests following his successful completion of the quest. The hero is expected to be boastful because he has earned this right and in both the *Táin* and *Beowulf,* boasting is the way that the hero can achieve immortality through songs written about him by the bard-scop-poet. Perhaps this is why the poet was a feared man in both Celtic and Anglo-Saxon societies: his gift with words and song could let a man's name live in glory or ignominy.

In ancient epics, certain warrior traits eventually fell out of practice, but because of Ireland's isolated location those warrior traits may have continued for many ages, even up to the introduction of Christianity in the fifth century. I refer here to the practice of cattle-raiding, fighting from iron-wheeled chariots, and the cult of the severed head.

I must pause here for a moment to explain something about cattle raiding and the two bulls for after all, that is what the *Táin* is about: the theft of a magical bull (Donn Cuailnge) that will allow a woman (Maeve) the equally magical climb to equality with her mate (Ailill) in a warrior society. The bulls, however, are much more than a symbol for equality. The story of the two bulls is extremely old and a bit complex. Simply defined, *donn* means "brown," deriving from the Celtic *dhuosnos.* But the adjective could also suggest "dark," for the character Donn, a mythical figure in Irish literature and folklore, is perennially equated with the shadowy realm of the dead. His name seems to be derived or at least suggested by the deity Dagda, the Irish equivalent of Zeus, Jupiter, and Odin. In some works, Donn is seen as the god of the dead in much the same fashion that Hades is seen as the god of the underworld in Greek mythology.

We find an early mention of Donn in the death tale of Conaire, who is killed by three red-haired men, the "sons of Donn, king of the dead at the Red Tower of the Dead." We have a natural reference, therefore, by which we may suggest that *donn* refers not only to "brown" but death as well. Additionally, the Brown Bull of Cooley is also "Dubh Cuailnge" in some texts ("Black of Cooley") and is seen by reference as a Black Bull. This, when compared to Findbennach, the White Bull of Connacht, suggests a war between the Light and the Dark. The word *donn* can also be seen as the opposite of *find,* which suggests "brightness" or "the power to illuminate." Additionally, *Findbennach* appears to come from the personage Find, suggesting a divine personification of wisdom. According to legend, Find emerged from crystal waters already fully mature with shining hair, speaking in verse. His wisdom brings him into conflict with the powers of darkness, thus his portrayal as a martial champion that finds his personification in Finn Mac Cumaill. But I digress. The purpose here is to explain the two bulls.

Two opposing beings of the Otherworld, the swineherders Friuch and Rucht, began to argue, each casting wicked spells upon the other's pigs. At last, their employers tired of their petty games and dismissed them. But by this time, Friuch and Rucht had built their argument into seething hatred for each other. They turned themselves into birds of prey and continued fighting, but neither was able to harm the other. Then they turned themselves into carp, stags, warriors, phantoms, and dragons, constantly searching each other out and grimly fighting. Eventually, they turned into maggots, one falling into a spring at Cooley where he was lapped up by a cow belonging to Dáire while the other fell into a Connacht spring and was lapped up by a cow belonging to Maeve. These two cows gave birth to bull-calves, the Donn Cuailnge and Findbennach, each stalwart and strong. The Donn Cuailnge is described as being so huge that thirty boys could ride on its back and so sexually potent that it could impregnate fifty heifers in a single day and those that did not calve on the following day would burst. Findbennach, by extrapolation, is given these same powers.

Although beheading one's enemies and retaining the heads as either trophies or offerings in shrines may seem barbarous by today's standards, literature must always be judged by the parameters of the time in which it first appeared rather than by modern sensibilities. Literature, after all, is a window into the past. Consequently, we should look at the practice of beheading among the early Celts as a way of controlling the soul or spirit of the defeated warrior. The ancient Druids believed that the soul or consciousness was located in the mind, and thus the cult of head-hunting became a vital part of Celtic society, for by taking the head of the enemy, one captured his spirit and consciousness, keeping it from being used against the victorious warrior.

We join the action in the *Táin* as we join the action in the *Iliad*— *in medias res*. It is important, however, to relate a few incidents not well covered in the *Táin* that may help the reader understand this epic.

The Ulster Curse, or the Pangs of Ulster, which made it necessary for Cúchulainn to defend Ulster's boundaries alone from the Connacht army led by Maeve and Ailill, came about when Crunniuc Mac Agnomain, a rich landlord who lived with his sons in the mountains, found his bed suddenly visited by a beautiful woman who mysteriously appeared out of nowhere. She identified herself only as Macha.

One day, he went to a fair in Ulster with Macha, who acted as his wife, and, after drinking more than he should, bragged that his wife was fleeter of foot than the king's horses. Although Macha warned him to cease his bragging, he continued with his boast until word reached the king.

The king demanded that the woman and her husband be brought before him. When they appeared, he told them that if the woman did not race his horses, then Crunniuc would lose his head. Macha protested that she was heavy with child and her time was near, but the king was adamant: either she raced the horses, or her husband died.

"I will race your horses," she said grimly. "But only evil will come out of this. My name and the name of my children will be given to this place. I am Macha, the daughter of Sinrith Mac Imbaith."

The race began and as the woman and the king's chariot neared the finish line, she felt the first pangs of birth and screamed out that all who heard that scream and their dependents would suffer from the same pangs for five days and four nights of their greatest difficulty, and that place would never know peace. She gave birth to twins: a son and daughter, and with her dying breath cursed Ulster for nine generations. The place became known as Emain Macha, the Twins of Macha. And from that moment on, those who had heard the scream suffered the same pangs. Strangely enough, Ulster, to this day, has not seen peaceful times.

Macha is seen as one of the Mórrígna along with Badb and Mórrígan, a sort of "triple goddess" of the battlefield who functions as goddess of war and symbol of promiscuity. The suggestion is that war and sex are interlocked, each an integral part of the other.

Badb appears sometimes as an old hag or *cailleach* (a shape-changer from old hag to young woman) and other times as a crow (the Badb Catha or "battle raven"). She represents the destructive element of battle, whose power is mainly psychological. When she appears on the battlefield, those whom she has chosen become confused and terrified. In the *Táin* she wreaks havoc among the Connacht men as a prophetess of doom.

Although she strongly resembles Badb, Mórrígan (the "She-Phantom") is a harbinger of death, but her prophecies are not always filled with doom as are Badb's. Hers is the most powerful sexual image among the three goddesses as can be seen when she appears to Cúchulainn as a beautiful woman, fervently demanding his sexual attention. She is also considered a fertility goddess for she is identified with Anu, "the mother of the Irish gods." Once while washing herself with one foot on the south bank and the other on the north bank of the River Unius during the great pagan feast of Samhain (Halloween), she met Dagda (the chief of the Gaelic pantheon of gods). Here, they mated over the water as part of an ancient fertility ritual. From their mating, this place has come to be known as the Bed of the Couple in County Sligo.

This translation derives primarily from the *Book of Leinster,* although I have had to consult other sources as well in order to prepare a complete story. The *Book of Leinster* provides not only the tale but, through the flamboyant use of florid adjectives, suggests as well the *intent* of the early taletellers with their vague references in epic similes. In translating, it is not only necessary to pay close attention to the literal detail of the original work, but to its connotations as well. When we consider the sexual imagery that is suggested by the appearances of the Mórrígna and by Maeve herself, a type of euhemerized divinity whose promiscuity is legendary, we become aware of the sexual attitudes the Celtic men had toward women. We can see this not only in the *Táin,* but in *Fled Bricrend (Bricriu's Feast)* where Maeve greets the heroes with

> *Mná finna fornochta friú*
> "Great breasts bared and bouncing."

We discover early in the *Táin,* during their bed argument, that Maeve had an arrangement with her husband, Ailill, whereby she could take a lover whenever she wished and she wished often, taking as many as thirty lovers a day—or Fergus Mac Roich once.

Fergus Mac Roich is also legendary with tales of his sexual exploits. Seven women were needed every night to satisfy him. That he is a sexual image is seen in the minor symbol of his sword, a magnificent weapon called In Caladbolg, a huge weapon that required two hands to handle and whose stroke was as swift as forked lightning and its fury as strong as the raging sea. This sword is the one that Ailill has stolen from Fergus's scabbard while he is dallying with Maeve while on the quest for the Brown Bull, suggesting the rendering of Fergus impotent, returning it to him only at the last battle.

An obscure verse-text of the early seventh century suggests that Fergus deserted the Red Branch so that he might be Maeve's lover, as she was the only one who could satisfy his sexual drive by herself. But the story of his exile in *Fochond Loingse Fergusa meic Róig* is probably more accurate in that Conchobar violated his word by promising safe passage to a woman (Deirdre) he desired and her husband, Naoise, then killed her husband so that he might have her. Deirdre, however, spurned him, killing herself by smashing her head against a stone. Accompanied by many heroes, among them Dubthach, the Beetle of Ulster, Fergus became enraged at Conchobar's arrogance and deceit and laid waste to Ulster and Emain Macha, torching it before leaving for Connacht and Maeve's court.

Other tales from the Ulster Cycle continue the action, and the reader is invited to pursue them. Chief among these are:

Cath Ruis na Ríg, "The Battle of Ros na Ríg," which is the story of Ulster's war for the raid after the Brown Bull. In this piece, Cúchulainn kills Coirpre, the king of Temair, in a classic battle.

Serglige ConCulainn ocus aenét Emireí, "The Sickness of Cúchulainn and the One Jealousy of Emer," explains about the goddess Fann's love for the Warped One and how she lures him into the underworld. Some scholars believe that this should be included in the *Táin* as it adds the traditional "underworld" element of the epic to the tale. However, I draw attention to the appearance of the Mórrígan throughout the work in addition to the appearance of Ferdiad's ghost to Cúchulainn while the boy-warrior is recuperating from his wounds. I suggest that Ferdiad's appearance (resembling the appearance of Achilles's shade in the *Odyssey*) and Cúchulainn's vision of the Mórrígan in "The Last Battle" is enough suggestion of the underworld, or Otherworld, to satisfy that epic element.

Aided Con Roi, "The Death of Cúroi," shows the tragic flaw of Cúchulainn when he uses treachery to murder Cúroi after he shamed Cúchulainn in battle.

Brislech mór Maige Muirtheimne, "The Great Slaughter on the Plain of Murtheimne," explains how Ulster's united enemies join forces to defeat the Red Branch.

Aided ConCulainn, "The Death of Cúchulainn," explains how Cúchulainn is killed by the sons of Coirpre, Cúroi, and Calatín and shows how even in death Cúchulainn refuses to give total victory to his enemies.

Dergruather Chonaill Chernaigh, "The Red Slaughter of Conall Cernach," explains Conall's revenge for the death of Cúchulainn.

These stories, although wonderful tales, are more in the fantasy range than what one would normally expect from an epic and, frankly, flawed tales not on the same level as the *Táin.* Although they do contribute to the overall story line, their usefulness to the national identity of Ireland is limited because of their dependence upon the supernatural. It is the same dependence that one sees in the inferior Greek plays where the use of the *mecchanae* saves the hero from impossible situations.

Two stories that are very interesting for study are sometimes grouped under the heading of "death tales" although they are not that so much as an attempt to explain the aftermath of Ulster. *Togail bruidne Da-Choca,* "The Destruction of Da-Choca's Inn," is concerned with the struggle by the warrior heroes for the successor to Conchobar following his death and *Siaburcharput ConCulainn,* "The Dream Chariot of Cúchulainn," explains how the spirit of Cúchulainn is called up by St. Patrick to help convert Lóiguire, then High King of Ireland, to Christianity. In the latter, we can see the merging of Christian elements into a pagan story in much the same manner that an ancient cleric did by inserting Christian elements into *Beowulf.*

For those who would like a further fictional treatment of Cúchulainn's life, Morgan Llywelyn's marvelous *Red Branch* is essential. Carefully researched and written, Llywelyn artfully blends modern fiction techniques with ancient writing to provide a complete story of Cúchulainn from birth to death.

According to legend, the *Táin* had been lost in time, although the name remained with vague references to it in several minor tales. Seanchán, who allegedly succeeded Dallán Forgaill as chief poet at the Convention of Drom Ceat in A.D. 575, went in search of it. Finally, he went to the grave of Fergus and intoned an incantation. A mist rose from the grave and rapidly grew in billowing clouds of gray, surrounding the poet for three days and three nights. When the fog disappeared, Seanchán explained that the spirit of Fergus had appeared to him in all his glory and told him the story of the *Táin*. Most of what is in the *Book of Leinster* allegedly comes from this.

But enough. Let Seanchán speak.

In scél fodessin is ní and fodechtsa.

—Randy Lee Eickhoff

Chapter 1

THE BED
ARGUMENT

ONE NIGHT AFTER THE royal bed had been laid in Cruacháin of the Enchantments in the province of Connacht for the rulers Ailill and Maeve, known as "She-Who-Makes-Men-Drunk," they began to argue while lying spent upon the richly embroidered pillows. In the comfortable rubble of their bedclothes Ailill nestled his head, damp from fervent lovemaking, upon Maeve's lap, admiring her naked breasts above him.

"It is true, my love, what they say about things being good for a woman if she is the wife of a wealthy man," Ailill boasted. He moved his heavy shoulders, twisting them to crush the sharp quill of a feather that poked him through the cushion he lay upon. He reached up and tweaked the nipples of her breasts, admiring how they leaped out for his attention. Maeve's breath quickened. Her lips touched his briefly, and he tasted honey on the tantalizing flicker of her tongue.

"Perhaps," Maeve answered. "But what made you think of that at a time like this?"

She lazily twined her long fingers through the thick hair of his chest, tugging gently. He pushed a heavy curl of her thick red hair away from her cheek and caressed it with the backs of his fingers.

"It just struck me how much better off you are today than the day I married you," Ailill said. "Far more fortunate with me than you were with your other husbands, Conchobar Mac Nessa, Tinne Mac Connrach, and Eochaid Dála."

"I was well enough off without you," Maeve said arrogantly, slapping him lightly upon the forehead. He grinned and tweaked her breast again. Her eyes became heavy, her pale skin blushing rosily beneath its alabaster, her red lips curling up toward her high cheekbones. Her long, flowing hair glowed golden-red in the pale light emanating from the guttering candles in sconces upon the polished wood of the walls and she swung it forward, brushing it lightly over his naked flesh.

"Then you must have kept your wealth well hidden," Ailill said huskily. "Your neighbors had made off with all of your plunder—except for the things that a woman has that are hers alone—before I came to your father's house to seek your hand. Your father was grateful, indeed, that I would bring my wealth and my armies into his family. Of course," he added slyly, caressing the roundness of her hip with his palm, "I found the prize well worth my trouble—even though there were other women with far richer dowries begging for my bed."

Maeve sat up, her eyes flashing with anger, her breasts heaving indignantly.

"Then you should have taken them for your wife!" she snapped. She slapped his hands away when he tried to caress her. "And what do you mean by suggesting I was a beggarly mist-wanderer? No! My treasure room bulged with riches. You forget that I had the High King of Ireland for my father: Eochaid Feidlech the Steadfast, the son of Finn, the son of Finnoman, the son of Finnen, the son of Finngoll, the son of Roth, the son of Rigéon, the son of Blathacht, the son of Beothacht, the son of Enna Agnech, the son of Aengus Turbech. My father had six daughters: Derbriu, Ethne, Ele, Clothru, Muguin, and myself, Maeve, who became the greatest of all. None were as graceful, more generous than I! I could easily defeat them in battle for I knew more about war than they. And my beauty drew men to my side as a candle flame draws a moth. My court dwarfed theirs: fifteen hundred soldiers served me, drawing their wages from my war chest. All were the sons of Exiles, and the same number of freeborn Irishmen. For every mercenary in my service, I had fifty-five others, and that was only my ordinary household."

She drew a deep breath, eyeing him arrogantly. "My father recognized my worth and gave me a whole province including this one that I ruled from Cruachain. That is why some call me Maeve of Cruachain. Many kings sent their sons to woo me. One came from Finn, the king of Leinster, Rus Ruad's son. And from Coirpre Niafer, the king of Temair, another of Rus Ruad's sons. The son of Conchobar, king of Ulster, son of Fachtna, came and others came from Eochaid Bec. But none could win my hand for I asked a harder wedding gift from them than had been asked by any other woman in Ireland: whosoever claimed my hand would never display meanness or jealousy or fear.

"I knew what I was doing, Ailill, for if I married a mean man, our union would most certainly fail. I am too full of grace and giving for one man. It would be an insult to my husband to have a wife more generous than he, but not if both were equal. Likewise, it would not do for a wife to be more spirited than her husband and I need a man my equal in temper. Nor could my husband be jealous for I have never slept with one man without another waiting in the shadows to take his place.

"That is why I chose you, Ailill, for you are not niggardly, jealous, or afraid. But apparently you have forgotten that I brought with me the highest wedding gift a bride has ever brought her husband: enough garments to clothe a dozen men, a chariot easily worth three times the price of seven serving maids, enough red gold to cover the width of your face and the equal of the weight of your left arm in white gold." She drew a deep breath, fondly slapping his hands away from her. "But this does not mean that you should feel as if you are a kept man. I would not have chosen you had you not been my equal. And if one has taunted you, saying that it is your wife who is the more important one in the marriage bed, you should ignore him," Maeve said patronizingly. "The one who would be insulted is me for suggesting I would settle for an inferior."

Ailill laughed and leaned back upon the cushions, moving away from another quill's stab.

"In this you are very wrong," he said. "I am a king's son and I have two kings for brothers: Cairpre in Temair and Finn in Leinster. They rule only because they are older than myself. Neither is better than I in grace or giving. The reason why I came here to claim your hand, Maeve, is not because you were wealthy, but because I had never heard in all of Ireland of a province being ruled by a woman. Now, I rule this province as the successor to my mother, Mata Muires, Mágach's daughter. You are my queen because who would be better than a daughter of the High King of Ireland? Not because of your wealth. And as for your generosity, well, Maeve, all know you enjoy men between your legs, drinking the honey-mead from your lips. As many as thirty a night!"

"You can make all the claims that you wish," Maeve answered haughtily. "But the fact remains that my wealth is far greater than yours."

"How delightful," Ailill said, laughing and shaking his head. "Surely you jest! No one owns more property than I or more jewels and riches. This is fact. I know it."

Maeve's lips thinned, her eyes glinting like gray ice. She leaned back away from his questing hands, her heavy breasts swinging tautly away, rosy nipples defiant. "Then," she purred, "let's have an accounting to see who is the richer."

"I think," Ailill said, laughing again, "you are making too much of this. But if you really want to do this, then we will. But later," he said coaxing, rolling his eyes up, the blue dancing with tiny lights.

For a moment, she resisted, then she caught her breath as his hands brought a rosy flush to her skin. "One night won't make any difference," Maeve relented, smiling roguishly at him.

And so, on the next day, they began with the challenge. Orders went out among the many rooms of the hall and servants scurried back and forth through the kitchens and the corn kiln and buttery, the ale-brewing house, the baking house, through the storage sheds and the guest houses, tripping over the rushes on the floor of the great hall, gathering the belongings of Ailill and Maeve. Servants first brought out the lowliest of their possessions: buckets and tubs, iron pots, washbasins, and ewers and drinking vessels, but all were found to be equal. Next came servants with caskets containing their rings for both fingers and thumbs, bracelets, and intricately carved gold brooches and pins mounted by fine jewels, followed by servants staggering under armloads of clothing dyed in solid colors: crimson, saffron, purple, blue, black, green, yellow, and plain gray. These were followed by clothing dyed in various colors: brown-yellow, checked, and striped. Shepherds brought folds of sheep in from the fields, their wool heavy and unshorn, and meadows and plains to be counted and matched and paired to be certain that they were of equal size. All, however, decided one to be equal to the other. Even Maeve's prize ram, worth the price of one bondmaid himself, was matched by another belonging to Ailill.

Next, their herds of horses and teams were led in from paddock and pasture. Maeve's finest stallion was easily matched by another from Ailill's herds. Then swineherders scoured the woods and gullies and refuse piles and drove in vast herds of pigs, but all were found equal. Maeve had a fine boar, but Ailill had another easily his equal. Finally, herdsmen rounded up their cattle from the woods and wastelands of the province and brought them in to be matched and measured, and they too were found to be of the same size and numbers with one exception: a great bull in Ailill's herd that had once been a calf of one of Maeve's cows. His name was Findbennach, the White Bull, and so proud was he that he refused to belong to a herd owned by a woman and moved in with

Ailill's herd. Maeve ordered her herdsmen to search for his equal among her herds, but their search was in vain, and Maeve's spirits fell into black melancholia as if she had not a single brass bracelet.

She had the messenger Mac Roth, a masterful maker of suggestions, called to her chambers and ordered him to find the match of Findbennach even if he had to search out every province in Ireland. Mac Roth, however, already knew where the equal of Findbennach lived.

"In the province of Ulster, in Cuailnge's territory, in the house of Dáire Mac Fiachna, lives the bull called Donn Cuailnge, the Brown Bull of Cooley," he said. "This bull is easily the equal of Findbennach; perhaps even better," he added.

Maeve's pulse quickened with excitement. One finger rose to wrap a long strand of her golden-red hair around it. She nibbled at her full lower lip. Finally, she leaned forward on her cushion, giving Mac Roth a full look at white hillocks on a much traveled land.

"Go there," she ordered him. "Ask Dáire for the loan of the Donn Cuailnge for a year. Tell him that I will give him fifty yearling heifers in payment for the loan of his bull at the year's end when I return him. If his people argue about losing the Donn Cuailnge for so long, I will give Dáire a portion of the Plain of Ai equal to his own holdings, a chariot worth the price of twenty-one bondmaids, and"—she paused, a lustful glint coming into her eyes; her nostrils widening—"and my own friendly thighs will be his as well."

Mac Roth immediately left with nine men, bearing Maeve's message with him, his mind crowded with envious thoughts of Dáire's luck, for Maeve's skill in lovemaking was well known among her household and troops, her bed being visited by thirty men a day until Fergus Mac Roich's arrival with the Ulster Exiles. Maeve found herself well sated by Fergus, whose own lust demanded seven women or one Maeve in his bed a night. When Mac Roth arrived at Dáire's house, he was well met as was his right for being the chief herald of all Ireland. After Dáire had treated him to a chalice of spiced wine, Mac Roth told Dáire of the challenge between Maeve and Ailill.

"Therefore," he concluded, "I am here to request the loan of the Donn Cuailnge to breed and match against Ailill's Findbennach. For this, you will be paid fifty yearling heifers upon the return of the Donn Cuailnge at the end of the year. If you come with the bull, you will also receive a portion of the fine Plain of Ai equal to your own lands, a chariot worth the price of twenty-one bondmaids, and"—he paused, his eyes twinkling knowingly—"Maeve's own friendly thighs."

Dáire felt the strength of his manhood rise with the last promise, for he had heard many stories about the lust of Maeve and her skill at pillow dancing. He clapped his great calloused feet together in delight as he rocked back and forth upon his cushion until it burst at the seams from his joy, feathers floating through the air like a winter snowstorm.

"By my beard!" he cried. "I care little what the Ulstermen may think! My treasure, the Donn Cuailnge, and I will accompany you to Ailill and Maeve in Connacht!"

Mac Roth grinned with pleasure at Mac Fiachna's decision. Dáire ordered his servants to see that Mac Roth and his fellow messengers were well cared for with clean rushes and fresh straw piled smoothly as bedding for them. He ordered his cooks to prepare the best of food and his steward to bring his best wine for them. Together, they celebrated the pact until they grew so drunk that their wits left them and they became loud with their boasts. But Mac Roth's men were not as tactful as their leader and Dáire's chief steward overheard two of them talking loudly:

"Ah, this is a fine way to treat guests! The man of this house is certainly one of the best hosts that we have met on our travels," one said merrily.

"Oh, yes, he is a good man. No doubt about that," the other said.

"Would you say there was a better host in all of Ulster?" the first asked drunkenly. Mead dribbled from his mouth, matting his beard as he drank from his bronze cup.

"His king, Conchobar, is by far better," the second replied. "All of Ulster bows to him. But it was good of Mac Fiachna to agree to give us the Donn Cuailnge. Otherwise, it would have taken four of our best provinces to carry it off from Ulster."

Another of the messengers drinking near them overheard this last and asked: "What are you two talking about?"

The first messenger looked at him and said: "I said that the man of this house is a good man whereupon our friend here agreed and when I asked if there was a better man in all of Ulster he replied, 'Certainly. His leader, Conchobar, is a better man and all in Ulster would bow before him.' Whereupon we agreed that this was a good thing for it would have taken four of our best provinces to carry the Donn Cuailnge away from Ulster."

The third messenger laughed and drained his goblet before replying.

"His mouth should spout blood for saying such a stupid thing! We would have taken the Brown Bull with or without Dáire's agreement. We would not have needed the strength of four provinces for that!"

The steward, who had been bringing them fresh wine and food, grew incensed at the ill manners of the guests and rudely slammed the pitchers of wine and trays of food in front of them without a word and went straight to Dáire Mac Fiachna's hut. Upon entering, he stared directly into Dáire's eyes and demanded:

"Did you or did you not give Maeve's messengers our most valuable treasure, the Donn Cuailnge?"

"I did," Dáire said, his brows knitting in wonder at the other's fury. "But only as a loan. And what is it to you? He is mine to do with as I wish," he added threateningly for never had a servant spoken to him in this manner before.

"You may be our king, but that was not what a wise ruler would have done," the steward said stoutly. "What our guests said must be true: if you had not given him up freely, then the armies of Ailill and Maeve, along with the cunning of Fergus Mac Roich, would have taken him anyway."

Dáire became angry at the steward's words. Stung by the insinuation that he was weak, he replied: "Gods' balls! Nothing leaves my lands unless I choose!"

"That is not what the others say," the steward taunted.

"Then they will leave and take with them only their empty words," swore Dáire, fuming.

The next morning, the messengers rose early and went to Dáire's hut, anxious to be away to Connacht with the Brown Bull.

"Greetings, Dáire," they said cheerfully upon entering his room. "We will be leaving shortly if you will tell us where we may find the Donn Cuailnge."

"No," Dáire growled abruptly, glowering at them. "And you may thank your gods that only my rule of hospitality keeps me from murdering messengers or travelers or any other wayfarers, for that matter. Otherwise, none of you would leave here alive."

"What is this?" Mac Roth said, an icy coldness driving away the last of the night's revels from his mind.

"You abused my hospitality last night with your brag that you and the armies of Ailill and Maeve, with the help of Fergus's cunning, would make me give you the Donn Cuailnge had I not agreed willingly to do so," Dáire said indignantly.

"Come now," Mac Roth replied, laughing. "Surely you do not pay attention to what drunken messengers say! It was the drink doing the talking! Ailill and Maeve cannot be blamed for the ill manners of their messengers."

"Sometimes wine brings the truth of men's thoughts out when lips would otherwise remain silent. How do I know that the Donn Cuailnge will be returned after the promised year is over? No, I won't give you the Brown Bull of Cuailnge, Mac Roth. Not now or ever. You may take these words back to Ailill and Maeve and tell them that it will do no good to send wiser messengers back to me," Dáire said firmly. He lifted a massive cheek from his cushion, farting horrendously in dismissal. The smell of rank onions filtered through the room.

And so Mac Roth withdrew with as much dignity as he could and returned empty-handed to Cruachain, the stronghold of Connacht, bringing his chastened men, now sober and fearful of their reception from temperamental Maeve. They traveled with heavy hearts through the cold, gray mist, fearful of the Connacht trull's rage. When Maeve asked them for Dáire's reply to her request, Mac Roth told her that Mac Fiachna had refused her offer.

Annoyed, Maeve asked, "Why?"

Mac Roth told her how the drunken brag of the other messengers had angered Dáire.

"Very well," Maeve said icily. "We do not have to smooth the knots and polish the knobs in this. I have no intention of sending other messengers to apologize for the poor tact and behavior of our first messengers." (Mac Roth breathed a silent sigh of relief.) Her eyebrows drew down in a fine line across her smooth, white brow, her eyes becoming flat and cold. "Dáire was well aware that if he did not agree to my offer, then I would bring my armies to his land and take what I had tried to gain by more peaceful means." Her lips tightened into an attractive pout. "The Brown Bull of Cuailnge will come to Connacht. I have spoken."

She did not give words, however, to the cold fury burning inside her at Dáire's refusal of her own thighs. This angered her as well and so it is best that we remember wars are often begun from the bed.

Chapter 2

THE RISING
OF THE
CONNACHTMEN

AND SO IT BEGAN.

Ailill and Maeve, angered by Dáire's refusal of Maeve's generous offer (more especially Maeve who had never before had her favors refused), assembled a massive army and sent word to the seven Maines, Maeve's sons who held the other three provinces under their rule, to bring warriors to Connacht. Ailill also sent fast messengers to his brothers, the rest of Mágach's seven sons: Anluan, Mugcorb, Cet, En, Bascall, and Dóchae, each commanding three thousand warriors. He also sent messengers to Conchobar's son, Cormac Connlongas, who led the three thousand Exiles from Ulster now living in Connacht, telling Cormac and his men that the time had come for them to repay Ailill's generosity for allowing them to live within the safety of Connacht's borders instead of being forced to roam the land as outlaws. Within weeks, all arrived at Cruachain Ai.

Cormac brought three companies with him. The warriors in the first company all wrapped speckled cloaks around them to tell their troop from the others. They wore their black hair clipped close to the neck and forest-green cloaks that fluttered around them like starling wings, held with silver brooches around their necks. Over their chests they wore tunics stitched with gold thread that fell to their knees. Each carried full-length shields and broad, gray-headed stabbing spears on slender shafts, and they carried their silver-hilted swords in white sheaths.

The second company wore dark-gray cloaks falling from their shoulders and red-embroidered tunics that reached their calves. They drew their hair back and tied it with red leather thongs. Their shields were brightly colored and edged in Druidic spells, sacred drawings around the edges. They carried five-pronged spears in their hands and wore gold-knobbed swords about their waists.

"I do not see Cormac yet," Maeve said wistfully to Ailill and Mac Roth from the brow of a hill where they had gathered in a clearing among burdock and brambles to watch the armies approach. Ailill turned away, smiling secretly from his place beneath a pavilion erected as shelter against the gray mist for he knew that Maeve's interest in Cormac was more than military. He pretended interest in the squalling children who mocked the march of their heroes, strutting in front of the pavilion with wooden weapons carved from hawthorn banging between stumpy legs, lips pouting, sullen and withdrawn as mountain goats.

At that time, the third troop appeared, each man wearing a purple cloak fastened with gold brooches filled with shining jewels around his neck and a red-embroidered hooded tunic that reached to his ankles. Their yellow-gold hair fell loose like a lion's mane around their shoulders. They carried curved, scallop-edged shields and thick spears like the pillars of a palace. At the head of the column rode a tall, handsome man, his bearing kinglike and haughty, his green eyes glinting like emeralds. Thick thighs clutched the sides of his prancing horse. A wide gold band encircled his high forehead; matching bands encircled his wrists. No beard graced his chin jutting proudly in front of him like a cliff.

"I see him now," Maeve said gladly, watching the man approach. She straightened her shoulders and smoothed the *sida,* the sheer silk imported from sea traders, down her side. Her nipples pushed visibly against the cloth. A tiny click could be heard in her throat as she spoke, and Ailill could tell what Maeve of the Friendly Thighs was thinking. He turned away so she would not see his smile erupt into a gleaming grin. He stared sternly at two warriors, their weapons held carelessly in thick hands, who stumbled drunkenly by on thick legs like huge, slow stones of a walking statue, singing a raunchy round about Manannán, the sea-god:

> *"Manannán and his three legs,*
> *the third but a peg . . ."*

No wiser than a clothespin, he thought, and made note of the markings of their heavy cloaks. He turned to watch as a troop of chariots clattered by, dust billowing from their wooden wheels, horses prancing, nostrils distended, gleaming redly. The horizon filled with armies marching into the valley below the pavilion, and still the armies arrived until four provinces of Ireland had gathered beneath the Druid's Hill at Cruachain Ai where the four fords of Ai, Athmaga, Athslisen, Athberena, and Athcoltna, came together. For over a fortnight they waited, eating and drinking, impatient to march, while the Druids and sages and prophets delayed, looking for a favorable sign. Fights broke out between the glowing red fires as quarrels rose between the warriors of the various armies, and Ailill's temper grew shorter and shorter as he went from camp to camp, settling arguments with a firm hand, seething with anger, supervising, checking for laggards and drinkers who let their mirth rob them of their good senses.

At last, tiring of the delay, Maeve ordered her charioteer, a jowly redhead, to yoke her prize blacks and take her to her Druid where she would consult with him. Ailill refused to go with her, saying: "You can go to the shadowy woods, if you wish, and listen to the prattlings of a fool pretending to understand secret portents. Frankly, Druid predictions give me a bellyache. I'll stay here and supervise the men. They could use more drilling."

Crom Deroil, the Druid, received her with a long face for he had just read the portents of the day in a quiet pool beneath a ring of oaks, his *fiodhneimheadh,* where he slept on his wattles of rowan from which he received his visions. He leaned on his ashwood cane and waggled his head. He belched and the stench of onions made her eyes water.

"You have news for me?" Maeve asked. "Tell me what you have found and let it be good news for me for no one is more dear to me than myself."

The Druid sighed, and took his carved sticks of hazelwood and threw them into the air, then leaned forward and peered among their tellings. He frowned and said, "A youth touched by the sun will oppose you. Whoever returns or does not return will matter less to you for be assured that you will return although many keenings will be heard in homes upon that day."

He blinked rapidly and belched again. He tried to smile and the stumps of his yellowed teeth showed beneath his thin lips in a grimace. He waited, knowing her words before she spoke them, and knowing that what he said would make no difference in her answer. A small cloud of flies buzzed around his head. He waved a brown-spotted hand, shooing them away.

"When should we leave?" she said *codladh grifin,* on pins and needles. She tapped a goad against her thigh, impatiently waiting for his answer. The old bastard's crazy as a loon, she thought.

The Druid shrugged and shook his head. He had heard her complaints for many years and it never varied. Impetuous! he thought. Not a lick of common sense in her pretty head. Fire instead of icy logic. But, he mentally shrugged, without the fire of youth we would still be crouching in cold caves. He sighed, saying: "It does not matter the day. What the gods have willed will be. You will return although many will not." Again, he waved the flies away.

Maeve returned to her chariot and bade her driver return to the ford of the four rivers where her army waited. He flicked the reins against the rumps of the horses, calling to them. The horses lurched, pulling the chariot away from the wood. One lifted its tail, dropping green horse apples behind him. The smell of rich manure filled the air. Maeve drew a deep breath.

"Many will curse me before this is over. All lovers and friends of those who will die will curse me for this army was gathered for me," she said, looking back at the wood.

The charioteer grew uneasy at this foreboding of doom and said: "Wait until I turn the chariot around so the sun will shine on our right. Then we will draw down the power of Lugh who will give us a safe return."

He slapped the reins against the backs of Maeve's black horses, admiring his mistress's great, white breasts the size of melons as she leaned forward, bracing herself against the chariot rail. The horses snorted and pawed the earth with their eagerness to be off, but he held the reins firm, holding them in check as a young woman suddenly appeared in front of them. She wore her yellow gold hair in three tresses: two winding up on her head while the third hung long behind her, touching her calves, swaying gently in the fresh breeze blowing in from the sea. She had fastened a speckled green cloak around her shoulders with a red-gold brooch. Sandals with gold clasps covered her long peasant's feet, the nails on them pink and even. She had a narrow jaw, two pitch-black eyebrows, and long, delicate dark lashes that cast shadows upon her cheeks. Her eyes had three irises. Her lips were the color of holly berries; her teeth white, gleaming shells. Her cone-shaped breasts were bare, the nipples red and erect, and a scarlet belt girdled her waist above her firm snow-white thighs. She carried a white-bronze sword inlaid with seven rings of red-gold in her hand and with it she wove strange symbols in the air that stayed for a moment, gleaming like silver, before disappearing. Two black horses, their night-black coats gleaming as darkly as her hair, drew her chariot, their nostrils flaming red, their hooves striking sparks from the flint rocks of the hill. She was well armed with throwing spears.

"What is your name?" Maeve asked, a touch of envy in her voice for the young woman was every bit as lovely as Maeve and younger, her skin glowing like the first night's snowfall. Her charioteer recognized the edge in Maeve's voice and hastily reached down between his legs for a jug of wine and her golden chalice. He spilled wine in her goblet and handed it to her. At times like this, she would shrivel like a prune and her blood would turn to dust from tension, but others would lose their heads. Absently, she took it, sipping.

"What do you want here?" she asked.

"I am Fedelm of the *Sídhe* of Rath Cruacháin," the woman answered. Her horses moved restlessly and she steadied them absentmindedly with the reins held firmly between luminous fingers.

"Where have you come from?" asked Maeve. She sipped the wine again, feeling its warmth settle comfortably in her stomach.

"From Alba, where I learned the *filidheacht,*" she said.

"You are one with vision? Have you then the *imbas forasnai,* the True Light of Foresight?" Maeve asked eagerly, for it would do good to know the luck of the future since her Druid had been unable to give her the words she wanted.

"Yes, I do," Fedelm answered quietly.

"Then look into the future for me and tell me what will become of my army," Maeve demanded.

The woman closed her eyes, concentrating. Tiny twin lines marred the surface of her broad brow. Her full lips moved silently, forming forgotten words, spells and enchantments that could move the forces of the woods and earth, the water and the sky. Thick-bellied clouds streaked with black gathered around the horizon and rushed toward them.

Maeve waited impatiently for a long moment, drumming her long fingers upon the arm of her wicker chariot, then demanded: "Fedelm, prophetess! Use your power! How do you see my army?"

"I see the Connacht host draped in crimson robes; I see it clothed in red," she replied hollowly.

Maeve's blood chilled at the sepulchral words. She drained the goblet and handed it without looking to her charioteer. He made a motion to refill it, but she shook her head, frown lines appearing deeply between her finely arched brows.

"This cannot be true," she said half angrily, half fearfully. "Everyone knows Conchobar suffers his pangs in Emain Macha with the rest of the Red Branch warriors. The curse of Macha still lies upon his shoulders and all of the Ulstermen from his mealy horse race when he forced her to run against his team while she carried twins in her womb. Even the pig-keepers and smiths and harp-carvers moan on their beds, their hands clutching their stomachs against the pain in their guts. My messengers have brought me word of this. Fedelm of the *Sídhe,* look again: how do you see my host?"

"I see them draped in crimson; I see warriors clothed in red," she repeated. Her red lips stood out from the chalk-white of her face. Dark smudges appeared under her eyes; she seemed to grow older and older, as if a *bocánach,* an air-demon, slowly drained the power from her.

"No! This is false prophecy," Maeve said angrily, a touch of panic in her voice. (Her charioteer moved nervously beside her, waiting half fearfully for her temper to flare.) "We far outnumber the Red Branch of Ulster. Celtchar Mac Uthidir still waits in Dún Lethglaise with a third of Ulster's armies. Fergus, son of Roich Mac Echdach, and his army of three thousand joined us here in exile. Again, Fedelm, prophetess: how do you see my host?"

"I see Connacht draped in crimson; I see it clothed in red." The words came faintly now, but Maeve suddenly brightened.

"Of course! Now, I understand," Maeve said. (Beside her, her charioteer breathed a deep, silent sigh of relief.) "Wrath and rage and wounds draped in red blood are common when armies clash. Look again, Fedelm, and tell us the truth: how do you see my army?"

"I see the host draped in crimson; I see it clothed in red," she said. Then, in a voice from beyond the grave, the words spilled from her lips:

"I see a battle: a man, broad and blond,
with blood about his waist, I trow

and a hero-halo girdling his head round.
Many victories fill his brow.

"Seven hard and heroic jewels
set in the iris of his eye.
A snarl covers his lips so cruel.
He wears a looped tunic of red dye.

"A noble countenance I see
works subtly upon women's ways;
a warrior of sweet coloring be
a form dragonish in the fray.

"His great valor suggests his name
Cúchulainn of Murtheimne,
the Hound of Culann, full of fame.
Where he is, I cannot see.

"But this I know: the whole host
is colored crimson by his glory.
Many hope to make their boast
of his death in their story.

"A giant on the plain I see,
battling the host on swards;
in each of his two hands he
carries four short swords.

"I see him hurling against the army
two *gae bolga* and a spear cast
and an ivory-hilted sword. I see
each weapon to its separate task.

"I see him moving to the fray:
take warning, watch him closely,
Cúchulainn, Sualdam's son! who bays
in pursuit after those who flee.

"Whole army troops he will behead,
making dense massacre in all.
Thousands will lose their heads.
I am Fedelm. I speak all.

"Blood pours from warriors' wounds
—total ruin—at his touch die
your many warriors. In tombs
the men of Deda Mac Sin lie!

"Torn corpses, wailing women cry
and the *beansidhés* bound
over fields where dead men lie
because of him—Forge-Hound."

She opened her eyes and stared calmly at Maeve, drawing deep, full breaths that made her breasts rise and swell. The charioteer covertly watched, hoping Maeve wouldn't notice the swelling between his legs. The years melted from her, the shadows disappearing from beneath her eyes, the wrinkles from her forehead, and the young woman soon stood in front of them once more. Maeve shook her head: this was magic far beyond what she had seen before.

"Be aware, Maeve of Connacht," Fedelm said serenely. "If you persist on traveling forward to Ulster with this mighty army, you will be left with torn corpses and women wailing their dirges because of the Forge-Hound!"

Maeve's charioteer moved uneasily at this, but Maeve threw her golden-red tresses back, turning her face into the wind so they streamed behind her like battle ribbons.

"Tell me, Fedelm," she said. "Is this what will be? Or what may be? If something is changed, will not the future also change?"

"I speak only what I saw," Fedelm said quietly. "I cannot answer for what you will do."

"Then," Maeve said triumphantly, "you cannot claim that the

future is locked in stone! Even our Druids do not proclaim that!"

"The future is what it will be, nothing more," Fedelm said. "A person believes what he wishes to believe."

"Then we will not begin today, but tomorrow," Maeve said. "That will change the flow of water across the sands of time."

And so it became the Monday after Samhain that they began their journey. The day loomed cold and wet, gray. Tempers flared as the warriors readied themselves to slog through the heavy mist, the gloaming, crushing heather with their heels.

Ailill gave them direction to march southeast from Cruachain Ai:

through Muicc Cruinb by way of Tóm Móna the ridge of peat,

through Turloch Teóra Crích, where the stinking lake marsh stands,

through Cúil Sílinne, where Carrcin Lake, named after Silenn, Madchar's daughter, lies,

past Fid and Bolga, forests and hills,

through Coltain, and across the river Shannon,

through Glúne Gabair,

over Mag Trego, the Plain of Spears,

through Tethba, both North and South,

through Cúil and Ochain,

and north by Uata,

through Tiarthechta to the east,

through Ord and Sláis the Hammer,

southward across the river Inndeóin, the Anvil,

through Carn,

through Ortrach the Dung Heap,

through the clear streams of Findglassa Asail,

through Drong, by the Duelt River,

through Deland,

through Selach,

through Slaibre of the Herds,
through Slechta, their way cleared by swords for the passage
   of Maeve and Ailill,
through Cúil Siblinne and Dub,
south past Ochaine Hill,
past Catha and Cromma and Tromma,
past Fódromma and Sláne,
and Gort Sláne, the pasture,
south by Druimm Licce, the Flagstone Ridge,
by Áth nGabla, the Ford of the Forked Branch,
through Ardachad, the High Field,
north by Féoraind,
past Findabair,
through Assi to the south by Airne,
and Aurthaile by the ridge of Druim Salaind,
by the ridge of Druim Caín, and Druim Caímthechta,
by the ridge of Mac Dega,
by Eódond Mór and Eódond Bec, the Great Dark Yewtree
   and the Lesser,
by Méthe Tog and Méthe nEoin, the Squirrel Neck and Bird
   Neck,
through Scúaip and Imscúaip,
through Cenn Ferna,
through Baile and Aile,
through Báil Scena and Dáil Scena,
through Fertse,
past Ros Lochad of the woods,
through Sale,
through Loch Mach, or Muid Loga,
through the great plain of Anmag,
past the great heights of Dinn
and the Deilt River,
and the Dublais River,
through Fid Mór, or Fid Mórthruaille, the Wood of the Great
   Sheath,

to Colptha River,
and the Cronn River in Cuailnge.

Until at last they came to Finnabair in Cuailnge where the armies from Connacht split up to search across the province for the Brown Bull of Cooley. But Fedelm, the *bánfáith* who read the future, did not come with them at that time for she had read what Maeve had asked, and beyond that she could do no more. We live by the myths imposed upon us, this and nothing more, actors in an endless play.

Chapter 3

THE CONNACHTMEN DISCOVER CÚCHULAINN

As THE ARMY FROM Connacht began marching from Cruachain to Cúil Sílinne near Carrcin Lake, Maeve commanded the driver of her chariot to make her nine chariots ready so that she might travel through the host and determine those who marched eagerly or reluctantly on the journey.

While Maeve toured her army, reveling in the lustful glances thrown her way, Ailill turned his attention to readying his tent for the night and making himself comfortable by having his bed and bedclothes precisely placed. He was not alone in his attention to his comfort. Fergus Mac Roich also paid close attention to the settling of his tent for, like all warriors, he knew the advantage of resting comfortably whenever one could. He ordered his tent to be pitched close by Maeve's, anticipating the frolic in the night when Maeve crept into his tent. He was followed by Conchobar's son, Cormac Connlongas, while Conall Cernach ordered his tent to be pitched next to Cormac's tent. Fiacha Mac Firaba, Conchobar's grandson through his daughter, had his men pitch his tent next to Conall's tent.

Before leaving, Maeve had ordered that her tent be placed on the other side of Ailill's tent. Finnabair, their daughter, had her tent pitched next to Maeve while next to her, Ailill Find's wife, Flidais Fholtchaín, who crept into Fergus's bed when Maeve had vacated it, had her tent pitched. Flidais quenched the thirst of the men of Ireland every seventh night with sups of milk.

When Maeve returned from her inspection of the army, she was furious and upset with the three armies from Galeóin, the Ulster Exiles descended from the Fir Bolg, the ancient ones. They were expert soldiers who had been so well trained in the arts of war that when Maeve rode through their ranks, they ignored her, giving their attention to their commanders instead. She told Ailill that these three armies should not be allowed to come with them on their march to Ulster.

"Why?" Ailill sighed, wondering if a night would pass without fault being found by Maeve on something. "What fault have you found with them?"

"Oh, I can find no fault about them. They are fine soldiers who had prepared their camp and were cooking their meal while the other troops were just making their camps ready. They had already finished eating and were listening to their harpers playing while the others were just beginning their meal. We have no other soldiers as good. This is the problem," she said. "They are too good at soldiering. When we defeat the Ulstermen, they will receive all the credit. This will be bad for the men of Connacht."

"But," Ailill said, frowning and trying to understand her logic. "The men from Galeóin are fighting with us. For all practical purposes, they *are* from Connacht. Their birthplace no longer matters; it is who they serve and now they serve Connacht. Their honor will be Connacht's honor. They have left Ulster and as everyone knows, you can't piss in the same puddle twice!" He gave a single irate snort of laughter.

Maeve's lips tightened. Her eyes narrowed and she said stubbornly, "Your sense of history is the sense of ignorance. Ulster is always Ulster. History's useful even when it's false. Now, listen to me: they can't come. Their power will only increase with their fame. That, I will not have. I'm a *feeling* creature creating my personal history. If they become too powerful, they may try to become rulers. This is dangerous, Ailill. One does not invite a wolf pack into one's own kennel. One wolf, perhaps two, but not a pack."

Ailill sighed again and shook his head, rubbing his temples wearily. "Then let them stay here and wait for our return. They can guard our borders."

"No," Maeve said stubbornly. "If we let them stay, they will seize our lands while we are gone. Surely you can see the wisdom in that. We do not need to have Ulster both at our back and in front of us as well."

"Well," Finnabair interjected, her fine brows drawing together in puzzlement. "What should they do if they do not go with us or stay at home to guard our borders?'

"Yes, what?" Ailill said, exasperated, echoing his daughter. "What *do* you suggest we do with them if we don't let them come with us and refuse to let them stay behind?" He longed to return to his tent where he could be warmed with a glass of spiced wine and rest away from the damp coldness of the coming night.

"Kill them," Maeve said indifferently. She pulled her cloak around her and started for her tent, but Ailill stepped in front of her, his face white with anger.

"That is an evil thing to say. Only a woman who thinks with her beard would think of that as a solution," Ailill said sharply, adding, "Even as a bad metaphor. What better way to fight Ulster men than with Ulster men. Set your wolves against each other!"

Fergus broke in on the argument, having come up on foot behind them. His head throbbed from too much wine the night before when eight maidens climbed into his bed without waiting in the other's shadow for him to finish. He scratched his big balls beneath his tunic as he listened to the argument, his eyes gritty from the dust of the march. At last he interrupted, speaking up for the Ulster Exiles that Maeve distrusted. His words dripped venom, the heavy scars around his cheekbones purpling with rage while his eyebrows, like tangled hazel and hawthorn amid the trunks of silver birch, quivered above eyes like two caves.

"This will not happen," he said lowly to Maeve. She drew up in anger, but he did not turn from the sparks flinting from her eyes. "You may think badly of these men because they did not pant after your loins when you rode naked between them, but they are our friends. They will be killed only after we are killed." He dropped his calloused hand upon the hilt of In Caladbolg, his mighty sword, for emphasis. Red coals burned deeply in his eyes.

Maeve's eyes narrowed at his defiance. Her nostrils drew down, white and pinched. Tiny muscles bunched along her jaw with her fury.

"That, we might just do," she said furiously. "You would threaten me? I have six thousand men who have pledged to follow me. My sons, the seven Maines, also follow with seven troops of three thousand each—may their luck continue: Maine Máthramail the Motherlike, Maine Athramail the Fatherlike, Maine Mórgor the Hard Duty-Minded, Maine Míngor the Soft Duty-Minded, Maine Móepirt who has no description although some call him He of the Honey Speech, Maine Andoe the Swift, and Maine Cotagaib Uli who has all the qualities of both Ailill and myself." Fergus laughed at her boast and folded his arms across his barrel-like chest.

"You are blind to all but your own desires," Fergus said calmly. He reached down casually and scratched his groin, his thick legs aspraddled, noting the hungry look leaping into her eyes. He grinned knowingly into them. "We have seven kings from Munster who support us and each of those kings has three thousand warriors who will willingly follow them in battle against you. I, too, have three thousand warriors *and* the Galeóin soldiers. But this is senseless talk," he continued tactfully, seeing that continued anger would only bring disaster down upon all. "There is another way that we can insure faithfulness and keep the Ulster Exiles from claiming credit for your success, thereby preserving your false Connacht pride. We can scatter the Galeóin warriors throughout the rest of the army. As we have seventeen armies of three thousand each with us, the Galeóins, our eighteenth army, can be scattered throughout the other armies. And," he continued with relish, "they will be able to help control the rabble and the young who have yet to earn the right to be warriors and the women— each king has his queen who travels in your court," he added slyly. "And well you know the Ulsterman's reputation for skillful swordplay."

"All right," Maeve said, grudgingly agreeing to Fergus's proposal. Her pink tongue flickered out to lick red lips, the lower dropping into a pout. "I will accept that as long as they are dispersed among the others."

"And," Ailill hastened to add, for he could see the anger in Fergus and wished to appease the hero-warrior. He had seen what Fergus could do with his mighty sword, the In Caladbolg, a gift from Leite from the elf-mounds, whose rainbow edge could cut through cold steel like rancid butter. "We will put Fergus over the entire army for he was king of Ulster for seventeen years until he was displaced by Conchobar."

Wisely, Maeve held her tongue and did not challenge Ailill's decision. If she had, Ailill would have drawn his armies back to Cruachaín and sent the seven Maines home with their troops, for he was weary of Maeve's waspish tongue and the way that she looked lustfully upon the battle-scarred Fergus.

The next morning, sated by her violent romp upon Fergus's cushions, Maeve rode contentedly among the army, with the Galeóins scattered among the others, as they began their march toward Móin Coltna, the moor. There, they found a hundred sixty wild deer in one herd. Silently, they surrounded them and at a signal, leaped forward, slaughtering them. But it was good for the rest of the army that the Galeóins had been scattered among them for only the Galeóins were capable of catching the deer—except for the five that managed to slip past the rest of the army. So the Galeóins showed their cleverness against the clumsiness of the Connachtmen.

At last, the army came to Trego Plain where they broke their march and cooked their meals. Here, Black-Tongued Dubthach, the Chafer of Ulster, stared deeply into the hot coals of the fire, his thoughts slowly turning and expanding into the cauldron of night. The others moved restlessly away from him, casting wary sidelong looks at his jet-black hair cropped carelessly around his shoulders, his bloody eye, the great spear of Cealtchair, its point gleaming red from its fresh bath in a vat of dark blood. A lone owl hooted, its call lonely and chilling in the night, and men stirred anxiously against what they saw as a bad omen. A raven swept through the darkness and some swore that its eyes glowed red like the Mórrígan's. Then a strangeness settled over Dubthach's face and, slowly, prophetic words began to spill from his lips:

"Listen closely now with dread
to how I see this war was born.
A dark march lies far ahead
toward Ailill's wife's Brown Horn.

"One man, himself a whole army,
moves to guard Murtheimne's herds.
Two pig-keepers, once friends, I see,
but now crows sip milk—cruel birds.

"The clay of the deep river Cronn
will rise red-stained and bar our way
to Ulster until his work is done
at Mount Ochaine in the north-way.

"Ailill orders Cormac: 'Quickly!
Rush to your son's side, then!'
Cattle feed upon the plains calmly;
while hard raiders kill brave men.

"In due time, the battle will start.
Maeve and one-third of our host
will face a youth who will tear apart
our men. You will hear his boast."

He raised his bloody eyes and looked with death around him, speaking hollowly, "Beware the Warped Man."

Immediately Nemain the War-Spirit moved among them in a magical shower, flailing them with hailstones, masses of fire streaking across the night sky, her words booming across the plain in loud laughter. Restlessly, they huddled in small groups by fires, taking comfort in each other's nearness, crouching beneath their shields. When they slept, dreams of Dubthach's brutal vision trampled through their sleep.

In the morning, groups of men roved restlessly among the warriors, telling them what Dubthach had seen, until Maeve dressed herself in her most becoming robes, her melon breasts seen but not seen, and left her tent to walk among them, calming them with her honeyed presence until they had finished eating and again began to march. Slowly, they forgot Dubthach's vision as they marched over the rough land until, at last, they arrived at Granaird in North Tethba where they spent the night.

While the army slept, Fergus, remembering his former friends, sent a warning to the Ulstermen. But the Ulstermen were still suffering the pains of childbirth from the curse of Macha, the daughter of Sinrith Mac Imbaith. All, that is but Cúchulainn and Sualdam, his father. Together, the two traveled to Iraird Cuillen where they settled in for many nights to watch for the arrival of the Connachtmen.

At last, Cúchulainn turned to his father, saying, "I can feel the warriors close tonight. You must ride and warn the Red Branch. Tell them not to stop upon the open plains, but to seek shelter among the woods and the valleys wrapped in mist until their sickness passes."

"And what will you do, my son?" Sualdam asked, gathering the reins of his chariot.

"I would go with you, but I have already promised Fedelm Noichride that I would spend the night with her." He smiled in anticipation of the lovemaking ahead of him, his silver-gray eyes shining at the inner vision of Fedelm, body slippery with sweat, glowing in the firelight like a white beeswax candle, breasts arching to his hands, her hands . . . Modesty surfaced beneath the memory and he blushed hotly, turning his face into the cold wind to cool the flush on his cheeks.

"Ah, well!" his father said, grinning at his son's embarrassment. "It is good for a warrior to have a woman before battle. Unless," he added, "there is a *geis* upon him that he spend the hours alone. But that is wrong for the gods to insist on such a thing for a man who battles with a woman in bed readies himself for battle on the fields. And Fedelm, ah, now that, indeed, is a battle worthy for a champion!" He laughed, then turned sober. "But it is bad that you leave Ulster to be trampled under the feet of its enemies!"

"If I do not, then I will have broken my word to a woman and there are those who will say that a woman's word is better than mine," Cúchulainn answered.

"Watch yourself carefully, then," Sualdam said. "For I do not trust the honor of the Connacht host." He turned his chariot, whipping his horses toward Emain Macha.

Some people later claimed that Cúchulainn did not spend the night with Fedelm Noichride, but rather with a young woman slave whom she kept for Cúchulainn to sleep with. But Fedelm of the Mountain Breasts had the lust of Maeve within her for the youth, and it is unlikely that such a woman would keep another for the bed-game. Before he left, Cúchulainn went into the oak wood and cut an oak sapling that he wove into a spancel-hoop of challenge and cut an *ogham* message into it before forcing it over a standing stone.

Meanwhile, Fergus, remembering his old friends, led the Connacht host on a wide detour to the south, trying to buy time for the Ulstermen to recover from their curse and gather an army. Ailill and Maeve, following in the vanguard, noticed the change in their direction of travel. Puzzled, Maeve said to Fergus:

> "Something seems strange
> with this road upon which our band
> travels. Our directions range
> across every kind of land.
>
> "Ailill and his army are minded
> of your friendship and think treachery
> directs you. Or have you not decided
> to lead us upon the determined way?
>
> "If you find yourself bound
> by old friendship to lead us astray,
> perhaps another one may be found
> to take us along our proper way."

Stung by her words, Fergus replied sharply:

> "Maeve, what troubles you?
> You will find no treachery in me.
> The land to where I lead you
> you chose: Ulster by the sea.
>
> "Are you suggesting something's amiss
> with our way? Another way would damn
> us. I am trying to lead us to miss
> Cúchulainn, the son of Sualdam."

At first, Maeve thought to give vent to her anger for the abrupt way Fergus spoke to her, but then she remembered the span of his broad shoulders and the clutch of his strong arms and his calloused hands upon her flesh in the dark of the night and swallowed her displeasure, allowing Fergus to continue as the head of the army. Soon, they came to Iraird Cuillen.

Err and Innel, with their two charioteers, Foich and Fochlam, the four sons of Urard Mac Anchinne, had moved out in front of the army with their musicians and servants to keep their rugs and cloaks and brooches from becoming soiled from the large cloud of dust being raised by the marching army. Suddenly, they came upon the spancel-hoop Cúchulainn had placed upon the standing stone. They climbed from their chariots and carefully walked the ground, noting where Sualdam's two horses had pulled the grass, roots and all, out of the soil while grazing. But where Cúchulainn's horses grazed, they had not only pulled up the grass, they had licked the soil down to the stone as well.

The four returned to their chariots and sat, waiting for the armies to come up while their musicians played soothing songs to take their minds from the difficulty of the march and slaves wiped their foreheads and arms with cloths soaked in sweet balm.

When Fergus Mac Roich came upon them, they rode out to give him the spancel-hoop they had found on top of the standing stone. As he read the *ogham* cut into the hoop, a tight smile played upon his lips beneath his whiskers. With a piece of his tunic, he wiped the dust from his face, turning as he heard a chariot coming hard behind him.

"Why are you waiting here?" Maeve asked impatiently as she rode up beside him.

Fergus gave her a grim smile as he handed her Cúchulainn's message. Her fingers grew warm from its touch and she felt the hero's fire smolder in her belly.

"We have stopped because of this spancel-hoop," he said. "The *ogham* message on the peg reads: 'Do not travel further unless there is a man among you who can make a hoop like this with one hand in one piece. Fergus, my friend, cannot be numbered as one of you.' This is the work of Cúchulainn."

He pointed at the barren plain where Maeve's horses nosed futilely, looking for a wisp of grass to eat.

"And his horses grazed the plain to stone."

Maeve reluctantly handed the spancel-hoop back to Fergus. He handed it solemnly to the Druids accompanying her, chanting:

"What do you see as the meaning
of this hoop? What does the crude
riddle say? How many left it lying
on the stone? A few? Or a multitude?

"Will our forces come to harm
if we continue on our way?
Come, Druids, don't give the alarm
but discover why it was here today!"

The Druids huddled together, hooded heads bowed, passing the spancel-hoop back and forth among them, muttering incantations, speaking to the ancient ones in fine, flicker-flash words lost in time with the ancient secrets. Finally, they answered: "What is certainty to us? We are Druids. But this we can tell you:

"A great champion made this ring
and left it to entrap our men.
This is an angry barrier to bring
against kings by one champion.

"Before we travel further, the royal host
must find one to challenge the one
who made this boast. Now, the host,
according to warfare rules, is done

"with travel until one can be found
among us who can skillfully do this day
what this man has done. We have found
no other way to continue on our way."

Fergus laughed and said laconically: "Well. Even pigs make aesthetic choices." He turned away from the breath of winter pouring from the Druids, ignoring them. He looked at Ailill. "You dare
not ignore this challenge and pass this point. If you do, the fury of
the man who cut this *ogham* message will find you wherever you
are: under the protection of a great king or locked behind the
doors of your own homes. Badh herself will not be able to protect
you from him! And if no one can answer the challenge of this hoop,
the man who did this will certainly have killed one of you by
morning if we stay here." He grinned mockingly at Maeve, watching her squirm, as she remembered the heat left by the Forge-
Hound's hands upon the oaken spancel-hoop.

Ailill grimaced at Fergus's news. His belly churned and he leaned
away from his charioteer, discreetly breaking wind. He pressed a
hand against the pain in his belly, pulled at his lower lip, considering the points, then became conciliatory and shook his head.

"This is indeed an ominous message," he said. "I have no desire to see one of our men killed at this time. Let us go through the
neck of the great forest south of here where sorrowful women live,
Fid Dúin, instead of trying to pass here."

The warriors took their great axes and labored hard, cutting a
road through the forest for their chariots. Their efforts were long
remembered throughout history by the name of the place: Slecht
na Gearbat, the Hewn Path of Chariots.

In some of the songs and chants that followed their efforts, it is
told that here, in the forest fortress of Fid Dúin, the warriors saw
the chariot with the beautiful young girl tending the reins of her
horses and it was here, not back in Connacht, that Fedlem gave
her prophecy to Maeve, who did not understand the truth of what
she said. And it is here that the girl said to Maeve when Maeve
asked her to look and see what would become of her army:

"It is too hard. I cannot see them because of the forest."

"Then," Maeve answered, angry that the trees would stand
against her, "this land will become plowed land."

And she ordered the cutting of the forest and the turning of it into crop land. Thus the name of the place has come to be called Slechta.

It is here that the Partraigi, the ancient ones who are the People of the Stag, live.

The army spent the night in Cúil Sibrille, now called Cenannos. When they awoke in the morning, the men discovered a heavy snow had fallen over them that rose to the height of their belts, shrinking their manhood and cracking the wood of the chariot wheels. The snow made it impossible to cook their meal despite the early hour when the men rose, bearded lips pursed in a pout, steam blowing from their nostrils.

But Cúchulainn rose later warm and content from his woman's bed in her lush room. Murals depicting past Ulster triumphs had been painted on the walls and bright drapes and beads hung everywhere, changing the room into a harvest of biffins and crabapples. Huge painted tables and chairs with armrests carved in intricate knots and sworls rested around the room on thick rugs. He took his time scrubbing and scouring himself clean, ignoring the lustful and admiring glances of the woman, before searching out the track of the army.

"I wish now that we had not gone to Fedelm Noichride," Cúchulainn said to Laeg Mac Riangabra, his charioteer. He shivered in the cold, huddling deeper into the thick warmth of his fur-lined cloak.

"Each man chooses his own steps," Laeg said dourly for he had been reluctant to roll from the bed and arms of the bondswoman who had been assigned to him.

"Perhaps," Cúchulainn said. "But who chooses the last?"

"The gods," Laeg said shortly.

Cúchulainn's silver-gray eyes darkened. "We betrayed Ulster with our night visit there for we allowed the army to go through without warning. See if you can discover from their tracks how many passed this way."

Laeg sighed and stepped into Cúchulainn's great Carbad Seardha, his scythed chariot, riding back and forth through the snow, vainly trying to do Cúchulainn's bidding, but failed.

"Their track is very confusing," he confessed, climbing back out of the chariot. "I cannot read it."

"I wouldn't be confused if I tried to follow it," Cúchulainn said. His words were quiet, assured, the words of one who knows his abilities although some would have claimed it boasting as did Laeg, who gave him a long look then gestured to the chariot.

"Get into the chariot, then," he challenged.

Cúchulainn climbed into the chariot, kicking away a bag of brain balls made from the lime-soaked brains of his victims. Laeg climbed in beside him and took the reins of the Gray of Macha and the Black of Saingliu whom only Cúchulainn could tame and Laeg drive. Cúchulainn had many gifts, among them the gifts of beauty and form and build, the gifts of swimming and horsemanship and of playing *fidchell* and *brandub,* and the gifts of battle and fighting, of conflict and sight, of speech and counsel, of birding and destruction. Cúchulainn began studying the track on either side of the scythed chariot. A long time passed as Laeg drove slowly back and forth along the trail.

"You, too, find it hard to determine how many men have passed," Laeg said.

"Perhaps, but it is still easier for me than you," Cúchulainn said. "You forget that I have three talents of sight and much training in matters like this. I have finished. Eighteen troops of three thousand each have passed here, but the eighteenth troop has been split up among the entire army. That is what caused you trouble: the Galeóins are the eighteenth troop."

Cúchulainn ordered Laeg to drive fast around the armies until he reached the stream now called Áth Gabla, the Ford of the Forked Branch. While Laeg held the horses tightly, Cúchulainn cut a forked ash tree with a single swipe of his sword and whittled a point on it, hardening it in a fire, then cut an *ogham* inscription on its side, and with one cast planted it firmly in the middle of the stream, anchoring it so a chariot could not cross the ford on either side. Then he stripped himself naked to wash in the stream.

The warriors Err and Innel, and their two brothers Foich and Fochlam, their charioteers, discovered him doing this and took advantage of his nakedness and challenged him, riding down upon him. Laeg tossed him his great sword and Cúchulainn easily defeated them, cutting off their heads and planting them upon the four points of the forked tree.

Their chariot horses, covered in crimson gore, raced away in terror from the carnage, their noses wildly distended from the blood-smell, galloping hard back to the army, the headless trunks of their owners and drivers red with gore and bouncing in the bottom of the chariots. The Connacht warriors went forward cautiously, fearing a large troop of warriors waited for them at the ford. But when they arrived, they found only the track of a single chariot and the warning tree-fork with the four heads of Err and Innel, Foich and Fochlam, stuck upon the points. Another *ogham* had been cut into the side of the trunk.

They waited until Maeve and Fergus and the Maines and the sons of Mágu came up. Maeve traveled always with nine chariots for herself alone: two before and two behind her and two on each side. In this manner, no clods of earth cast up by the hooves of horses, nor dust raised by chariot wheels, would settle upon her.

"Are these the heads of some of our warriors?" Maeve asked as the Connacht army arrived at the ford. Her eyes widened at the sight of black blood dripping into the crystal waters.

"Yes," Ailill said glumly. "And belonged to four who were among our best."

An *ollamh,* sent to the tree, returned from studying the *ogham* cut into the tree trunk and told Ailill what it said: a single man had thrown the fork into the ford with one hand and forbade the army to pass unless another could be found to duplicate the feat. Fergus, again, was excluded from the challenge.

"Amazing how swiftly these four warriors were killed," Ailill said sourly, examining the bodies, free from cuts save where their heads had been severed cleanly by one blow. He lifted a hand, frozen in death, still clutching a sword and examined the clean edge of the blade. "I do not think they even swung a blow." He belched and made a face and spat, the phlegm spotted with soured wine from the noonday meal.

"You should not be surprised at that," Fergus said acidly. "They were not as great as you think: many of Ulster's boy-troop could have defeated them in single combat. What you should wonder about is how that fork was riven from its trunk with a single stroke (I believe the base was made with a single cut) and driven into the ford like that. The man who did this did not dig a hole to plant it; he threw it with one hand from the back of his chariot."

"Move it out of our way, Fergus," Ailill ordered, reaching for the jug of wine in his chariot. He rinsed his mouth and spat.

Fergus shook his head in annoyance. "To do that would not be honorable. The challenge has been made and one should answer the challenge."

"We do not have time for such nonsense," Ailill said harshly. "Move it out of our way."

Again, Fergus tried to warn Ailill that to do so would bring dishonor upon the Connacht army, but Ailill refused to listen to him. At last, Fergus shrugged and said, "Then give me a chariot, and I will take the fork out and insure that the base has only one cut upon it."

He stood up in the chariot and whipped the horses forward, but the tree was anchored so firmly that the wheels of the chariot ripped off the wicker cage when he tried to pull it out. The tree was so deeply planted that fourteen chariots broke down under Fergus.

"That's enough!" Maeve snapped. "If you weren't with us, we would probably be on our way back home now with the Brown Bull on our lead."

Fergus gave her a long, level look that drove deeply inside her, then called for his own chariot. He hitched the tree to the spear hoop of his chariot, then spoke gently to the huge brown horses, urging them forward. Their mighty muscles rippled under their gleaming coats as they strained against the deeply sunk tree until it slipped from its mooring with a loud *slumph* and slid through the water to dry land. Then, all could see it had been cut from its roots with a single swing of a hero's sword.

"We need to meet in council and discuss among ourselves about what type of people we are nearing," Ailill said as he examined the base of the fork. He ran his fingers wonderingly along its smooth plane. His stomach soured. He grimaced and turned to the others.

"Pitch the tents. All of you prepare your meal," he ordered. "It is time for us to eat for I know that most of you could not prepare a meal last night with the heavy snow falling. Have the warriors make music and then rest. Bring your meal to council for I would hear more of the stories about the people who live before us." Fergus shrugged and turned to direct the setting-up of tents, again having his pitched on the other side of Maeve's, away from Ailill's tent.

It was here, by the ford of Áth Gabla, that many heard for the first time about the feats of Cúchulainn.

"Tell us, then: Did Conchobar do this?" Ailill asked Fergus when the exiled Ulsterman entered his tent. He waited impatiently as Fergus shook the dusting of snow from his cloak and washed his hands and face in a bronze bowl of water. He seized a jug of wine and drained it in one draught, belched, and wiped his lips with the back of his hand.

"Well?" Maeve demanded. Fergus smiled arrogantly at her.

"No, Conchobar did not do that," Fergus answered. "Conchobar would cross the border only with an army of three thousand chariots bristling with arms around him. The man who did this deed is Cúchulainn. He struck the trunk from its base with one stroke and killed the four with the same ease. He is the one who has come to the border with only his charioteer for company."

"One man?" Maeve asked increduously. "What sort of man could do that?"

"A man who makes maidens dream gratefully of the loss of their maidenhead and men to quail in fear from his name," Fergus answered. Maeve's eyes sparked with interest. Ailill grunted in annoyance.

"Tell us about this man, this Hound of Ulster," Ailill said. "How old is he? What sort of man is he?"

Fergus dropped onto a cushion and settled himself comfortably, his thick-muscled legs sprawling out between them, before beginning.

"It is said that he came in his fifth year to Emain Macha in search of arms to serve in Conchobar's boy-troop. When he was seven, he went to study the art and craft of war with Scáthach and court Emer. When he was eight, he took up the call of arms. Now he is seventeen."

"He is the best, then, that they have in Ulster?" Maeve asked. She nibbled her lower lip, remembering the oaken spancel. Fergus grinned at her.

"Oh, yes. He is the strongest. The strongest of all," Fergus said. "You will find no warrior more difficult to defeat. No other sword has a point more sharp than his, the Cruaidin Cailidcheann, and if the point is bent back to its gold handle with rings of silver, it springs back, straight and strong. It can cut a hair on water and sever a man in twain so cleanly one half will not miss the other for a long time. No shield is as strong as his Dubhan, the Black One. And as for his spear, the Gae Bolga, no one can throw it to rip a man apart except Cúchulainn. No sword slashes harder, no raven has more desire for man's flesh, no hand more deft, no warrior more fierce, no one his own age one-third as good, no lion as fierce, no barrier, hammer, gate of battle, no challenger of armies finer than he. No one in Ulster can measure up to him. His youth and vigor, his apparel, horror, eloquence, splendor, fame or form, voice or strength or sternness, cleverness, courage. No one to deliver as many blows in battle, no one with his fire or fury or sense of victory, no one whose presence spells doom as much, no one better at stalking, scheming or slaughter in the hunt, no one as fast or alert or, yes, as wild and no other can perform the battle-feat of nine men on each point. There is no one like Cúchulainn," Fergus said with satisfaction. But Maeve laughed loudly at his description for she did not believe that such a man could ever exist.

"Come now," she said merrily. "You make too much of this. He is only one man with one body. He can still suffer the pains of being wounded. He can still be taken. Besides, you yourself said he was only seventeen. I thought we were talking about a man, but he is only a youth with many manly deeds yet to come."

"It would not be strange for him to do those deeds now," Fergus replied quietly. "You do not understand the ways of warriors despite what you may think." Maeve frowned at him and started to speak, but Ailill shook his head, motioning her to silence. "Why, he had already accomplished several deeds when he was much younger than now that men would have been proud to claim if they could have done them."

And Maeve thought on this and as she thought, the lust rose in her thighs until they trembled. She squeezed them together to keep her desire from showing, pulling her cloak around to cover her lap from its wetness.

"Then tell us this boy-warrior's story," she demanded, reaching for a goblet of wine to wet the sudden dryness in her throat.

Chapter 4

THE TELLING
OF THE
YOUTH OF
CÚCHULAINN

SERVANTS MOVED QUIETLY AMONG the advisors in Ailill's tent, serving fresh and salted pork to those reclining upon cushions along with fish seasoned with cumin, and honey-baked salmon. Ale and mead flowed freely, but some took advantage of wine that had been traded from ships.

Fergus settled himself comfortably. He spat into the fire and leaned back on his elbows upon the rug that had been laid for his comfort. A servant handed him a jeweled cup of spiced wine. He sighed happily: the whole evening lay before him like a meadow. He took a long drink, sighed, belched, smacked his lips with relish, and began:

"Cúchulainn was raised by his father, Sualdam Mac Roich, and mother, Deichtine, Conchobar's sister, in their house of oak on the high, grassy plains of Murtheimne. While still a small boy, he heard stories about the one hundred fifty boy-troop in Emain. It has always been so, you know. Conchobar spends one-third of his day watching the boys at play, one-third in which he plays *fidchell* (he cheats, you know, moving his men when you look away and then pretending he has yet to move when you look back. A trifle, perhaps, but a character fault, nonetheless), and another third drinking strong ale until sleep comes upon him. Ah, Conchobar!" he sighed. "I miss the *fidchell* board and those days! Good days, they were, lazing in the sun beneath the ash tree at the end of the boys' playing field. Honey bees, the soft wind—"

"I hope," Maeve said, interrupting his meditation, "that you do not miss them too much. It would not be good for you if we thought you were deliberately leading us away from Ulster."

Fergus fixed a strong eye upon Maeve. "Do not come upon me with your queenly ways, Maeve! I was a king long before Ailill consented to let you pretend to rule. Aye! Don't be babbling your lips with idle threats! Only a horn blow keeps my warriors from falling upon your Connacht petty prissies and then what army you'd have left wouldn't be enough to empty your piss-pot!"

Maeve started up, but Ailill raised his hand, pain showing between his eyes. "Enough of this bickering! If you wish to stay in the council of warriors, then mind your place," he said to Maeve. He ignored her as she pressed her lips tightly together and leaned back upon her cushions. "And you, Fergus! Ulster warriors are surely better men than to rise to a woman's quarreling words! Get on with your story, man!"

"No greater warrior lives in Ireland than Conchobar," Fergus said slowly, enjoying the sparks coming from Maeve's eyes, for he knew that Conchobar had once been her husband, but it had not been Maeve who had left him despite the Connacht woman's pretense. "And I say this even though he forced me into exile ten blue winters ago. Now, where was I? Oh yes.

"One day, Cúchulainn, lonely with no other children to play with, begged his mother to allow him to travel to Emain Macha and join the boy-troop there.

" 'You can't go that far,' Deichtine said. 'The way is far too dangerous. Wait for the new moon. Some Ulster warriors will undoubtedly be traveling there, then, and you may go with them if you wish.'

" 'I cannot wait that long,' Cúchulainn said impatiently. 'Please: point the direction toward Emain Macha.'

" 'You have to travel to the north,' his mother said at last in exasperation. 'But the road is long and hard and Sliab Fuait is between here and there. You must be very careful when you travel through there as there are many in that area who do not take well to strangers.'

" 'I still will try it,' Cúchulainn answered stubbornly.

"And so he left the oaken home of his parents armed only with a toy shield made from sticks woven together, toy javelin, and his hurling-stick and ball. As he traveled, he played a game by throwing the javelin high in front of him and running to catch it before it struck the ground.

"At last, he came to Emain Macha, high on a hill and surrounded by a deep ditch topped by a palisade of timber. There, he saw the boy-troop playing in the field. Excitement filled him so that he forgot himself and ran up to Conchobar's boys without asking for their pledge of safety. He did not know that no one, not even Conchobar or myself went onto the boys' playing field without first requesting a promise of safety from them. That is the tradition of the boy-troop, you see. One started by Conchobar himself. The pledge teaches respect and manners, you see.

" 'I can see that this youth comes from Ulster, but yet he challenges us by coming among us without permission. He should know better,' said Follamin, Conchobar's son.

"The boys on the field shouted warnings at Cúchulainn, but he ignored them and continued making his path toward them. They threw one hundred fifty javelins at him, but he deflected them with his stick-shield. Then they drove their hurling-balls at him, but he caught them all upon his chest. They threw their hurling-sticks at him, but he eluded every one of them except for those few that he pulled down as they flew past, anger building in him.

"It was now that we saw the man beneath the boy's skin." Fergus's voice became quiet. The others strained forward, trying to catch his words before he spoke them. "The warp-spasm, terrible to behold, came upon him. Each hair seemed hammered down like spikes into his head, the end of each tipped with a fire-spark that burned like brimstone. One eye squeezed shut like the eye of a needle while the other opened as wide as a goblet's mouth. His lips peeled back to his eyeteeth until his gullet showed and his jaws gaped wide to his ears. Then, the hero-halo rose up in a shimmering cloud from the crown of his head and he charged the boys although they greatly outnumbered him. The boys hesitated at the spectacle, then Badb whispered in their ears and they fled in terror from him.

"He knocked fifty of them unconscious to the ground before they got to the gate of Emain. Nine of them flew past Conchobar and myself where we played *fidchell* as if they had wings upon their feet. But he leaped after them over the *fidchell* board, knocking the pieces to the grass. Conchobar caught his wrist as he flew by, pulling him around, but such was his fury that even Conchobar could scarce hold him. I leaped over and grabbed his other arm, holding with all my strength against the rage of the youth. Slowly the warp-spasm left him.

" 'You have damaged some of these boys badly,' Conchobar said sternly when the youth reappeared.

"He pulled free from Conchobar's grasp, saying, 'I am in the right, friend Conchobar. I left my home and my mother and father to join with them, but they did not accept me. They threw their javelins and hurling-balls and hurling-sticks at me. They have only received what they sought to give me.'

" 'Who are your parents? What do they call you?' demanded Conchobar.

" 'I am Sétanta, son of Sualdam and your sister Deichtine,' the boy answered. 'I did not expect to be treated in this manner when I came here. The boys' hospitality is lacking in manners.'

" 'Why didn't you place yourself under protection from the boys by asking them to receive you?' Conchobar asked curiously.

" 'I did not know that was the way things were done here,' said Cúchulainn. He threw his long hair back from his eyes and held himself proudly erect, treating Conchobar as a warrior would. 'But now, I ask for your protection and hospitality.'

" 'Very well,' said Conchobar, trying to repress a smile. 'You may have it.'

"Cúchulainn turned to chase after the boys through the house, but Conchobar again stayed him.

" 'What do you plan on doing to them now?' he asked.

"Cúchulainn gave him a puzzled look. 'Why, I plan to offer them my protection,' he said.

" 'I see,' Conchobar said. His eyes became hard, and when they looked like gray stones, no warrior would dare to ignore his words. 'Perhaps it would be wise for you to offer it here and now. Just in case something should go wrong when you talk with them. Those boys, too, are under my protection.'

" 'I promise,' Cúchulainn said promptly, giving his word.

"And he kept it when all of us went out to the playing field where the foster mothers and fathers of the boys whom Cúchulainn had struck down were helping the wounded boys to their feet."

Fergus took another glass of wine to ease the dryness in his throat from talking. The others waited impatiently, seeing that he had more to tell them about the warrior they were facing. At last, he began again:

"Once, when he was a young boy, he could not sleep at all in Emain Macha. Concerned over his welfare, Conchobar called Cúchulainn, red-eyed and irritable, to him.

" 'Tell me, Cúchulainn, why is it that you cannot sleep here in Emain Macha?' he asked.

" 'I must have the same level under both my feet and my head,' he answered. 'Otherwise, I cannot sleep.'

"So Conchobar arranged for two blocks of stone to be sized and cut and dressed for Cúchulainn and a special bed be built between them for him.

"Tired, Cúchulainn lay down and immediately fell into a deep sleep for it had been a long time since he had last slept. After a while, a man attendant was sent in to awaken him. When the man touched him, Cúchulainn lashed out blindly at him, striking him in the forehead with his fist, driving his forehead back into his brainpan. He threw his arm aside to push himself erect and knocked the stone block flat with his arm."

"That was a warrior's fist. A born-warrior's arm," Ailill mused. Pain flickered over his face. He farted and the hard lines relaxed. He sighed in relief.

"Yes," Fergus answered, leaning back from the smell rising from Ailill's cushions. He absently scratched his chest through his tunic with a horny thumb. "But it was a lesson well learned for from that time on, no one has awakened him. He is left to awaken by himself. It is a *geis* that all must obey.

"Another time when he was playing ball in the playing field east of Emain, he defeated all one hundred fifty boys who had challenged him. He always won," Fergus continued. He twirled his wineglass between thick, calloused fingers. "I watched him work: every time they laid a hand upon him, he would work with his fist, knocking them senseless fifty at a time. When the rest of the Red Branch saw what he had done (myself included, I admit, and Conchobar himself), they rose in fury against him. He ran and hid under Conchobar's bed. We should have left him there, but never had the boy-troop been so destroyed! In anger, we ran after him. When we came into the room, he suddenly straightened up from under the bed, lifting it high and heaving it into thirty warriors, knocking them to the floor, stunning them. The others circled him and bore him back by sheer numbers. But by then, his fury had cooled us and no punishment was given him for we knew that he had been the intended victim of the boy-troop. At last, Conchobar and I made a peace between the boy-troop and Cúchulainn. We had to do this, you see. Otherwise . . ." Fergus shrugged, leaving the rest unspoken. With a sudden movement he took another drink of wine, draining his cup, then held it out to a servant to refill. He sighed and stretched his feet out to the fire. He was getting old and his feet needed to be warmed now and then. He sighed again and scratched his head, frowning as his fingers slid through oily hair. He sniffed the ends of them and grimaced and made a note to have his bondmaids wash it.

"Well?" Maeve said impatiently. "Is that it?" She shook her head, her lips curling in derision. "It appears that this is only a child's tale, a fantasy of a boy who would be a warrior."

Fergus laughed. He reclaimed his cup from the bondmaid and took a large drink of wine, swallowing it in installments. "You know little of what makes a warrior. Much more than playing a woman's game."

She flushed. "I have had many dealings with warriors," she began heatedly, but Ailill interrupted her.

"Yes, yes, yes, yes! But for now, be quiet! We are not here to listen to your bed boasts," he said sternly. "Go on with your story, Fergus."

Fergus nodded, took another drink and stared deeply into the past, rolling his tongue along his teeth, remembering.

"Then, there was the time when Eogan Mac Druthact challenged all of Ulster to a battle. While Cúchulainn slept, the Red Branch answered Mac Druthact's challenge. They were ill prepared for this and soundly beaten. Conchobar and his son Cúscraid Menn Macha, the One Who Stammers, were left for dead with other warriors heaped around them. The wailing of the warriors and the women over the lost battle woke Cúchulainn. He stretched, throwing his arms out, and cracked two stones beside him. Bricriu of the Bitter Tongue saw this so it is true," Fergus added. "He rose and went out to Emain's gate where he met me, covered with wounds." Absently, he ran a thick forefinger down a ridged scar on his heavily muscled forearm.

" 'I am sorry about your wounds. May God help you, friend Fergus,' he said. He looked around, concern frowning from his brow. 'Where is Conchobar?'

" 'I don't know,' I answered, feeling faint from my wounds. I wanted a healer then, and not to spend idle time chatting with a youth.

"So Cúchulainn left me and went out into the black night, turning his steps toward the slaughter field. A *bocánach* flew across the silver sickle moon, cackling. I shuddered as I looked back upon the ground I had just left, black from blood soaking into the earth. Cúchulainn seemed not to notice the ground or smell the fetid stench rising like mist around him. The moans of the dying rose around him like notes from a *cruitire,* a black harper. I thought I saw flames lick in the distance from the fire-breath of a *péist,* but I was feeling faint from my wounds for I am sure now that the *Súil Bhalair,* the Eye of Balor, had fallen upon me during the fighting. Cúchulainn chanced upon a half-headed man bearing half a corpse upon his back.

" 'Help me, Cúchulainn,' the man said. 'I am hurt and carry half of my brother upon my back. Carry it for me awhile.'

" 'No,' answered Cúchulainn.

"He meant to speak more, but the man threw his brother's corpse at Cúchulainn. He dodged the corpse and grappled with the man. They strained against each other, sinews snapping with their efforts, and then the wounded man threw Cúchulainn to the ground.

"I watched this from afar, surprised that a wounded man could best Cúchulainn, but suddenly, I heard a voice: the Badb calling from a pile of corpses: ' 'Tis a poor warrior who lies down at the feet of a ghost!' Whereupon Cúchulainn rose with his hurling-stick in his hand and struck the half-head from the man's body, driving it like a hurling-ball across the plain of battle. And then I knew the man to be an *aithech,* a churl of the Fomorians, lords of darkness and death.

" 'Conchobar!' Cúchulainn yelled, his voice booming across the plain. 'Are you on this field of battle?'

"Faintly, Conchobar answered. He cried out again, but I could not hear his words. Cúchulainn followed the sound of his voice and finally discovered him lying in a trench with earth piled up around him, hiding him in its breastworks.

" 'Why do you walk among the dead on this slaughter-field?'

Conchobar asked painfully. 'Are you trying to learn mortal terror?'

"Cúchulainn did not answer but reached down and pulled him from the ditch. Conchobar gasped with pain as the young boy lifted him from that breastwork of earth. Six of the strongest Ulstermen could not have dragged him from that ditch, but Cúchulainn did it with ease. He lifted Conchobar to his shoulders and Conchobar noted an old *seantán* standing against the dark line of the woods a short distance away and said:

" 'Take me to that shack and light a fire therein for me.'

"And Cúchulainn obeyed, kindling a great fire in the hearth for him. He settled Conchobar before the fire and Conchobar sighed with pleasure for he had grown very cold lying in the ditch with Badb's breath blowing over him, waiting for someone to pull him free.

" 'Ah,' he said. 'Now, if only I had some cooked pork I might find some life within me.'

" 'Then I shall go and get one for you,' Cúchulainn said simply.

"And he left the shack and entered the forest that stood behind the house, searching for a pig among the bramble thickets. He came upon a hard-faced man by a cooking-pit where he roasted a boar while bearing his weapons in his huge hand.

"He struck out at Cúchulainn, but he was no match for the youth. Cúchulainn dodged his first stab, then attacked and killed him easily, driving his fist into the man's brainpan, then used the man's sword to take his head as well as the boar back to Conchobar.

"Conchobar ate the entire boar, then rested for a bit, warming his wounds before the fire. At last, he told Cúchulainn that he was ready to return home. On the way back, they found Cúscraid, Conchobar's son, heavy with wounds. Cúchulainn did not pause, but lifted Cúscraid to his back as well and carried both him and his father back to Emain Macha."

Fergus hawked and spat. He wiped his lips with the back of his hand and combed the snarls from his beard with his fingers, thinking. At last, he smiled.

"I remember another time if you all are not too tired from hearing about Cúchulainn's feats," Fergus said. He glanced around the circle and saw with satisfaction that none expressed a desire for him to remain silent. He grinned and took another sip of wine before beginning.

"Once when the Ulstermen were in their pangs—this affliction was borne by the men only, not the women or children or anyone not from Ulster, which excluded Cúchulainn and his father—no one dared to spill an Ulsterman's blood while they were suffering from their pangs for if one did, why then, the Curse of Sinrith Mac Imbaith would fasten itself upon that one and they would begin to grow old before their time or else die shortly after.

"As it happened, twenty-seven raiders came from the Faichi Islands and broke through the rear gate while we lay helpless with our pangs. The women began screaming as the raiders came upon them, stripping their clothing from them and assaulting them. Naked bodies rolled in the dust, firelight flickering redly from the sweating bodies. Our women fought, but they were no match for the strength of the raiders. The boy-troop heard their screams from their playing field and raced to help them. But when the boy-troop saw those dark men, they ran away. All but Cúchulainn. He did not hesitate, but attacked them with throwing stones from his sling and his hurling-stick. He killed nine of them although he suffered more than fifty wounds himself from their swords and battle axes. When the raiders saw he was still determined to fight, they fled for their lives. And remember: this was all before he was five years old. Small wonder, then, that a man would have such little trouble cutting off the heads of our four warriors, right?"

"Yes," Conall Cernach, one of the listeners, answered. "Yes, we know about the boy, those of us who have followed Fergus into exile. I knew him better than most for I fostered him. It wasn't long after these deeds that he performed yet another."

While Fergus replenished himself with more wine, Conall took on the job of *seanchaí,* the storyteller.

"One day Culann the Smith decided it was time to entertain

Conchobar. You have to remember that under the rules of hospitality, it is only natural and good for each person to entertain his king sometime after Samhain. But Culann had no land or property with which to sponsor the type of feast usually given to Conchobar (he had only what he could earn with his tongs and hammer although a wheelwright is highly valued among the people), so he was forced to ask Conchobar not to bring too many of his *laochra* with him. Conchobar knew this and, thinking kindly of Culann, left with only fifty chariots of his best champions to accompany him. But before he left, he went by way of the playing field to say goodbye to the boys. When he arrived, he saw that Cúchulainn was playing ball against all one hundred fifty boys and beating them.

"When they played for the goal, Cúchulainn peppered the goal with his shots and all were helpless to stop him. When it came their turn to shoot against Cúchulainn, he turned all their shots aside. When they tried to wrestle with him, he pinned all hundred fifty and when they thought to play the stripping game with him, he left them naked while not one could even pluck the brooch that held his cloak to his shoulder.

"Conchobar was truly surprised at this and asked the other boys if they thought there would remain the same differences between their abilities once all reached manhood. All claimed sheepishly that the differences would remain the same so Conchobar impulsively invited Cúchulainn to come with him to Culann's feast.

" 'I would like to finish this game, friend Conchobar. You go ahead and I will follow when I am finished,' Cúchulainn said.

"So Conchobar went on ahead but by the time he arrived at Culann's house, he had forgotten that he had told Cúchulainn to come after him after the boy-troop had finished the game

" 'Are you expecting anyone else to come?' Culann asked. 'I inquire only for politeness for I have a savage hound that takes three chains to hold him back with three men on each chain. I use him to guard my house and will release him outside the gate to guard us while we feast.'

" 'No,' Conchobar said absently, his eye following a round-rumped bondmaid whose saucy eyes spoke bed invitations. 'No one is following me.'

" 'Good,' Culann said. 'Then release the hound to guard our cattle and stock,' he ordered his servants. 'Be certain that you close the gate after, though.'

"The servants did as they were told. Later, when the boy came up the road, the savage hound spied him and set upon him, baying his hunting call, slobber dripping from his huge fangs, madness gleaming from his eyes. But Cúchulainn was still playing with his hurling-stick and threw his hurling-ball up into the air and stroked it, hurling his javelin after it and catching both before they hit the ground. Conchobar and his company heard the savage growls of the hound and rushed to the parapets to see what was happening. When they saw the hound nearly upon the boy, they became horrified, but there was nothing for them to do for they were not able to reach the boy in time to keep the hound from him. The hound leaped for his throat, but Cúchulainn tossed his stick and ball aside and caught the hound by its throat beneath its shaggy head; squeezing the apple flat with one hand and grasping its back through its thick fur with the other, he smashed it against the nearest pillar of the house with such force that its limbs leaped from their sockets. This I saw although some claimed that he had smashed his hurling-ball down through its mouth with his hurling-stick, tearing its guts out its anus. But I tell you that it happened the way I saw: he simply smashed the hound against the pillar as if it were only a mouse from the field.

"The Ulstermen threw open Culann's gates and rushed out to greet him. Some of the warriors leaped from the parapet, so excited were they at this exhibition of strength. Together, they raised him to their shoulders and carried him in triumph to Conchobar, cheering that the son of the king's sister had escaped harm or death.

"But Culann was not happy at the outcome although he remembered the rules of hospitality and made Cúchulainn welcome.

" 'For your mother's sake, you are welcome,' he said. He bowed to Conchobar. 'I am sorry that my feast has turned out so badly. Now my life is wasted and my household is like a wasteland since my hound has been taken away. He meant nothing to you, but he guarded my property and my honor and kept my stock from being taken from me by rogues. Alas! Now we shall be defenseless for I cannot afford the *curadh* to guard my property.'

" 'I am sorry for causing you grief,' Cúchulainn said magnanimously. 'I will raise a pup for you from the same pack that fostered your hound. And until that hound ages enough to become the guard for your property, I will be your hound and guard your property and all of the Murtheimne Plain.'

"These were strong words and from the mouth of another youth would have been taken for boasting and therefore frivolous. But Cúchulainn was sincere and all there could see his sincerity and Culann agreed to his terms.

" 'Then your name shall become Cúchulainn, the Hound of Culann,' Cathbad the Druid said to the youth.

" 'I prefer my own name, Sétanta,' Cúchulainn said, frowning at the Druid. 'Why is it that Druids always want to change a person's name?'

" 'A child bears a child's name until he becomes man enough to carve out his own with his deeds,' Cathbad said. 'Sétanta will remain unknown for it is a name given by a mother while Cúchulainn will live forever in the memory of men,' Cathbad replied.

" 'Then that is a good name, indeed,' Cúchulainn said. And from that day on he was called by his new name.

"So is it any wonder that a boy who could do this in his sixth year could do what he did today to our men while seventeen?" Conall Cernach asked the gathering.

"There was yet another deed," Fiacha Mac Firaba said, taking on the role of storyteller. "Not long after this happened, Cathbad the Druid was staying with Conchobar Mac Nessa, his son, with a hundred studious men at his feet, trying to learn the lore of the Druids from him. (This was always the number that Cathbad taught: when one left, he made room for another.)

"One day during their lessons, a student asked him how that day would bring luck. (As you all know, each day is made for certain things and these things the wise Druids are privy to.) Cathbad answered by saying any warrior who took up arms for the first time that day would find his name enduring in Ireland forever as a symbol of mighty acts and deeds.

"Cúchulainn overheard Cathbad's words and straightaway went to Conchobar to claim his weapons. When Conchobar asked him by what authority he claimed his weapons, he said, 'My friend Cathbad.' "

Fiacha paused, frowning. "That's the trouble with Druids. Always speaking in vagaries," he said.

"They call it wisdom," Ailill said impatiently. "Go on. Or else this story will take the entire night."

Fiacha shrugged and continued. " 'I see,' Conchobar said. Knowing Cathbad to be wise and able to see down the days yet to come, Conchobar gave the boy a shield and spear. But when Cúchulainn tried these out, they broke from his strength. One by one, Conchobar gave Cúchulainn set after set of the weapons that he kept for the warriors who might break theirs, but each set fell apart in Cúchulainn's hands. At last, Conchobar gave Cúchulainn his own weapons and when Cúchulainn discovered how fine these weapons were and how strong they remained in his hands, he saluted Conchobar with his own weapons and pledged himself to him.

"At this moment, Cathbad entered the room and saw Cúchulainn holding his new weapons.

" 'Is this boy newly armed?' Cathbad asked in alarm.

" 'He is,' Conchobar answered proudly. 'He carries my own weapons for none other are worthy of him.'

" 'Then his mother will know sorrow,' Cathbad said, shaking his head.

" 'What?' Conchobar exclaimed. 'Did you not send him to me to receive his arms?'

" 'I did not,' Cathbad said. Conchobar turned in anger to Cúchulainn.

" 'Devil, why did you lie to me?' His lips were white with his anger and his shoulders and legs trembled from his fury.

" 'But I did not lie to you, king of warriors,' Cúchulainn said. 'I overheard him in his instruction with his students when one of them asked him what this day would bring. This was south of Emain Macha,' he said and Cathbad nodded when Conchobar looked at him for confirmation, signifying that it was so. 'It was then that I came to you.'

" 'That is true,' Cathbad said, 'but I think you were so eager to receive your arms that you did not listen to what else I said: that he who does arm himself for the first time today will certainly achieve fame and greatness, but his life will be very short. Very short, indeed.'

"Others might have flinched from this news, but not Cúchulainn. He grinned at Cathbad and said, 'Well, then, that is a fair bargain. I will accept that. I will be content even if I have only one day left on earth. For that is the only immortality that we are given.'

"The next day, the same student asked Cathbad what luck that day would bring for someone.

" 'Who mounts his first chariot today will find his name living forever in Ireland,' Cathbad said.

"And Cúchulainn overheard this, too, and went to Conchobar saying, 'Friend Conchobar, I claim my right for a chariot!'

"And Conchobar, seeing the spirit of the boy, weakened and gave him a chariot. Cúchulainn clapped his hands between the shafts of the chariot and the spars broke cleanly at his touch. He tested twelve other chariots in this same manner until at last, Conchobar gave him his own chariot to use. That one survived the test. Cúchulainn gleefully mounted the chariot beside Conchobar's own charioteer, Ibar by name, who turned the chariot around the courtyard with its right side to the sun to bring luck to Cúchulainn.

"When he had finished making the rounds, Ibar said to Cúchulainn, 'You may step down now.'

"At this, Cúchulainn laughed. 'You may think your horses are precious,' he said to Ibar. 'But I am even more valuable. Take me around Emain Macha now.'

"Reluctantly, Ibar drove the chariot through the gate and down the road at Cúchulainn's urging to where the boy-troop practiced on their playing field. When they saw Cúchulainn in the chariot, they all cheered him and Cúchulainn told Ibar:

" 'Whip the horses forward.'

" 'To where?' Ibar asked.

" 'Wherever the road takes us,' Cúchulainn answered.

"Amused by now at the young upstart, Ibar struck up the horses, pointing their noses down the road. Soon, they came to Sliab Fuait. This was the place that had fallen to Conall Cernach to guard on that day. It was the province boundary where each of Ulster's warriors, those of the Red Branch, are supposed to care for and make welcome all men who come that way with poetry upon their lips and to fight with any others who try to cross the boundary. But it is the place where many evil men come as well for it is the main road to the Red Branch. Conall was there to keep Emain Macha safe from surprise. To be chosen as that guard was a great honor.

"When Cúchulainn arrived in his new chariot, Conall greeted him with the words that one normally used in greeting his friends.

" 'May you be rich in the future,' Conall said. 'May your victories be many and your triumphs great.'

"Cúchulainn stepped down from his chariot and grinned at Conall. 'Friend Conall,' he said. 'Go back to the fort and leave me here to watch for you.'

" 'Well, you might do for looking after men whose lips drip poetry, but you are still too young to challenge warriors,' he teased. 'And,' he added, 'you are lacking the niceties in speech by which friends greet each other. You are not fully a warrior yet.'

"Cúchulainn felt a moment's annoyance, but quickly pushed

down the irritation he felt for Conall. 'Well said, friend Conall! And I apologize if my words were too eager in greeting. But I may never have a chance to challenge warriors. At least,' he added, 'not for a long while. Still, there is a chance, a chance. Let's wander down to Loch Echtra where warriors often camp by the lake.'

"The day was hot and the thought of a cool hour or two spent by the shores of the lake appealed to Conall. He grinned at Cúchulainn. 'Now there is a happy thought,' he agreed.

"They set off in their chariots, Cúchulainn in his while Conall put his horses next to those of Cúchulainn. Cúchulainn played with his sling, bouncing stones off stones, off trees, knocking a hornet's nest from an oak, a knob off a blackthorn. Suddenly, Cúchulainn whirled his sling overhead and dashed a stone against the shaft of Conall Cernach's chariot, smashing it. Conall pulled hard on his reins to keep the startled horses from running away. He looked sternly over at the youth.

" 'Why did you break the shaft of my chariot with that stone, boy,' he asked dangerously. Anger glinted from his eyes, but Cúchulainn did not flinch from them.

" 'To test my hand and aim,' he answered. He gestured towards Conall's broken chariot. 'I am sorry that you will have to return to Emain Macha now, friend Conall, but you are fairly useless with that chariot. Go on back and leave me here in your place as guard.'

"For a moment, Conall was tempted to take the boy's chariot from him, but something about Cúchulainn made him withhold the sharp retort threatening to erupt from his lips.

" 'If I must, I must,' Conall growled.

"While Cúchulainn continued on with his journey, Conall lashed the chariot's shaft together with leather lacings and slowly drove back toward Emain Macha.

"When Cúchulainn got to Loch Echtra, he was disappointed to find no one there. His charioteer hid his grin behind his hand and pretended to be as disappointed as the youth. He sighed and slapped the reins against the horses and shook his head.

" 'Well,' he sighed. 'I guess there is nothing else for it but to go back to Emain Macha.' He glanced up at the sun. 'If we hurry, we might get back for the drinking.'

" 'No,' said Cúchulainn. He pointed to a blue mountain in the distance. 'What is that peak called?'

" 'Sliab Mondairn,' the charioteer said glumly, realizing that Cúchulainn had no plans for a quick return. 'Most men try to avoid it.'

" 'Take me to it,' Cúchulainn ordered.

"His charioteer whipped up the horses and they traveled across the dusty plain to the mountain. When they arrived, Cúchulainn looked up and saw a large pile of white stones on top of the mountain. He asked the charioteer what they were.

" 'That is where a watch usually stands,' the charioteer answered. 'It is called Finncarn, the White Cairn.'

" 'And the plain below?' Cúchulainn continued, turning to his left.

" 'Mag mBreg, Breg Plain,' the disgruntled charioteer answered. 'Many battles have been fought there.'

"Cúchulainn carefully turned, numbering the forts and watchtowers between Temair and Cenannos. He made the charioteer tell him about all the fields and fords and homes and forts that could be seen from their vantage point. At last, he came to the fort of the three sons of Nechta Scéne who bore the names of Foill the Deceitful, Fannall the Swallow, and Tuachell the Cunning who were born from the Scéne River mouth. Fer Ulli, the son of Lugaid, was their father and Nechta Scéne their mother. They bore a grudge against the men of Ulster for members of the Red Branch had killed their father. Cúchulainn knew their names and stories for he was a bright pupil when the *seanchaí* told of battles and glory while *cruitire* played their harps.

" 'Those are the ones who claim to have killed as many Ulstermen as are now living?' Cúchulainn asked. The excitement of battle began to surge through his veins. His hands trembled and the flesh on his inner thighs quivered.

" 'They are the ones,' the charioteer said grudgingly. He did not

like the way Cúchulainn quivered beside him or the drumming
of his fingers upon the chariot rail. Secretly, he tugged at the left
rein, causing the off-horse to dance nervously, turning the chariot
away from the three sons of Nechta Scéne.

" 'Take me to them,' Cúchulainn ordered.

" 'Do you think it is wise to be courting danger alone?' Ibar
asked. Cúchulainn turned his head, staring at him. His irises
seemed to expand and Ibar felt his will leave him, falling into their
depths.

" 'We are not looking for trouble,' Cúchulainn said quietly. 'But
neither will we avoid it if it should come toward us. We are of the
Red Branch of Ulster and we will not shame that house by leaving before we have had words, pleasant or otherwise from them.
They have the obligation of hospitality upon them.'

"Ibar reluctantly turned the gate-horse and drove toward the
stronghold of the sons of Nechta Scéne. He tried to take the road
that would have led past their watchtower and the road upon
which they had pledged free travel, but Cúchulainn quietly corrected his direction. He turned the horses to where the bog and
river met, south and upstream of the stronghold. They came upon
the pillar-stone on which the three sons of Nechta Scéne had hung
their spancel-hoop of challenge. Cúchulainn took it from the pillar-
stone, read the *ogham,* then curled his arm around his waist and
uncoiled and threw the hoop far out into the river where the swift
current could carry it away from the pillar-stone, challenging the
three sons to mortal combat.

"The three sons had observed this and started down from their
stronghold toward him. Cúchulainn did not wait on them, however; he lay down by the pillar-stone to rest, telling Ibar not to
awaken him unless all three came.

" 'If one or two come, do not bother to wake me,' he ordered.
'But if all three come, then you may awaken me. But do so carefully, standing well back,' he cautioned. And Ibar agreed, for he
well knew about the *geis* of Cúchulainn governing that he should
not be awakened by anyone.

"Ibar watched fearfully and silently cursed Cúchulainn as a rash boy as the three sons neared them. He knew the stories about them, about their bloodletting and the terror they brought upon their foes when the battle-seizure came over them and their weapons became covered with blood-red gore. He knew also that they not only killed warriors who challenged them, but the charioteers of the warriors as well, adding their heads to those that ran around the parapets of their stronghold. When black clouds gathered over the stronghold, the spirits of the dead heroes spoke from the severed heads in wails that chilled the blood of all. Nervously, he yoked the chariot, the coupling rings slipping with nerve-racking frequency from nerveless fingers suddenly as clumsy as stone. As the three sons neared, he carefully pulled off the skins and coverings that Cúchulainn had arranged over himself, marveling at the youth calmly sleeping upon the deep, soft grass, oblivious to the threat coming upon him.

" 'Who is it that sleeps at our approach?' the first of the three demanded fiercely as they came up to Ibar.

"He trembled at the battle-stench rolling from them, but forced his fear down and away, trying to dismiss Cúchulainn's throwing of the spancel-hoop of challenge into the river as the frivolous actions of a vainglorious boy who saw himself as a hero with a man's laurels draped around his shoulders.

" 'Oh, no one,' Ibar said carelessly. 'Just a little boy who has been allowed out in his chariot for the first time today.'

"The three laughed at this. One arrogantly stepped forward and looked at the sleeping Cúchulainn. He turned and sniggered, pointing down at the youth whose face, free of wrinkle and whisker, remained serene and peaceful.

" 'This is not a way for him to become a warrior,' he said, adding carelessly, 'His luck is gone if he remains here.' He laughed and gestured away toward Ulster. 'Take him and leave our lands and do not bring your horses here again to graze our grass.' He grinned at the others. 'It is a good day to be gracious. We owe a life now and then to the gods.'

"Ibar stretched forth his hands, showing the tail of the reins slipping through his fingers. 'I have the reins, here,' he said. Then he felt ashamed of his eagerness to be away from the three sons. 'Why should you act this way toward us? Look: the boy sleeps like a boy should. Why should you expect him to be a warrior when no beard sprouts from his chin?'

" 'Because this is a boy different from other boys,' Cúchulainn said, leaping to his feet. 'This is a boy who came to fight!'

"The warrior who stood beside him laughed loudly, the sound of his laughter ringing off the dark pine-draped hills surrounding the ford. A cloud moved over the sun, changing its glow from gold to blood red as if Lugh was smiling upon the boy.

" 'This is a barefaced boy who wishes to be a warrior,' the warrior said. He prodded Cúchulainn in the chest with a thick, greasy forefinger. Foul breath wafted over his rotting teeth. 'It will be a pleasure to teach him a few manners.'

"Cúchulainn laughed, but in his laughter could be felt politeness. He leaned back from the cloudy breath and grinned. 'If you are willing, my wishes may make themselves known in the ford. There,' he said, pointing.

"Ibar nudged the young warrior, whispering, 'Be careful with him. He is called Foill because he is very wily in the ways of the warrior. If your first thrust does not kill him, you may spend the rest of the battle thrusting in vain at him.'

" 'I swear by my people's oath that he will not use his tricks to his advantage today,' Cúchulainn said grimly. 'Nor will he use his tricks on any more Ulstermen! When Duaibhseach, Conchobar's broad spear, leaves my hand, he will feel it and my strength and think it to be that of an outlaw!'

"And Cúchulainn unleashed his heavy spear with all of his might. Foill tried to dodge, but so swiftly did the spear fly that it had pierced him and broken his back while he was still thinking which of his many warrior tricks to employ against the youth in front of him. Cúchulainn gave a shout of triumph and immediately claimed his trophies, taking Foill's head with a single swordstroke.

"A shout of anger rose from the other two and the thin one moved swiftly towards Cúchulainn. His face contorted in fury as he banged his sword against his shield. Foul epithets roared toward them.

" 'Be careful as well with this one,' Ibar warned. 'His name is Fannall and he is light upon the water as if he were a swallow or a swan.'

" 'That trick, too, will not be used upon any Ulstermen after today,' Cúchulainn said. 'You have seen how lightly I walked the pool in Emain Macha.'

"They met in the ford and Fannall danced lightly upon the water, but he was not as light as Cúchulainn and the boy killed him easily and took away his trophies including his head.

A battle scream rose from the thin lips of the third. He roared down up then, a battle-ax swinging in his hand. Grim lights danced from its red-stained edge.

" 'This one,' Ibar said hurriedly, taking heart at the skill of Cúchulainn he had seen displayed that day, 'is called Tuachell and he lives up to his name: he has never been touched by any weapon. He is the cleverest of the bunch.'

" 'Then I will use the *del chliss* on him,' Cúchulainn said. 'That is a wily weapon itself and will red-riddle him before he can attack.'

"And Cúchulainn's weapon split Tuachell in twain and he died looking at his guts pooled around his feet. Cúchulainn went up to him and cut off his head, taking his weapons as trophies as well. He brought them back and gave them to Ibar to attend.

"Suddenly a scream rent the air behind him from the mother of the three, Necta Scéne, as she drove toward them. Madness flared from her eyes, her red mouth gaped wide in blood fury. Cúchulainn took the three heads into the chariot with him, saying:

" 'These heads will remain with me until we reach Emain Macha.'

"Ibar whipped the horses, turning the chariot toward Emain Macha. Cúchulainn laughed and said, 'You promised us the best driving among all the charioteers. I think we'll need it now, with Necta Scéne chasing us.'

"Ibar looked over his shoulder at the nearing chariot of Necta Scéne and uncurled the lash over the backs of the horses, not touching them, but letting them know the whip was there. They traveled toward Sliab Fuait and so rapid was their flight across Breg Plain that the horses overtook the wind and birds flying above them. Cúchulainn could unleash a stone from his sling, stunning one and catching him before he hit the ground. Slowly, Necta Scéne fell farther and farther behind until, at last, she sadly gave up the chase and turned back to care for the bodies of her children lying bleeding and headless upon the ground.

"When they arrived at Sliab Fuait, Cúchulainn saw a herd of wild deer in front of him and told his charioteer to stop. Ibar quickly brought the horses to bay, speaking softly to them until they stopped their impatient dancing upon the earth.

" 'What kind of cattle are those beasts who seem to dance upon the air?' he asked.

" 'Not cattle, but wild deer,' Ibar said.

" 'How would the Ulstermen like to receive one? Dead or alive?' he asked.

" 'Every one of them has brought home a dead one,' Ibar said. 'That is not so unusual. But a live one, well, that would give them pause for thought. But it is senseless to talk like this: no one can catch them alive.'

" 'I can,' Cúchulainn said, and so simple was his speech that Ibar did not doubt him. 'Use your goad upon the horses and drive them over the bog.'

"Ibar whipped up the horses and drove them until the wheels of the chariot sank deep into the bog and the mire reached near the shoulders of the horses. Cúchulainn stepped out of the chariot, treading lightly, and caught the stag nearest him, the most handsome of all. He drove the horses from the bog and calmed the frightened stag before lashing him between the rear shafts of the chariot.

"Next, they saw a flock of swans and again Cúchulainn asked which would be better, to bring the swans with them to Ulster alive or dead.

" 'Only the most expert take them alive,' Ibar said.

"Immediately, Cúchulainn threw a small stone at the swans and brought down eight of them. He threw a bigger stone and brought down twelve more, using the stunning-shot both times instead of the killing-shot.

" 'All right,' Cúchulainn said with satisfaction. 'Now gather our birds. I would gather them except if I do, I am afraid that this wild stag will turn upon you and try to free himself.'

" 'But I cannot go,' Ibar said, trying to keep the horses from bolting. 'These horses are so maddened that I will not be able to get past them. The rims of the chariot wheels are too sharp for me to climb over and the horns of the stag fill the space between the chariot's shaft. I cannot get past him.'

" 'Then step out onto his antlers,' Cúchulainn answered. 'I will fix him with a stare that will frighten him so that he will not move.'

"And this he did. Cúchulainn took the reins from the charioteer's hands and tied them to the chariot rail while Ibar gingerly walked over the deer horns and gathered the birds. Cúchulainn tied the swans to the leather thongs used to tie weapons to the chariot and in this manner, they returned to Emain Macha with the swans fluttering above their heads, a wild stag docilely following behind, and the three heads of Necta Scéne's sons securely lashed to the rim of the wicker chariot.

" 'A man advances upon us in a chariot!' cried the watch. 'There is such a fever upon him that he will spill the blood of the entire court.'

"Now, you may think that Cúchulainn was showing bad manners when he turned the left side of the chariot toward the city in brazen challenge, but the blood-lust was still upon him and he did not know that they had arrived at Emain Macha.

" 'I swear by the oath of the Red Branch that I will spill the blood of everyone in this court unless someone is sent to fight me!' he yelled. Ibar tried to calm him, but such was the battle-fury that Cúchulainn could not hear his soothing words, wrenching the reins from the charioteer's fingers and tumbling him from the chariot with a well-aimed kick.

"Conchobar, who had run to the wall at the watch's shout, could see the tremor of battle upon Cúchulainn and the foam of madness around his lips. But he also remembered the youth's shyness when in the presence of women and he turned to his court, ordering all of the women to strip themselves naked and go out to the young warrior.

At first, the women were reluctant to do this, but when they were told the young warrior was Cúchulainn, they eagerly tore their clothes from their bodies, exposing their breasts and the dark triangle of their lust. They raced through the gates, laughing and calling to Cúchulainn with Scandlach, the wife of Conchobar Mac Nessa, she whose body builds strong lust in the most celibate of warriors, leading them, dancing lightly across the grass to Cúchulainn's chariot.

" 'Then come and fight with us!' Scandlach laughed. 'Here are warriors worthy of the spear between your legs to battle you!' She pulled her long hair high over her head, large breasts bubbling, wide hips shaking saucily. Nubile women, maidens and wives, danced around him, red and gold and black beards winking with pleasure at him.

"Immediately, Cúchulainn hid his face from them and they tore his tunic from him, stripping him when no other had been able to, and when his manhood became apparent, they paused in wonder, mouths slackening with eagerness. The warriors of Emain Macha took advantage of the moment and seized him, plunging him into a vat of cold water to clear the fire of battle-lust from his veins. The water boiled and the vat burst from the sudden heat of the water. The warriors seized him again and thrust him into yet another vat. The water boiled with bubbles the size of the strongest warrior's fist. Again they thrust him into a vat of cold water and this time, the water rose to his temperature, but no higher, and the blood-lust left him and he saw where he was and that he was naked. He tried to hide his nakedness against the shouts of laughter and crude invitations as to what to do with the man-sized pole between his legs. The women looked enviously upon him, their loins becoming weak as they considered his seven toes on each foot and seven fingers on each hand, the seven pupils in his royal eyes and seven gems sparkling from each, and four dimples showing deeply in each cheek: blue, purple, green, and yellow. His hair hung behind, bright yellow like the top of a birch tree.

Scandlach hip-swayed her way to him, men wistfully eying her naked beauty and envying Conchobar. She gave Cúchulainn a green, hooded cloak threaded with gold to hide his nakedness, with a silver brooch to clip it to his shoulder.

"Then he was taken to Conchobar and took a seat beside Conchobar's knee, signifying his devotion to the king and he has held this seat ever since.

"Now, I ask you," Fiacha Mac Firaba said, "if one who could do this in only his seventh year would find it easy to triumph over our warriors today when he is fully seventeen years old?"

And Maeve breathed deeply at his words, envying the women of Emain Macha.

Chapter 5

DEATH STALKS THE CONNACHTMEN

ALL REMAINED SILENT LONG after Fiacha Mac Firaba's words had joined the air. At last, Ailill broke the trance into which all had fallen with the tale of Cúchulainn.

"That is, indeed, a fine story," he said. He paused to clear his throat. He rubbed his hand across his forehead, his vision suddenly blurry, and he realized he had drunk more than he realized. "We can see the greatness of this warrior who opposes us. But now, let us leave."

But they had to wait until morning, and that night it snowed again, the drifts piling up against the sides of their tents. Then, as abruptly as it began, it quit and when they stepped out from their tents into the cold, early morning, the sun, a blood-red ball, hung ominously in the opalescent light. Tiny crystals filtered through the air. The warriors labored to breathe in the fairyland surrounding them. Dark mutterings rose.

"The *Tuatha Dé Danann . . .*"

Fergus moved among them, prodding them with his goad, pushing them, cajoling them, cursing them and their superstitions although secretly promising himself to leave a copper armband at the next hollow hill they found to guard against mischance.

"Ah now, boys!" he wheedled. " 'Tis only morning frost, nothing more! If the Badb now had been doing the asking—or the Mórrigán," he added hastily—"why then your heads would already be dangling like the Donn's balls from the wicker rail of his chariot! Break camp now! Marching will warm your blood and tighten your bellies!"

And, grumbling, they went to Mag Muceda, the Pig-Keeper's Plain, and found that here, too, they could not escape Cúchulainn, who had cut down an oak tree and laid it in their path, cutting an *ogham* message into its side with his sword: "No one may pass this oak until a warrior leaps it in his chariot on his first try."

"Make camp," Ailill ordered resignedly.

"No horse will leap that thing except that blasted Gray and Black of his'n," Dubthach said sourly. He hawked and spat. "Mark my words! Easier to find acorns on an ash tree than find a nag in this bunch to scale that!"

"It'll take two," Fergus corrected absently, gauging the distance with a practiced eye.

"All the more," grumbled the Beetle of Ulster. He held his nose between thumb and forefinger and blew delicately onto the ground. "I got a bad feeling about this."

"You got a bad feeling about everything," Fergus said.

The Connachtmen pitched their tents and set to, trying to leap the tree. Thirty horses died in the attempt and thirty chariots were smashed. The place has been called Belach nAne ever since. At last, they reluctantly gave up trying to leap the oak and waited until morning when Maeve called Fraech Mac Fidaig, one of the greatest of the Connacht warriors, to her tent.

"Fraech," she said. "We must find a way around this obstacle that has been placed in our path. Since none among us can seem to leap over the oak, I want you to take your chariot, find Cúchulainn, and challenge him to mortal combat. If you defeat him, then we may pass this *ogham* without worry. And, if you do this for me," she said, wetting her red lips with her tongue so they glistened in the dim light of her tent, "then you shall have the thanks of my bed."

Excited about the possibility of lying in the white arms of Maeve, Fraech of the Weak Chin left her tent and found nine others willing to accompany him in his search for Cúchulainn. Together, they set out and after a short time of searching along the riverbank, they discovered the young man washing himself in the river. He appeared slim, his youth so evident that Fraech took heart in his challenge.

"Wait here," he said to his fellow warriors. "This is definitely to our advantage. I will attack him while he is in the water. He may be strong on land, but the advantage will be all mine there."

So saying, Fraech stripped himself naked, exposing his brawny chest to the early morning sun, and entered the water, wading up to Cúchulainn. The youth smiled as he watched the warrior approach and said:

"That's close enough, my friend. If you come any closer, I will consider this a challenge and then be forced to kill you. More's the pity," he added politely.

Fraech laughed at the youth's brashness and said, "Despite your words, I intend to come closer. I'm afraid you'll have to fight me," he taunted.

"Then," Cúchulainn said magnanimously, "choose how you wish to fight."

Fraech paused at this and carefully eyed the youth, noting his stature. He remembered the stories told about the youth's expertise with weapons and said, "Let us fight without weapons; my strength against yours."

He leaped immediately after his words upon the youth and they clasped each other fiercely, muscles straining to throw the other beneath the water's surface. Fraech tried an old trick, but Cúchulainn knew the counter to it and Fraech went under. Cúchulainn held him for a minute under the water, then pulled him gasping and sputtering to the surface by his hair the color of milk-weed pods.

"Now, will you yield and let me spare your life?" Cúchulainn asked. But Fraech felt humiliated, having lost to the youth after his boasting words to his fellow warriors and refused to yield.

"No," he gasped. "Not in a pig's arse! I am not through yet."

And he strained again against the youth's muscles, but Cúchulainn thrust him again beneath the waves and held him there until Fraech's lungs filled with water. That ford is still called Áth Froich.

Cúchulainn pulled the limp body of the warrior up and carried him to dry land and turned him over to his followers. Silently, they carried him back to their camp where the entire company raised lamentations and wails at their champion's death. Then they saw a group of women dressed in forest-green tunics, white legs shimmering in the soft light, coming to gather Fraech's body, and they recognized them as the women of the *Sídhe*. They gave a great cry as the women silently gathered Fraech's body and bore him away into the *Sídhe*. The hill where they took him has been called Síd Froich to this day.

At that moment, the bearing away of Fraech, Fergus grimly gathered his reins and leaped his chariot across the oak tree.

According to some, the Connachtmen left Síd Froich and went to Áth Meislir where Cúchulainn slew Meslir and five other warriors while others claim that they went to Áth Taiten where Cúchulainn killed six Dúngals of Irros. It does not matter for the feats of Cúchulainn were so numerous against the Connachtmen that six here or there are of little consequence. Wherever it was that Cúchulainn slew the six, the army eventually arrived at Fornocht, the Naked Place, where Maeve set her young hound, Baiscne, after Cúchulainn who tore the hound's head from his shoulders with a stone from his sling. This place is still called Druim Bais-cne.

Angry at her hound's death, Maeve turned upon those around her, shaming them as Cúchulainn drove away in his chariot.

"Why do you wait here, lolling in your chariots instead of chasing after this demon that kills all of our best?" she demanded.

Stung, they put the goad to their horses and raced recklessly after Cúchulainn over high plains and stones until their chariot shafts split. The next day at a place called Támlachtai Orláim, Orlám's Burial Place, just north of the Dísert Lochait sanctuary, Cúchulainn, looking for wood to repair his own chariot, came upon the charioteer of Orlám, one of Ailill and Maeve's sons, cutting wood-shafts from holly.

"What are you doing here?" Cúchulainn asked, mistaking the charioteer for an Ulster warrior. "Are there more Ulstermen here in advance of an army?"

"Ergh. None of them be dirtying their hands with ax and adz," he said derisively. "More to find them in their tents dreaming of diddling. I'm cutting wood-shafts for the chariots we smashed chasing that running deer, Cúchulainn," the man explained. He chuckled, the sound like dust. "Please help me with them. You can do either cutting or trimming."

"I would rather trim," Cúchulainn answered. He took the holly-shafts the other had cut in his hand and drew them through his clenched fist, stripping them clean of knot and bark. The charioteer watched this in awe.

"This is not the way one normally trims branches," the charioteer said.

"Who are you?" Cúchulainn demanded.

"Fertedil, Orlám's charioteer," the man replied, jerking his thumb to where Orlám lay sleeping under an ash tree. "He is a son of Ailill and Maeve. And who are you?"

"The running deer you called Cúchulainn. But you do not need to worry," he added quickly as the other blanched at his words. "I have no quarrel with charioteers."

Cúchulainn then awakened Orlám and after a short fight, slew him, cutting off his head. He lifted Orlám's head high and shook it in warning at the Connachtmen below the brow of the hill upon which he stood, then placed the head upon Fertedil's back and said:

"Carry this back to your camp like I have placed it. If you do not," he warned, "then I will strike you with a stone from my sling."

"Now, hold that stone tightly," the charioteer whined. "I'm only him that does what he's told. They snaps their fingers and I jump. Don't ask where, just jump." But he followed Cúchulainn's orders until he neared the camp and came upon Maeve and Ailill. Then, he disobeyed Cúchulainn and took the head from his back and told Maeve and Ailill what had happened to their son. Maeve looked at Ailill and shook her head.

"This isn't at all like catching birds," she said.

"Did you think it would be?" he asked, annoyed that she would be so careless as to underestimate Cúchulainn.

"I did not think one warrior, and a boy at that, could cause so many problems for us," she answered.

"And he told me," Fertedil broke in anxiously, "that if I didn't carry Orlám's head on my back all the way into camp he would strike me with a stone."

His words registered upon his own ears and he looked fearfully around from where he stood between Ailill and Maeve outside the camp. At that moment, Cúchulainn hurled a stone from his sling, shattering the charioteer's head. His brains spattered those around him and he fell dead to the ground. He was one of the few charioteers that Cúchulainn killed, for only those who did wrong felt the warrior's wrath.

When Cúchulainn returned to the ford, three sons of Gárach waited for him: Lon, called the Blackbird, Ualu, called the Prideful, and Diliu, the fiercest of them all, called the Torrent. Three charioteers also waited for him: the three foster-sons, Meslir, Meslaech, and Meslethan, who couldn't bear the thought of Cúchulainn killing two foster-sons of the king and a son by blood, lifting the head of the latter and shaking it in insult at all. Between the six, they had decided to rid the Connacht host of the scourge of Cúchulainn by defying the rule of fair fight and all attacking him at once. They had even cut three chariot shafts of aspen to affix to their chariots that all might come at him at the same time from different directions, hoping to confuse him and striking before he realized what was happening. But their plans went for naught: Cúchulainn killed all six.

Following this, Cúchulainn swore an oath in Methetaht to hurl stones at Ailill and Maeve whenever he found them within range of his sling. The next day, he hurled a sling-stone south across the ford of the river and tore the head off Maeve's pet squirrel as it sat next to her neck, chattering softly into her ear. Blood spattered her white cheeks and ran down between her heavy breasts, soaking into the fine gown of white she had chosen for the day. That place became known as Méide Tog, the Squirrel Neck. This saddened Maeve and the next day when Ailill's pet falcon sat on his shoulder, Cúchulainn tore its head off, too, with a sling-stone, splattering his dark beard with blood. The host named that place Méide ind Eóin at Áth Srethe, Bird-Neck Ford. That afternoon, Reuin drowned in the lake that is now named after him.

Infuriated, Ailill went to see his sons, the Maines, saying, "He cannot be far off if he can do these deeds with his sling. Find him! And bring back his head!" His stomach burned and he clutched it, glaring at his sons, belching in pain.

Stung, the Maines rose to search out Cúchulainn, only to fall back as Cúchulainn smashed one in the head, pulping his brains, with a stone from his sling.

"Ah yes," jeered Maenén the Jester. "That was quite the way to rise up against him after all your boasting! Now, if I had risen up against him, why I would have knocked *his* head off with a stone."

And promptly fell dead as Cúchulainn shattered his head as well with a stone.

Ailill pulled the army back from the ford to take stock of the men he had lost: Orlám, first, on the hill which now bears his name; Fertedil, who stood between Maeve and Ailill as they spoke on Orlám's death; the three sons of Gárach on their ford, and Maenén on his hill.

Angered at the deaths, Ailill seethed for a long moment, then said hotly: "Dagda's Balls! I swear that I will cut in two any man who speaks lightly of Cúchulainn from now on. Let us bypass this place and travel by day and night until we arrive at Cuailnge. If we wait on this man, he will easily kill two-thirds of our army."

The Connachtmen then rose up and made haste. While they were readying themselves for traveling, the harpers of Caín Bile, who were Druids of great knowledge, came out of the red waterfall at Es Ruaid to soothe their spirits with their magic songs. But the warriors did not recognize them, and thinking them to be Ulster spies, chased after them, roaring challenges, until the shape-changers formed themselves into deer and fled far to the north among the Liac Mór stones.

Lethan, raging Cúchulainn's slaying of his foster-son Meslethan at Áth meic Gárach, waited at the ford of the river Níth in Conaille to challenge him, but his wait ended in his death as Cúchulainn easily slew him, cutting off his head and leaving it with its body. They called that ford Áth Lethan from that time on. In the ford before Áth Lethan, so many chariots were shattered in the rear guard when Cúchulainn caught up with them that it became called Áth Carpat, the Ford of Chariots. On the small shoulder of land that lies between these fords, Mulca, Lethan's charioteer, fell when he wheeled his chariot insultingly to place the left side toward Cúchulainn. Now it is called Guala Mulchai, Mulcha's Shoulder.

Slowly, Cúchulainn whittled down the massive Connacht army as it fled across Breg Plain toward the home of the Brown Bull,

sending many warriors to their graves and giving names to places
that had no names before.

Now, Mórrígan, the goddess of war, came to a standing stone in
Temair Cuailnge, forming herself into her raven shape and saying to the Brown Bull:

> "Dark One, you seem restless.
> Is it because you, too, guess
> that sons of Connacht daughters
> gather for certain slaughter?
> The old Wise Raven, I see
> the infesting army of enemies
> ravaging our fair fields
> in wild packs, seeking yields
> from our rich green plains;
> warring armies, their feet stained
> with the blood of our host.
> Cattle moan for their lost
> masters while hungry ravens
> rage over Cualinge, craving
> flesh, our sons' death!
> Our kinsmen's death!
> Death! Death! Death!"

And the Brown Bull listened to Mórrígan and moved his fifty
heifers to Sliab Cuilinn with his herdsman Forgaimen following
closely in wonderment behind them after the Brown Bull threw
off the one hundred fifty men who always played on his back,
killing two-thirds of them, tearing a trench through the land of
Marcéni in Cuailnge, the earth flying behind him in great clouts
from his heels.

And behind him came Cúchulainn, following the Connacht
warriors from the loomy waters of Saili Imdorchi until they came

to Sliab Cuinciu in Cuailnge. Cúchulainn killed no one during this time, but when he arrived at Sliab Cuinciu, he swore again that if he ever found Maeve again, he would hurl a stone from his sling at her head.

He tried several times to get to her, but she had learned about Cúchulainn's vow and never left her tent unless her army surrounded her, holding their shields around and over her like a barrel. One day, Lochu, one of Maeve's bondmaids, a favorite of Ailill who took her to bed when Maeve played her night-games, carried an urn down to the river to collect water. Many others went with her and Cúchulainn, thinking she was Maeve, swiftly fired two stones at her and killed her in the place known as Réid Locha, Lochu's level ground, in Cuailnge.

Chapter 6

FROM FINNABAIR TO CONALILLE

ACCORDING TO SOME, THE Connachtmen divided their force at Finnabair in Cuailnge and laid waste to the countryside, torching haystacks and wooden huts, burning fields of oats and rye, in frustration at not being able to kill Cúchulainn or find the Brown Bull. If this is true, it was a most desperate move to take and one that would surely anger Cúchulainn. But a passionate woman thinks more with her loins, and Maeve of the Thirty Men was one of the most passionate. Maeve demanded not only the firing of the fields and homes, scorching the ground where the snow had not fallen, but she demanded that her men bring all the women and boys and girls and cattle in Cuailnge to Finnabair. Even then, she was not satisfied.

"You have still failed," she said angrily, her voice shrilling like a harridan. "Where is the Brown Bull among you? Is there not one man among you who has a mind more than lousewort? Men!"

They drew back, alarmed at her anger, watching while she threw rouge pots and copper perfume bottles, staining the walls of her tent. She smashed a cushion hard against a table, filling the air with goose feathers. At last, the boldest among them stepped forward, saying: "We have tried, Maeve. The gods themselves know this. But we can find no trace of him anywhere in the province. He has vanished."

"How," she said through gritted teeth, her eyes glowing like brimstone, "could a bull, of that size, with ballocks like wheelbarrows and a pizzle like Dagda's spear, simply vanish into the air?"

"Magic," the man said firmly.

"Magic?"

"Magic," he repeated. "Yes, magic. Much magic lies in the country of Ulster. The very stones speak philosophies to those who can listen with the right ears."

Maeve pondered his words for a minute, walking furiously back and forth. At last, she dismissed them and summoned one of her herdsmen, Lothar, who knew more about cattle than cattle did themselves.

"The army cannot find the Brown Bull," she said. "The fools. They claim magic is at work in Ulster. Do you have any idea where he might be?"

Agitated at Maeve's question, Lothar tried to avoid speaking, but she sternly commanded him to tell her what he knew. Shaking with fear (for he well knew her wrath—a silver cup had gouged a chunk of flesh from his forehead in one of her rages), he answered: "Well now, I have heard that on the same night the Ulstermen took to their bed with pangs tearing at their guts, the Brown Bull left with his sixty heifers to Dubchoire, the Black Cauldron in Glenn Gat of Osiers. Mind you," he hastened, shrinking back from the sudden glow springing to her cheeks, "this is only scatterwords, flibbertigibbeting rumors, words passed from the slit trench when men squat to relieve their bowels."

"It's enough," Maeve said decidedly. "There's always smoke where there's fire. If he isn't there, someone will know where he has gone."

She stormed from her tent, yelling for her guardsmen. They hurried to her, shifting back and forth from foot to foot nervously. "Ready yourselves," she ordered. "Pair yourselves and each pair take a shackle of osiers and catch that black-hearted beast. Bring the Donn back to me or leave your head where the Hound can find it. Matters not acorns or thistles to me."

They left, shaking their heads at their orders, for they knew the bull was as fierce and wild as the boy-warrior making war alone upon them, and that is why this place is now called Glenn Gat, the Valley of Osiers. There they found him, mounting one of his heifers, big ballocks swinging like a grainer's basket. Carefully, they drew a circle tight around him, tentatively driving him toward Finnabair.

At first, sated from his mating, the Brown Bull moved sedately with his heifers obediently following, but when he saw the cowherd Lothar at Finnabair, he furiously attacked him, raking out the herdsman's entrails with a long, sweeping hook of his horns. When they smelled the blood steaming upon the ground, the sixty heifers grew wild-eyed, nostrils rolling back to the red membrane, and attacked the camp. Fifty heroes died when they tried to turn the Brown Bull; then he vanished. The others slowly emerged from slit trenches and from behind bushes and rocks, mud and manure dripping wetly from their ears. Sheepishly, they avoided Maeve's eyes as she surveyed them in disgust.

"Well?" she demanded. But none could tell her which direction the Donn Cuailnge took for all had become a part of the sod while he raged through the camp. In disgust, Maeve again turned to her herdsmen and asked them if they knew where the bull had gone.

"He is back in the fastness of Sliab Cuilinn," they said, all eyeing the others to make sure they were in agreement.

So the Connachtmen headed for Sliab Cuilinn, ravaging Cuailnge, scorching the earth where they could, taking the crops and the riches of that place with them, raping the women after killing their husbands. But when they arrived at Sliab Cuilinn, they still could not find the bull.

Now the elements themselves began to oppose them, to fight them, for their cruelty and the senselessness of their battle. Even the river Cronn rose up against them, rising to the heights of the trees, keeping them from passing, and the men began to speak uneasily among themselves, wondering if the gods had placed a curse upon them.

Maeve fumed beside the riverbank, ignoring the half sugges-tions by Fergus, who finally left her in disgust for two bondswomen eager to share his bed, swinging by Ailill's camp stores to snare a bottle of honey-mead made from the first settling of the season.

When morning thrust bloody fingers through the river mist, Maeve ordered some of her warriors to ford the river. Ualu, the most famous of those who had not the wisdom to avoid her black mood, was first to try it. He shouldered a large, flat stone to help him push his way through the raging water, but the river overwhelmed him, stone and all, and he drowned. Later, after the river subsided in its fury, they found his waterlogged corpse, belly-white, and buried him there, covering his grave with the stone he carried. It still stands there beside the road by the river. Lia Ualonn, Ualu's Flagstone.

Here Cúchulainn killed Cronn and Caemdele and a hundred warriors died when they struggled together with Roan and Roae, the first two writers of the *Táin*. And this is why the story was lost for so long until others found it and began its song again. All to-taled, one hundred twenty-four kings died by Cúchulainn's hand beside the river until the army left in despair, traveling up the river until they reached its source.

There they started to cross between the spring that fed into the river and the mountain from where the spring drained when Maeve called them back, electing to cross over the summit itself. This was an insult to the Ulstermen, and the Connacht army, re-membering the boy-warrior's terror, marked their track well, tear-ing up the earth to form the pass Bernas Bó Cuailnge.

The Connacht host went over Bernas Bó Cuailnge, driving all

their cattle before them and trailing their camp behind them. They spent the night in Glenn Dálimda in Cuailnge at the place now called Botha after the huts they built there. The following day they moved to the Colptha River. Here they tried recklessly to force their way across, but it, too, rose up against them, driving them back from its banks and carrying a hundred of their charioteers toward the sea. The place where they drowned is called Cluain Carpat, the Meadow of the Chariots.

The Connachtmen were forced to move along the Colptha River up to its source, then across to Bélat Aliuin. There they passed the night between Cuailnge and Conaille at Liasa Liac, named after the stone shelters the armies built to house their calves. After a brief rest, they crossed to Glenn Gatlaig. There the Gatlaig River rose up against them. Before that time the river was called Sechnaire, but since then the people have called it the Gatlaig, after the osiers the Connachtmen used to carry their calves. From there, they traveled to Druim Féne where they spent the night.

Maeve waited impatiently as they brought their spoils back to her. As they unloaded their tribute from their chariots, she said:

"We must divide up the army again. Our army is too large to advance down one road. Three or two abreast gives the Hound too much of an advantage. And one . . ." She paused significantly, eyeing the men to see if one would rise to the unspoken challenge. None answered. "Well, so be it. Ailill will take half of the army across the Midluachair Road. The rest of us will go with Fergus by way of Bernas Bó Ulad."

"What?" Fergus exclaimed in protest. "That leaves us the most difficult way. We will have to cut a gap through the mountain to move the cattle for they will not be able to go up and over it. That is a way for goats!"

A tiny smile crept over Maeve's lips at Fergus's complaint. She gave him a knowing look and Fergus sighed deeply and turned away. He walked heavily toward the encampment of his men to make the arrangements to lead his men up and over what is now called Bernas Bó Ulad.

Ailill looked from Maeve to the retreating Fergus, noting the familiar rosy blush climbing up the white column of her neck, recognizing the look of familiarity that had been exchanged between them.

Now, Ailill took Cuillius, his charioteer, aside, whispering to him: "Watch Maeve and Fergus for me. Be careful! The old witch is wise and at times, I think Macha herself sits on his shoulders, watching his back. See if you can discover why they are becoming so intimate with each other."

Cuillius waited, pretending to repair the shaft of his chariot, wrapping it with green cowhide, covertly watching Maeve and Fergus as they spoke quietly together. Then they were gone like wisps of mist, and he looked for them, finding them at Cluithre where they had lingered beside the stream alone as the army moved on. Cuillius crept closer, taking pains to walk quietly over the grass and gravel. But his precautions were not necessary: they would not have heard a troop of soldiers driving a herd of cattle before them. He watched as they moved nakedly together, the sun creating a soft halo around Maeve's white body, shining bright off the web of wide scars along Fergus's shoulders and back. Then, he spied Fergus's sword, the In Caladbolg, carelessly tossed on the ground and carefully drew it out of its sheath. He smiled as he crept away and took it to Ailill.

"Well," Ailill said, a smile teasing his lips as he took the sword from Cuillius's hands. "So, this is why Maeve wished to change our plans. Hmm. I wonder if Fergus's sword cries out for its sheath."

"Well, indeed," Cuillius answered. He took the sword from Ailill's hands and held it high in the air so that the sunlight glinted off its sharp edge, creating a rainbow of colors that arched high towards the sun.

"Here is your proof. There is no other way that I could have gotten that warrior's sword unless he was riding the two-backed beast."

"You are right," Ailill said. "There is no way." And they grinned at each other, knowing Maeve's weakness for warriors.

"I suppose there is nothing wrong with this," Ailill said, trying to keep the laughter out of his voice. "I suppose you could say that Maeve is justified in doing this to keep him from leaving."

He took the sword back, hefting it for a moment, considering, then handed it back to the charioteer, saying:

"Keep it oiled and clean, then wrap it in clean linen and place it under your chariot seat. Fergus will not think to look there."

Meanwhile, Fergus, sated from his romp with Maeve, found his empty scabbard. His manhood wilted quickly.

"This is terrible," he said, digging his fingers desperately through his beard. "Terrible, terrible, terrible!"

"What's wrong?" Maeve asked lazily, watching him claw through the brush. Dead leaves flew through the air, a storm of mottled gold and brown.

"I wronged Ailill," he moaned.

"Oh," Maeve said, suddenly uninterested. "Is that all?" She arched her back, throwing her rosy-tipped breasts high toward him invitingly. But he ignored their beckoning, rooting like a maddened boar beneath a blackthorn.

"Stay here," Fergus cautioned. "I must go among the trees for a moment. It may take me a long while," he added. "Piles."

Maeve frowned, not seeing that his sword had been taken. She chewed her lower lip petulantly as he disappeared, taking his charioteer's sword with him. When he was out of her sight, he paused and cut a limb from a white oak tree, quickly carving a wooden sword from it. This is how Fid Mórthruaille, Wood of the Great Scabbard, took its name. He returned to Maeve. She raised her eyebrows at the sight of him fully dressed, the wooden sword in the scabbard by his belt.

"Come," he said roughly. "Dress yourself and let us go back to camp."

"But—" she began.

"It's getting late," he said.

Slowly, Maeve dressed in her garments, teasing Fergus with her white body and the golden red of her lust as she slowly picked up her garments from where they had been thrown in her lust. But Fergus did not respond to her nakedness, pulling worriedly at his beard as he wondered where his sword had gone.

At last, Maeve was ready, and Fergus bundled her roughly into his chariot and drove back to the great plain where the armies had met and made camp. As soon as he discovered their return, Ailill sent for Fergus to play *fidchell*. When Fergus entered the tent, Ailill glanced at his scabbard and broke into a great gale of laughter.

Stung, Fergus answered:

"Better to be laughed at
when anger strikes after the act,
my sword's edge maddened
by Macha's curse quickened
the blood in our pulses to try
our Galeóin swords and fly
ourselves through the dark
driven to meet them, stark
spears flying fast to them,
stark swords clashing with them
while the army leaders stand still
upon the brow of Ness's Boy's Hill
and watch the armies struggle in fury
to slice warriors' necks and bury
their blades deep in their bellies."

Ailill grinned and said teasingly:

"Why are you so wild-spoken
without your weapon? Taking

liberties with a certain royal belly
by a certain ford? Belly slapping belly
in an old dance? Did you work your will
or did she hers? Do Maeve's oaths still
bring tribes of men to hear your luck
in bedding her? Your cries sucked
dry in passion's heat, the desire
of a woman whose lustful fire
no man can satisfy? He who battles
such a woman can only herd cattle."

The blood rose in Fergus's face, but Ailill ignored it, saying: "Now, sit and we will play *fidchell*. I do not care what you do with Maeve. Many others have plowed that field before. You are welcome to bury your sword in her scabbard."

He laughed again and drank deeply from his jeweled goblet, then wiped his lips and said:

"For you play *fidchell* and *buanbach*
better than you make the two-backed
beast. *Fidchell* is far more interesting
with a king and queen each questing
to rule the game with their eager
armies against the other's meager
rank and files. Forming iron companies
around the other's iron companies.
You may think that you may take
my place, but you cannot make
yourself into me despite your thick rod.
Queens and women all like brave men's rods.
The fault comes from their sweet swellings,
like valiant Fergus, with his bellowings
that brings loving lust to his groin.
and lustful and deep-rod-gorings

of women all over Connacht's rich lands
means little despite his many gold bands."

Fergus crossed to the small table and sat and they began to play *fidchell,* advancing the gold and silver men back and forth over the bronze board. After a while, Ailill said:

"You play well, but death should not
come to this sweet king, This is not
to make you think this mad board
is like the mighty Maeve who accords
her charms by whim on who pleases
her the most with lustful teases.
I move against Fergus. There! Take care!
Do not make your move on lust or air."

Fergus glared at him, then forced a laugh and answered:

"A pity, my friend, that we hack
at each other before we act
with rightful speech in public places
while false words make empty spaces
and we play at games of war,
kings killing kings, in mock war."

They played throughout the night, each moving his men fiercely, trying to gain a position. The next morning as light ran bright into the tent, Ailill spoke:

"Before our army one warrior stands
unleashing his deeds upon our bands
of Connachtmen whose bright red blood
pours down from hacked necks in floods
and great men are dark-driven down
into graves the beardless hero found."

Maeve frowned at Ailill, her white shoulders gleaming in the bright light as she brushed the night knots from her hair. She bit her lip at one snarl, then said:

"Might Mac Mata's chariots crash
down from the rocky heights to smash
the beardless hero waiting at the ford
while our men form in mass in accord
to their ranks to carry off women
as they carried off cattle before them?
Do not call down violence just yet
until our weary warriors can get
their needed sleep and dream dark dreams
of slashing swords by the crystal stream
and men's battle-deeds in the murk
where fearful things seem to lurk.
Let them dream of oxen driven
from the fields and women shriven
from their beds as our men turn
from Cuailnge's fields now burned."

Fergus moved restlessly at these words for he knew what such destruction would mean to the Ulster people. He said:

"I can see huge heads stuck
on Cúchulainn's chariot. His luck
will make great-hearted heroes swear
to their people about queens who dare
to make war after a bedside squabble
about riches. Meaningless drivel!"

Stung, Maeve answered:

"Then let it be as you have said.
What Ailill and I argued in bed

has now come to pass. Use the power
Ailill has put into your hands and shower
the waiting foe with our army's yoke
until the beardless hero is broke."

The armies moved onward until they came to the Cronn River. Here, Ailill's son Maine spoke to them, begging to be allowed to race forward to battle Cúchulainn:

"Let me ride swiftly out, Father,
to do fair deeds before going farther.
Let the horned herds stand fast
until I can drive my chariot past
them to the battlefield and sweep
the waiting warrior into the deep."

Fergus shook his massive head, saying:

"Such foolishness will only mean
your beheading by the silver stream.
You are no match for the beardless boy
in whose hands you are a child's toy.
His howls on the plain summon rivers
and shake woods. Brave men shiver
at the sight of his shape-change.
Your death will not make a change
in what will happen. Ailill will be hurt
and Maeve mocked. Deep black dirt
will be the home after our battle
for our enemy's mighty horned cattle."

He paused, his mighty brow furrowing in thought. Then he said: "I think it would be best if I were to lead the Exiles forward to make sure that no one plays foul against the youth. I suggest that

you send the cattle forward, then the armies, and follow us with
the women in the rear."

Maeve shook her head and said warningly:

"Listen well, Fergus! Do not make
any false moves or else your mistake
will be your undoing. Guard well
these cattle or a battle roar will swell
over the Plain of Ai. The army's track
will follow the cattle's track."

Fergus answered heatedly:

"Spare us such shameless talk!
My warriors have never balked
at battle or doing what we swear.
No limp or soft son follows me
to the struggle in Eman. No more
will I strike blows by this shore
for your sake if you send men
breathing down my neck. Then
you will be alone and we will see
who will do your work besides me."

They traveled forward in silence until they came to the ford upon
the Cronn River. There, Cúchulainn came down to meet them.

"Laeg, my friend. I think the Connacht army is here at last," he
said to his charioteer.

Laeg grinned back, saying:

"I promise by the gods to do great deeds
in battle here. We will drive our steeds
well upon the foe. The silver yokes
and golden wheels will be broke

and we will crush the kings' heads.
Our presence will make them dread
coming across our fair lands
with their pitiful warrior bands."

Cúchulainn laughed loudly at this and said:

"Well said, friend Laeg! Now set
our course headlong to them. Let
them feel Macha's triumph and dismay
about our mighty power while I flay
our way across their path
with my vengeful wrath."

Cúchulainn raised his well-muscled arms high. Sunlight glinted
from his warrior's bracelets. He threw back his silver-streaked
hair and said:
"I summon the water to help us, the air and the earth! Bring
now before us the Cronn River:

"Let the waters of Cronn River rise high
for Murtheimne and make our enemies sigh
in dread until our warriors' work is done
high upon Ochaine's mountain in the sun."

And the waters heard Cúchulainn's summoning and rose in
fury high to the treetops.
Maine saw this and the son of Ailill and Maeve forgot the warning of Fergus and forced his chariot out into the forefront of the
army to challenge Cúchulainn. But Cúchulainn met him well in
the ford and killed him there, slaughtering as well the thirty horsemen who followed him and another thirty-two warriors who came
after them into the water.
The army made camp at the ford while Lugaid Mac Nois Allchomaig took a bodyguard of thirty horsemen to talk with Cúchu-

lainn. The youth met him at the ford, greeting him respectfully.

"Welcome, Lugaid," he said. "I regret that you are with the ene-mies of my people. I wish it were otherwise. In fact, if a flock of wild birds grazed among the grains on Murtheimne Plain I would give you a whole one for yourself and share another with you at dinner. If salmon swam up the weirs or through the river-mouths, I would do the same, cooking them with three herbs: watercress, marshwort, and sea-herb. I would also stand with you at the ford in battle."

"I know. I know, beloved son," Lugaid said fondly. "May a wealth of strong men follow you."

Cúchulainn glanced at the warriors with him and said, "I see you have a fine army with you."

Lugaid laughed. "You could hold them back single-handed."

"Perhaps," Cúchulainn said. "If they came one by one against me. I have right and might to help me against them. But tell me, friend Lugaid: do my enemies fear me?"

"By the gods! They do not dare to step away from the camp to piss alone or even in twos, waiting until the bladders of twenty or thirty are swollen enough to go together," Lugaid said, laughing at the thought.

Cúchulainn grinned at the picture Lugaid painted with his words, then said: "Tell them that I have decided to use my sling against them. But I am curious, Lugaid: what is it that you want?"

The smile disappeared from Lugaid's face and he said somberly: "I want you to spare my men."

"I see," Cúchulainn said slowly. He pulled at a lock of his hair for a moment, then nodded and said: "Very well. I promise that I will spare them, but they will have to have a sign among them so I know them from the others. I will do the same for my friend Fer-gus if he will place a sign among his men as well. And," Cúchu-lainn added, feeling magnanimous, "you must tell the healers that they, too, will be safe with a sign—provided that they swear to use their powers to save my life if I have need of them. And," he added, "send me food at night. But do not let others join you who are not your men."

"This I promise," Lugaid said and turned away from the boy-warrior to make his way back into camp. He found Fergus in Ailill's tent and drew him aside to tell him about Cúchulainn's words. Ailill frowned at this.

"Why are you two whispering?
Our men are steadily disappearing
one by one although Maeve's needs
inspire some men to attempt great deeds.
So. The youth is to choose among us,
is he, who will live or die? Let us
all take our best men to our tents
and all be safe from stones that dent
our heads. From your secret meeting,
Lugaid, I would guess our time is fleeting."

Lugaid looked at him with contempt. "Cúchulainn has given my men and the men of Fergus leave to wear the safe sign. I have given my word that I will not take advantage of his generosity. I will not dishonor my name because you are afraid of his sling and stones."

Ailill glared at Lugaid and hot words rose to his lips, but Fergus forestalled them with a calming hand.

"Friend Lugaid," he said. "Will you return to Cúchulainn and ask him if he will allow me to take Ailill and his three thousand warriors among my own? Take an ox, a pig that has been well salted and cured, and a barrel of wine with you as a gesture of my good intentions."

With misgivings, Lugaid did as Fergus asked and returned to Cúchulainn, giving the words of Fergus to him along with the gift of ox, pig, and wine.

"I do not care where he goes," Cúchulainn said indifferently. "He may do what he wants, but certain of his men will die anyway. This is in the hands of fate. Unless," he added, "he returns to his own lands."

Lugaid went back to Ailill's tent and gave them Cúchulainn's words. Ailill merged his troop with those of Fergus and they spent the night, uneasy with the thought of what might come upon them in the dark. Likewise, according to some, did they spend other nights. How many, we are not told, but even so, Cúchulainn still killed thirty of Ailill's warriors with huge stones that could build a wall from his sling.

At last, Fergus approached Ailill, warning him that he was making a big mistake.

"If you do not move soon, the pangs will soon leave the men of Ulster and they will come hard upon you and grind you to gravel. Besides," he added, looking around at the high ridges with a warrior's eye, "this is not the place to make a stand and fight. If you would save some of your men, then follow me."

And with that, Fergus broke camp and moved his force east toward Cúil Airthir. Ailill hastily followed him, but the wrath of Cúchulainn still descended upon his army after the boy-warrior returned from delivering his report to Conchobar, numbering the women captured and the cattle stolen.

Thirty warriors fell at Áth Duirn, the Ford of the Fist, before they reached Cúil Airthir that night. Before they could even pitch their tents, Cúchulainn killed thirty more with stones from his sling. With relief, they fled inside their tents, hiding behind the flimsy hides out of the boy's sight.

The next morning, Ailill's charioteer, Cuillius, was killed with a stone from Cúchulainn's sling while he was washing his chariot wheels in the ford. The place was called Áth Cuillne, the Ford of Cuillius and Cúil Airthir from that time on. Ailill gathered his forces and marched away from that place, reaching Druim Féne in Conaille by night. There they rested.

Chapter 7

THE
DUEL

Cúchulainn continued his guerrilla warfare against the Connachtmen, slaying a hundred men a night with his sling from Ochaine Mountain.

On the morning of the fourth day, Ailill called his advisors from the troops to his tent, saying:

"Our army is in danger of being totally destroyed," he said. "Now, what I propose is to have a message delivered to Cúchulainn. I will give him a part of the Ai Plain that is equal to the entire Murtheimne plain. I will also give him the finest chariot that can be found in Ai with a harness of his design. I will also deliver to his house twenty-one bondmaids and due compensation for anything of his that we may have destroyed whether it be something of the household or cattle. But he will swear allegiance to me, foresaking the half-lord that he now serves for I am far more worthy of him than the Ulsterman who dares to call himself a king."

Servants moved silently among them with platters of cheese and hard bread made from coarse flour and pitchers of warm milk against the damp cold of the morning. The advisors looked among themselves, wondering who would deliver the message. At last, Fergus spoke: "And who will deliver this message to the youth? For surely, that man will be placed in the greatest danger."

Ailill looked among them, then selected Mac Roth whose speed was such that he could cover all of Ireland in one day. Mac Roth set out to Delga, carrying the message from Ailill and Maeve to where Fergus thought the elusive and wily Cúchulainn could be found. That night, a heavy, wet snow fell upon the plains of Ireland and the dark, mutinous Shannon waves, turning all of the provinces into a snow-white blanket. Cúchulainn and his charioteer saw Mac Roth's approach from a long way off.

"A man approaches," Laeg said. "He is large and proud. A linen band holds his yellow hair from his face. He carries a terrible club, and a sword with an ivory hilt hangs from his waist. He has wrapped a red-threaded tunic with a hood about him."

"I wonder which of Ailill's warriors he might be," Cúchulainn mused.

"I do not know," Laeg answered. "He is dark, but handsome with a broad face. I see now that he wears a bronze brooch in his brown cloak and a tough triple shirt is next to his skin. Well-worn shoes cover his feet and he holds a peeled hazel-wand in one hand."

"A herald, then," Cúchulainn said. "I wonder what he wants?"

Mac Roth drew up in front of Laeg and looked past him to where Cúchulainn squatted haunch-deep in the snow, wiping spots from his shirt with handfuls of fresh snow.

"Which man do you serve?" Mac Roth asked Laeg.

Laeg nodded toward Cúchulainn, watching carefully, for he did not trust any of Ailill's men, thinking that all of the Connachtmen were treacherous.

"He," Laeg said.

Mac Roth approached Cúchulainn, but did not recognize him for the youth who had unleashed the terror among Ailill's army. He asked Cúchulainn whom he served.

"I serve Conchobar Mac Nessa," Cúchulainn said carelessly. He continued to wash his shirt in the snow.

Mac Roth frowned at what he determined to be insolence. "Your words do not say much," he said.

"They say enough," Cúchulainn answered.

Mac Roth's hand toyed with the hilt of his ivory-backed sword, then remembered his mission and reluctantly took his hand from his sword.

"Where can I find Cúchulainn?" he said roughly.

"Why do you want him?" Cúchulainn countered.

Mac Roth gritted his teeth, then shrugged. If this youth wanted to be impolite, he could teach him his manners after he had finished with Ailill's command. He gave him the message.

Cúchulainn shook his head, the silver streak flashing in the dim light from his mane of hair that fell to his shoulders.

"If Cúchulainn were here, you would know that he would never sell the brother of his mother for service in another king's guard," he said.

"There is more," Mac Roth said. "Ailill will give Cúchulainn the noblest women in his service and the naked body of Maeve along with all of the cattle who bear no milk if he will leave the Connacht army alone at night, leaving his killing for the day."

"No, I cannot agree to that," Cúchulainn answered. "Our free-women will have to become grinders if you take away our bond-women and our children will cry for milk if there is no milk to be had."

"Then," Mac Roth said, "we will leave both the bondwomen and the milk cattle as well."

Cúchulainn smiled and shook his head. "But then the Ulster-men would beget slave-sons upon the bondwomen and use the milk cattle for meat."

"Then what is it you want?" Mac Roth asked frustrated, for he had by now realized that he spoke to Cúchulainn. Tactfully, he took his hand from the hilt of his sword and toyed with the golden torque around his neck.

"You will have to find someone who knows what I want," Cúchulainn said cryptically.

Mac Roth returned to Ailill's tent with Cúchulainn's message. Ailill looked around the tent among the warriors present and tapped his hand impatiently upon the carved arm of his oaken throne. His stomach began to burn again.

"Is there no one who can guess at what this man wants?" he demanded.

"I know," Fergus said.

"Then speak," Ailill said impatiently.

"You will not be happy," Fergus warned him. Ailill beckoned him to continue. "Very well. Cúchulainn will agree to leave you alone at night if you come upon him one at a time in the ford and agree that no cattle will be taken from the grass around the ford for a day and a night after each combat."

"That is all?" Ailill asked. He frowned suspiciously at Fergus. "And how is it that you would know this?"

"You do not understand," Fergus explained patiently. "He will gain time from this arrangement. Soon, the men of Ulster will have recovered from their pangs and will come to his aid. Indeed," he murmured more to himself as he looked into the flame of the torch casting light into Ailill's tent, "I wonder why it is taking so long for the Ulstermen to recover."

"I see," Ailill said softly. He chewed on the end of his mustache for a moment, then shrugged. "I agree. It is better to lose one man every day than a hundred every night. Take that message to Cúchulainn, Fergus. Tell him that I agree."

And Fergus left to take Ailill's message to the boy-warrior with Etarcomol, son of Eda and Léthrenn, the foster-son of Ailill and Maeve, at his heels. He paused and turned to the young man who followed him.

"I think it would be much better if you stayed in the camp," he said skeptically to Etarcomol. "You are far too proud and too aware of your friendship with Ailill, who, incidentally, does not know that you are sniffing around Maeve's loins. This is not the place or time for an insolent youth."

"Will I not be under your protection?" Etarcomol asked, his lips tightening, suppressing his anger at the words of Fergus.

"Very well. But do not insult him while we are talking," Fergus said. "Otherwise, no good will come from our meeting."

The small party went to Delga in two chariots. Laeg looked up from the game of *baunbach* he played with Cúchulainn and glanced over the youth's broad shoulder and noticed their approach.

"Two chariots are coming," he said. "A great, dark man wearing a purple cloak with a gold brooch and a red-threaded hooded tunic rides in the first chariot. He holds a curved shield with a light gold scalloped edge and a stabbing spear wrapped tightly from neck to foot. He carries a sword the size of a boat rudder at his thigh."

"A useless rudder it is," Cúchulainn said with a laugh. "That man is Fergus and there is no sword in the scabbard but a wooden imitation. I have heard the stories men tell when they leave the camp to piss, talking about how Ailill's charioteer caught him while he slept after making love with Maeve and stole his sword."

Fergus came up to them and Cúchulainn grinned at him.

"Welcome, my friend," he said politely. "If salmon swam in the rivers, I would give one to you and share another. I would give you a wild bird if a flock landed on the plains and share yet another with you after baking it with watercress, sea-herb, and marshwort. I would give you a drink from the pure water that flows through the sand and take your place in battle and watch over you while you slept."

"As I would you," Fergus said roughly. "But I did not come to share food with you, although I know how you keep your board."

"Then give me your message," Cúchulainn said politely, and Fergus did.

"I will think upon this," Cúchulainn said.

And Fergus left, looking backward at Etarcomol, who kept his eyes insolently upon Cúchulainn.

"What are you staring at?" Cúchulainn asked.

"You," Etarcomol answered. His lip curled with insult.

"You can see all with one glance," Cúchulainn said, giving the young man a chance to leave with honor. But Etarcomol did not listen to the gentle warning under Cúchulainn's words.

"You're right," he said. "I don't see anything to fear here—no horror or terror that makes men quake in their sleep at night. Only a boy who plays at war with wooden weapons."

"Brave words," Cúchulainn said. "But I will not kill you for your insulting ways for the sake of Fergus who gave you safe passage when he came."

His brow lowered threateningly and Etarcomol looked into his eyes, feeling himself fall into the abyss that looked back into his from the death-promise of their depths.

"Be aware, though," Cúchulainn continued. "If you had not come under his protection, I would have ripped your bowels out by now and scattered your quarters from here to your camp."

Stung, Etarcomol forgot the caution of Fergus and said: "I don't need any of your empty threats. I will come first against you tomorrow in the single combat we have agreed to with Fergus's plan."

He turned to his charioteer and commanded him to drive back to camp. As the chariot rattled back over the rough ground toward camp, he told his charioteer what he had said to Cúchulainn.

"Did you make that promise? That you would come tomorrow?" the charioteer asked.

"I did," Etarcomol said.

"You will not get the better of him tomorrow," the charioteer said. "Perhaps it would be better for you to take advantage of this day."

"I have said what I have said," Etarcomol said in a huff. "Drive on back to the camp."

But when they came to Methe and Cethe, he shook his head, saying, "I have sworn in front of Fergus that I will fight Cúchulainn tomorrow, but that's too long to wait. Turn back."

The charioteer did his bidding, his guts quaking inside him. Laeg saw the chariot turn and said to Cúchulainn: "The youth returns with his left chariot-board against us. Most insulting, wouldn't you say?"

"I can't refuse that," Cúchulainn answered. "Such an insult would be unbearable anywhere. Let us go down and meet him."

Together they drove down to the ford in Cúchulainn's chariot. Etarcomol proudly watched their approach, making his weapons ready to battle.

"You are the one pushing this," Cúchulainn said warningly. "I don't want any part of this for you are still under safe-bound by the honor of Fergus."

"You have no choice in the matter," Etarcomol said arrogantly. "Either fight or die."

He swung his sword at Cúchulainn, who easily slipped the blow. Cúchulainn drew his sword for a return stroke, but instead, cut the ground under the youth's feet. The would-be hound-slayer tumbled onto his back, the cut sward landing with a hard *plop!* on his belly, a subtle warning.

"Now leave," Cúchulainn said softly. "You can see that you are no match for me and I do not want to wash your blood from my hands. I would have cut you to pieces long ago had it not been for the protection of Fergus."

Stung, the humiliated Etarcomol threw the winter-hardened sod-brick from his belly and leaped to his feet. Tears glinted in his eyes.

"I will not leave! This isn't over!" he sobbed with fury. "Either I'll cut your head from your shoulders or you mine!"

"Then you will lose your head," Cúchulainn warned, his blade dancing in his hand as he easily fended off the youth's attack. He touched him twice on the chest, pressing, but not nicking the flesh in warning. "Don't be foolish, now. Leave it alone."

In a rage, Etarcomol attacked, swinging wildly, good sense taken from him by his fury. Again, Cúchulainn easily avoided the young man's rush, turning his blade from him with an easy flick of his wrist. His sword danced in the light, touching Etarcomol here and again there, warning him with the pressure of the blade that stung, but did not cut, the flesh. Suddenly, with a quick movement, the point of his sword flickering like fireflies, he cut through the youth's tunic. The two halves split and fell away, leaving Etarcomol naked, his goad hanging heavy and limp between his legs in the cold air.

"Now leave!" Cúchulainn ordered. "You can tell by now that you are no match for me. Why be foolish? The brave man is the one who knows when to withdraw."

"No!" Etarcomol shouted, swinging his sword with both hands as he charged Cúchulainn.

Again, Cúchulainn dodged the young man's onslaught, this time shearing off the youth's hair as he swept by, his sword edge cutting through the youth's proud locks as neatly as a razor without nicking the skin. Again, he warned the young man to leave. Again, the young man refused and renewed his attack upon Cúchulainn.

At last, Cúchulainn met the young man's charge, deflecting the blow and cleaving him from crown to belly. The sword slipped from the young man's nerveless fingers. He tried to push his guts back into his belly, then fell forward dead, his intestines slipping out onto the winter ground like thick, white worms. Etarcomol's charioteer became frightened at this and turned his horses, racing fast back to camp.

Startled, Fergus watched the chariot clatter past him and when he saw only the charioteer in it, a great fury shook him. He caught Etarcomol's chariot and made the charioteer follow him. He then turned his chariot and raced back to Cúchulainn.

"You damned demon!" he shouted. "You have disgraced me! That boy was under my protection! Do you think my cudgel is so short that you can treat me as a eunuch?"

"Fergus, my friend, this was not of my doing alone," Cúchulainn answered.

"You are partially to blame
for this young man seeking fame.
You ran from the Ulster land
with an unfamed sword in your hand.
I honor mighty men, but this boy
in my hands was only a toy
and foolishly gave up his death-petals
after I thrice warned him with the metal
of my blade. Do not use hard words, Fergus,
for I do not want further battle among us."

Cúchulainn knelt humbly on one knee while Fergus thrice circled him furiously in his chariot, working himself into battle-madness.

"Why don't you ask Etarcomol's charioteer who was at fault?" Cúchulainn said.

Fergus's eyes flickered angrily toward the charioteer who flinched from their red madness.

"No, it wasn't you," the charioteer said to Cúchulainn, his legs trembling before the fury in Fergus's eyes. "He gave you no choice."

"Etarcomol vowed that he wouldn't leave until he had my head or I his," Cúchulainn said. "This is after I gave him three warnings by showing him he was not my match." He gestured toward the carefully oiled, lime-bleached locks lying on the ground beside the cut tunic. "But he would not leave even then. What would you have done, friend Fergus?"

Fergus pulled his horses in and sighed, swallowing his fury. He pawed at his beard with thick fingers, then shook his head, the fire dying from his eyes.

"Yes, yes, yes," he sighed. "I can see that you had no choice. I tried to warn the young pup against his arrogance, but he would not listen to me. Be at ease, Cúchulainn. There is nothing more between us in this regard."

And saying that, Fergus climbed down from his chariot and pierced Etarcomol's two heel-cords with a ancelring, tying a leather thong to it. He climbed back into his chariot and dragged the unfortunate would-be warrior back to the camp in this ignoble manner. When Maeve saw this, she became furious with Fergus and his treatment of the overproud youth.

"This is a brutal treatment for a dog," she said. "Warriors deserve better." She looked at the scraped and bleeding body, shorn of its hair, and the limp goad, remembering the attentions the moonstruck youth had lavished upon her.

"Warriors, perhaps," Fergus said bluntly. "But he was an ignorant whelp and deserves nothing less since he was so foolish with his pride as to challenge the great Hound of Culann. And," he added, "to press that challenge when thrice Cúchulainn tried to show him his weakness."

They dug a grave for him and planted a memorial stone over him with his name cut deeply into it with *ogham* markings. Then they made the proper lamentation for him. This is called An Amadán.

That night, Cúchulainn kept his sling beside him and slew no more. Women and maidens were sent to him, bearing his food.

After the burial, all met again in Ailill's tent. Lugaid blew warm breath upon his fingers stiff with cold and said: "And what man will you send forth to battle with Cúchulainn tomorrow?"

"Let us wait until the morrow to tell," Maine, Ailill's son, answered.

"After this, I do not think we will be able to find someone willing to go against him," Maeve answered, sighing. "Perhaps we had better ask Cúchulainn for a truce while we see if one can be found."

Lugaid agreed to this and left the tent, returning to his own fire. Ailill sighed, turning to Maeve, watching as she readied herself for bed, admiring her white shoulders and rosy-tipped breasts.

"Well," he said. "Who do you think we can find to fight with Cúchulainn?"

"I don't know," Maeve said, frowning prettily, her white teeth gently pressing against her full lower lip. "He certainly does not seem to have any match in Ireland. Perhaps Cúroi Mac Dáiri will come to fight with him. Or Nadcranntail."

One of Cúroi's people overheard this through the thin wall of the tent and said loudly: "Cúroi will not come. He has said before that he has sent enough men here to be killed."

"That leaves only Nadcranntail," Maeve said. She looked at Ailill. "In the morning, send a messenger to him, begging him to come for the honor of Connacht."

Ailill nodded agreement, then stretched out his arms, pulling the naked body of Maeve hard against his own. They fell back upon the cushions, tightly locked in love-fury.

The next morning, Ailill sent a messenger to Nadcranntail. The warrior-hero listened to the message, then said; "I will do as they ask, but they must give me their daughter Finnabair as my prize."

He had his charioteer pack his weapons in a wagon to be driven to the camp from East Connacht. He did not travel with his weapons, so anxious was he at the thought of possessing Finnabair, and traveled ahead of the wagon in his chariot. When he arrived, he went straight to Maeve's tent, bursting in upon her, large and hairy and sweating. Tiny blackheads dotted his nose and the flesh on his cheeks above his beard shined greasily.

"You may have our daughter," Maeve said, after greeting him and listening to his proposal. "But only if you will go against Cúchulainn."

"This I will do," Nadcranntail promised and grinned, his teeth showing like large yellow stones streaked with lichens.

Lugaid overheard the promise of Maeve and Nadcranntail's

promise as well and went in the night to tell Cúchulainn what he could expect on the morrow.

"I do not think you will be able to resist Nadcranntail," Lugaid said. "He is a mighty warrior."

"The fight has yet to begin," Cúchulainn answered, and rolled himself into his cloak to sleep.

The next morning, Nadcranntail left camp and since his weapons had not yet arrived, took only nine spears made from holly with him, their points sharpened and charred into hardness. Cúchulainn ignored his approach, playing a game he had invented, catching birds between his thumb and forefinger, then releasing them so that they fluttered and danced above his head. His chariot stood nearby, but far enough that he could not readily grasp his weapons. Seeing this, Nadcranntail threw one spear at Cúchulainn, who leaped up into the air and danced delicately upon its point while his hands continued to play with the birds, catching them and releasing them as they fluttered around him.

Nadcranntail quickly threw the other eight spears at him. As the ninth spear sped from his hand, the birds took fright and flew away. Cúchulainn ignored the spears, stepping lightly upon their points in midair as he raced after the birds. It was nothing that he had not done many times before, but the Connacht warriors watching from a distance could not see everything and to them, it appeared that the Cúchulainn was fleeing before the fury of Nadcranntail, refusing to do battle.

"Look at your brave Cúchulainn running away from me," Nadcranntail boasted as Maeve rode up beside him in her chariot.

"And why not?" Maeve murmured, admiring the breadth of his shoulders. A pity he does not wash, she thought. "You are a true warrior, much better than the others who rode with us. Before such a man, a youth does wisely to flee."

But Fergus and his fellow Exiles from Ulster were troubled by this for it suggested that all Ulstermen would do well to flee before Nadcranntail. Fiacha Mac Firaba was sent to Cúchulainn to protest his flight from the Connacht hero.

"Tell him," Fergus commanded, "that he did a noble thing when he showed his bravery before the warriors. But he had better hide now, after fleeing from Nadcranntail, for he has shamed not only himself with his action, but all of Ulster as well."

"Who boasts that I ran away?" Cúchulainn asked angrily when Fiacha told him about the words of Fergus.

"Nadcranntail," he answered.

"What has he to boast about?" Cúchulainn asked puzzled. "Is there another who can dance upon the points of his homemade spears as I did? It would have shamed me to fight a man who did not carry proper weapons with him instead of the wooden toys such as children use. All of Ireland knows I will not kill an unarmed man. If he wants to make good his brag, then let him come again to meet me on the morrow between Ochaine Mountain and the sea. The time does not matter; as early or late as he wishes. I will wait for him there and we shall see who runs away."

Fiacha returned to the Connacht camp, bearing Cúchulainn's words with him while Cúchulainn went to the appointed place between Ochaine Mountain and the sea to wait for the warrior. As he passed, he saw a great standing stone as big as himself and picked it up, wrapping it under his cloak next to his body. In this way, he slept upright so that he would be ready when the warrior came upon him.

The next morning, Nadcranntail came fully armed, the wagon with his weapons having arrived in the night. Fergus traveled with him and when they came upon the plain between Ochaine Mountain and the sea, Nadcranntail turned arrogantly to Fergus, demanding to know where Cúchulainn hid.

"There he is," Fergus said, pointing to where the youth slept, wrapped in his cloak next to the standing stone. Cúchulainn heard his words and opened his eyes, yawning.

"You do not seem to be the man I saw yesterday," Nadcranntail said doubtfully for he had been too far away when he had thrown his holly spears to see Cúchulainn's features in order to recognize him now. "Are you really the warrior Cúchulainn?"

"What if I am?" Cúchulainn asked.

"Why, I won't be able to fight you," Nadcranntail said, laughing. "What kind of warrior would I be who takes a lamb's head back to camp claiming it to be a lion's head? You have no beard. A warrior such as Cúchulainn must have a beard as full and thick as my own if his reputation bears any merit."

"You have guessed correctly," Cúchulainn said, for he wanted Nadcranntail to fight him with all of his fury and not with the contempt he was showing. "I am not the one you seek. You will find him behind that hill."

As Nadcranntail turned to the hill, Cúchulainn ran rapidly to Laeg.

"Make a false beard for me to wear when I go out to meet that man," Cúchulainn demanded. "He refuses to fight anyone who does not have a beard as full as his own because to do so would demean him."

Dutifully, Laeg obeyed Cúchulainn, taking hairs from the tails of Cúchulainn's horses, weaving them quickly into a beard as full and thick as Nadcranntail's own. Cúchulainn tied the beard to his chin, knotting the ends behind his ears, then went to meet Nadcranntail on the crest of the hill.

"Ah!" Nadcranntail said in delight as Cúchulainn approached. "Now, this is more like it! A worthy opponent, indeed, who will fight according to the rules."

"Agreed," Cúchulainn said. "Name your rules."

"Throwing spears," said Nadcranntail, adding, "and no dodging!"

"No dodging," agreed Cúchulainn, "except upward!"

At that, Nadcranntail made a quick cast without warning and Cúchulainn leaped high to avoid the spear. It struck the standing stone behind him and the point shattered like frost.

"Foul!" Nadcranntail raged. "You dodged my throw!"

"Try mine as well," Cúchulainn said. He threw his spear, but as his arm came forward, he twisted his wrist, sending the point high into the air. It dropped down onto Nadcranntail's skull, driving through it, pinning him to the earth.

"Woe! Woe!" he cried. His fingers touched the shaft of the spear. He shuddered and said: "You are undoubtedly the best warrior in Ireland to have made such a cast. I beg of you, let me go and tell the twenty-four sons waiting for me in the camp about this and I will return to be beheaded. If you pull this spear out of my head now, I will surely die."

Cúchulainn was not a merciless warrior, and agreed, warning Nadcranntail to be sure that he returned. The wounded warrior wended his way to camp, bearing his death-wound with him. His sons and other warriors came out to greet him, looking curiously at the spear standing from his skull.

"Where is the head of the young warrior?" they asked.

Nadcranntail listened to their words, knowing he had failed in his brag. Ashamed, he said: "Warriors, you will have to wait. I must tell my sons things of concern to them, then I return to fight again with Cúchulainn."

Having said this, he took his sons aside, speaking lowly to them. Then he turned back to the hill where Cúchulainn patiently waited. When he came close, he broke his vow by suddenly throwing his sword at the boy. Cúchulainn leaped high to dodge the treacherous toss. Then the warp-spasm came upon him with his fury. He turned around in his skin and one eye bulged from his head while the other slitted. His hair stood straight from his head and the hero-halo rose wrathfully from his brow. He leaped onto the rim of Nadcranntail's shield, striking down at the wounded warrior, slicing his head from his shoulders and striking again, cleaving him through the neck and through his groin. The treacherous Nadcranntail fell in quarters to the ground. Then Cúchulainn raised his voice in his warrior's chant:

"Nadcranntail has fallen, see where he lies.
But if more of you, too, wish to die,
bring forth a third of Maeve's men
who would wish to challenge me, then."

But none dared venture forth while the warp-spasm was upon him and hid in their tents until Cúchulainn went down to the sea to wash Nadcranntail's blood from him. Only then did they withdraw fully from Ochaine Mountain, keeping its mass between them and the boy-warrior, who rested after his battle in accordance with the agreement he had made with Fergus.

Chapter 8

THE BULL
AND THE
MÓRRÍGAN

WHILE AILILL AND HIS warrior advisors brooded over Cúchulainn's slaying of Nadcranntail, Maeve left with a third of the Connachtmen for the Cuib district to search for the bull. Unknown to Ailill and the others, Cúchulainn followed closely, reckoning her to be the more dangerous, for a woman set upon her way is far more treacherous than a man who is bound by a code of honor. And Cúchulainn did right to follow her for it was Maeve's plan to scorch the lands of the Picts and Ulstermen from the side of the Midluachair Road as far north as Dún Sobairche.

It was here that one of Maeve's warrior chieftains whose hero-halo would pale beside Cúchulainn's found the bull surrounded by fifteen heifers and began to drive him back to where Maeve's men made ready to burn the land. But they had forgotten Cúchulainn in their anxiety to please Maeve of the White Shoulders and when Cúchulainn found Buide Mac Báin at the head of sixty of Ailill's men, all wearing hooded cloaks and coming from Sliab Cuilinn, he came up to them, demanding:

"Where did you get these cattle? By what right do you drive them along this way?"

"We found them at that mountain," Buide Mac Báin said, turning to point at the hazy mountain behind them. He looked boldly at Cúchulainn, thinking him to be only a brash, beardless youth. "And we drive them by our own right."

"And their herdsmen," Cúchulainn said gently. "What have you done with them?"

"There was only one attending the bull and heifers," Buide said brusquely. "We brought him with us. Now step aside, youth, as we have men's work ahead of us."

Arrogantly he pushed by Cúchulainn for he did not know the beardless youth to be the feared night-terror who had struck so many dead, as the youth wore no beard and Buide was one who thought men's might mated merrily with the length of one's beard. Cúchulainn reached the ford in front of them in three great strides, saying to the leader:

"What do they call you?"

"I have no fear of a youth with no beard! As for my name, I am Buide Mac Báin. Note well the name and stand aside!"

He shook his weapons fiercely, holding his ground between Cúchulainn and his men who drove the bull and heifers around the pair and across the ford.

"Then, Buide Mac Báin," cried Cúchulainn. "Here is a spear for you!"

And a short spear flew from his fingertips as if by magic. Buide Mac Báin tried to deflect the spear, but it slipped past his guard and into his armpit, the point severing his liver, and the bearded warrior-hero fell dead in the shallow waters of the ford that came to be called in his name: Áth Buide. But by the time Cúchulainn had decided the battle with his short spear, the men had driven the bull into the Connacht camp.

Cúchulainn's legend began to grow now, and men began to speak warily in tight-knit groups in the closed corners of the camp, exchanging stories about the youth's prowess and how he might be defeated. A story grew how his weakness must lie within his javelin, the Gae Bolga, since he had not been seen without it near at hand. At last, Ailill's poet, Redg, made his way to Cúchulainn's camp high in the trees to test the story.

"You are welcome," Cúchulainn said politely to the poet for he well knew the strength of the poet lay in the stories that he could tell about those who displeased him. "What may I do for you?"

"I want your javelin," the poet said.

Cúchulainn shook his head regretfully, saying, "I will give you any gift that I can but that."

"I don't want anything else from you," Redg said rudely. "You have asked what it is that I wish and that is what I wish. Do you not know me for who I am? Ailill's poet, Redg. My songs are many and are sung across the land."

Without thinking, Cúchulainn lashed out at the poet, staggering him with a blow for demanding what Cúchulainn could not give. A trickle of blood oozed from the corner of the poet's mouth as he grinned a bloodstained smile at Cúchulainn, saying, "You know the power that lies in songs. Give me your javelin or I will strip your good name from you and you will live forever with shame attached to your name."

Cúchulainn knew well what Redg could do and he knew that the poet would do as he said. So he gave the poet his javelin, sending it through his head with a flick of his wrist, the copper point of the javelin resting at another ford well to the east of where they stood.

"Ahh!" cried the poet. "Now, that was a stunning gift!"

And he fell to the earth and died and the place was named Áth Tolam Sét, the Ford of the Stunning Gift, and where the javelin at last came to rest is now called Umarrith, Where the Copper Point Fell.

Many tried to slay Cúchulainn after Redg fell in Cuib: Nathcoirpthe near a grove of trees now bearing his name; Cruithen in the ford now called after him; the herdsmen's sons who tried to drive the bull at a cairn now called by their names; and Marc fell on his hillock, Meille on his hill, Baeve in his tower, and Boguine by his marsh.

Cúchulainn then discovered that Maeve's army was drawing him farther and farther from his home and turned back again to Murtheimne Plain. There, he killed the men of Cronech at Focherd when he discovered them making camp where he had forbade them to go. Ten cup-bearers and ten warriors fell there.

Meanwhile, Maeve returned from the north where she had been destroying the small forts of the province and laying their crops and fields to waste. Her triumphs were many: she had attacked Finnmór, the wife of Celtchar Mac Uthidir, and taken fifty women for the use of her men when she captured Dún Sobairche in Dál Riada. But where this is now, no one knows. So fierce was her desire for revenge against Cúchulainn that she destroyed every place in Cuib where she rested her horsewhip and many places are now named the same: Bile Maeve, Maeve's Whip. Every ford she crossed or every hill where she paused is now called Maeve's Ford or Maeve's Hill.

She met the men who drove the bull at Focherd where Ailill had taken his troop. The herdsman who had been captured with the bull tried to escape with the bull to return it to its people, but Ailill's men drove the herd after him into a narrow gap from which he could not climb, beating their spearshafts upon their hide-shields, and there, the hooves of the cattle and horses pounded him into dust. Forgaimen, the herdsman, lies crushed into the earth there still and so the hill bears his name. Maeve and Ailill and the army of Connachtmen might have rested there easily that night had only someone been found who could have kept Cúchulainn back from that ford.

First, the warrior advisors sent for Cúr Mac Daláth to fight Cúchulainn. This was a warrior so fierce that when he drew blood from any man he faced, that man would die within nine days. Several times, he had done this in jest and the stench of blood seemed to ooze from his skin so that few would sit with him around the fire.

"This is a good choice," Maeve said to her advisors. "If he kills Cúchulainn, then we have won. But we will win just as well if Cúr Mac Daláth is killed, for that, too, will be a burden from our shoulders: there is no pleasure sitting, sleeping, or eating beside him. He carries the smell of dried blood with him wherever he goes."

She did not add that she had once taken Cúr Mac Daláth to bed only to force him from it when her gorge rose in her throat from his rank kisses.

Cúr took his assignment with relish, carefully sharpening his long sword, which took two servants to carry, and dressing himself in his tunic, stiff with ancient blood, that made all those downwind of him gag from its stench. Eagerly, he climbed the hill, his beetle-browed eyes searching anxiously for the feared warrior whose tales he had heard with misgivings around many campfires. Carefully, he followed Cormac Connlongas into the hills to spy upon the warrior to see his strength, his weaknesses. But when he saw the beardless youth with whom he was to fight, he spat in disgust.

"Why am I so insulted?" he sneered. He looked boldly upon the youth. "You compliment my skill with arms!"

He turned away in disgust, muttering, "Had I known it was one like you that I was supposed to fight, I would have sent a boy from among my company."

"Your boast is not unusual," said Cormac Connlongas. "Still, we would think it a victory if you drove him off. Despite his age," he added.

Cúr sighed and eyed the boy again. His displeasure shone from his eyes.

"Well, I said I would do it. But get us ready to leave early in the morning. Killing this young deer won't take long so we should be well rested for our journey," he said.

The next morning, Cúr rolled grumbling from his blankets

and brashly ordered the troops to ready themselves for travel as his coming fight with Cúchulainn would undoubtedly make the journey easier going than it had been coming. He gathered his weapons, tossing his shield carelessly over his shoulder, and set out to climb the hill to the forest where he had seen the youth.

As he approached, Cúchulainn was exercising, putting himself through his moves, the special feats of arms that only he had mastered: the apple-feat, the sword-edge and sloped-shield feats, the javelin-and-rope feat, the body-feat, the cat feat, the heroic salmon-leap feat, the pole-throw and the leap over a poisoned stroke. He practiced as well the chariot-fighter's crouch, the throwing of the Gae Bolga, speed, the chariot-wheel feat, leaping upon the shield-rim, holding one's breath, snapping one's mouth, and the hero-scream. He worked his sword in precise strokes, then practiced with his sling, throwing the stunning-shot. He had Laig throw lances that he leaped lightly upon, playing with the shaft with his toes and standing upon its point. He practiced tying a warrior with a single cast of his rope.

Cúr saw him practicing his warrior's tricks and disdainfully attacked him without warning, not bothering with a warrior's courtesy for he did not think Cúchulainn to be worthy of such a warning. But such was Cúchulainn's concentration that he did not even know he was under attack. So precise were his moves that Cúr's strokes and warrior's tricks were useless against him. Finally, Fiacha Mac Firaba, who had made the long climb beside Cúr to bear witness to the rude warrior's claims, cried, "Watch out, Cúchulainn, for the warrior attacking you!"

Cúchulainn glanced behind him and immediately threw the apple he held in his hand. The apple flew behind Cúr's shield rim and struck him in the center of his forehead, driving through and breaking through the bone at the back of the brute's head. Fergus watched this with a slight smile upon his lips, for although he did not like being held hostage by Cúchulainn's might, he had liked less Cúr's bragging. He traced his way back down through the tall pines with satisfaction to where Ailill and Maeve's host waited impatiently for word about Cúr's duel. When he stepped into the clearing, all looked up with hopeful faces that quickly fell.

"Now you must honor the pact that you made with the boy-warrior," he said, concluding his story of what had befallen Cúr. "You must wait for a full day before you send another against him."

"Yes, wait we must, but not here, not here," repeated Ailill despondently. He turned away from Fergus, saying, "Let us return to our tents and make plans for the next warrior to send to him."

Obediently, the others followed him. They waited while Ailill drank deeply the bitter brew placed before him, draining vessel after vessel of warm ale. Fergus kept pace with him, surreptitiously watching to see that Ailill did not drink a separate mug without him.

"It is obvious that those who go to face my foster-son are doomed men," Fergus boasted as the ale loosened his tongue. He blearily eyed the others sitting a respectful distance from him and the brooding Ailill. "Ah, yes. Trying to find one to go against that youth is madness. Madness!" His eyebrows wagged like quaking mountain slopes.

"Be quiet, fool," Ailill growled. "Life is fundamentally risible. We'll find someone. We just have to think."

"Think," Fergus said, rolling the word around in his mouth with relish. "Think! Drying work best left to the passionless Druids who give up everything for an interesting idea. Give me a coarse soldier every time! Cut! Slash! Hack!"

"If words were grass, yours would not feed a goat," Ailill said.

"A king's words," Fergus said, winking roguishly at the others.

"I certainly hope your sword is as sharp as your words," Ailill said pointedly.

Fergus flushed dark red and buried his nose in his goblet, ignoring Ailill. The others tactfully began to slip out of Ailill's tent until only he and Fergus remained. At last, Ailill looked up and together they made plans.

The next day, Láth Mac Dabró was selected to challenge Cúchulainn and he, too, fell as easily as did the blood-spattered warrior before him. Again, Fergus returned to tell them of the warrior's fate and remind them of the pact that they had made with the boy-warrior. Láth Mac Dabró came after Cúr Mac Daláth and Foirc Mac Trí n-Aignech, the descendant of the three Swift Ones, and Srúbgaile Mac Eobith came after Láth Mac Dabró, and all were killed as quickly as Cúr in single combat.

After the last, Cúchulainn said to his charioteer, "Return to the Connacht camp, Laeg, and find Lugaid Mac Nois Allchomaig and ask him if he is the next one to come against me tomorrow."

Laeg tugged at his forelock, agreeing, and went to the Connacht camp. There, he found Lugaid and put Cúchulainn's question to him.

"Welcome," Lugaid said. "No, I am not the one to challenge Cúchulainn on the morrow. That chore has gone to another: Ferbaeth—may his weapons be cursed and blunted! A former friend of not only mine, but Cúchulainn as well. Ah, Cúchulainn! One man against the might of Ireland! I do not envy his position. Still, I do not feel right about all of this for many brave men have died for a queen's whim! But Ferbaeth will fight for they have promised him Finnabair of the Anxious Thighs if he does and the throne over his own people."

Laeg returned to Cúchulainn and told him what he had learned. Cúchulainn stared into the coals of the fire, the minor light of Lugh, and read the future there.

"You do not seem to be very happy with the answer you received from Lugaid, friend Laeg," he said.

"I'm not," Laeg said curtly.

And Cúchulainn laughed.

But what Cúchulainn did not know was that Ferbaeth had been called to Ailill and Maeve's tent for dinner and placed by Finnabair's side. She fed him dainties from her plate and teased him until he felt lust rising within him. Then he was told that she, Finnabair of the Anxious Thighs, had picked him to fight as their champion against Cúchulainn for they knew that he had trained as well as had Cúchulainn at Scáthach. At first he refused, but the wine they poured into his chalice was thick with honey and the perfume of Finnabair was strong in his nostrils as she rubbed her heavy and creamy breasts against him and her tongue was like honey in his mouth when he kissed her roughly and listened to her moan as she tasted his urgency. She told him he was the best out of those who filled the fifty wagons who followed the army. At last, Finnabair took him with her to her tent.

"This is not an honorable thing to do," Ferbaeth said roughly. "Cúchulainn is my foster-brother and I have sworn to be faithful to him forever."

He looked at her fine, naked limbs, glowing like marble in the tent-lights, and sighed.

"Still, I must meet with him tomorrow and kill him, hacking his head off to present to Maeve on a silver tray. Do you not find this strange?"

"You will do what you have vowed to do," Finnabair said, blowing softly, warmly, into his ear.

"Yes," he answered, his rough hand caressing her smooth flesh.

"You will do as you have promised," Maeve said, for she had followed them to the tent and joined with them in their merrymaking. And so they passed the night.

The next day, Cúchulainn rose, bothered by a dream that he had and sent Laeg to the camp of the Connachtmen to learn what he could. Laeg found Lugaid squatting beside a fire, staring into the coals, and brought him back with him to Cúchulainn.

"So," Cúchulainn said softly after hearing Lugaid's tale, "it will be my brother Ferbaeth who will come to meet me on the morrow."

"Yes," Lugaid replied, avoiding the youth's eyes, staring into Lugh's minor light.

"A cold day," Cúchulainn said, shivering and huddling closer to the fire. Lugaid looked closely at him, but saw only resignation and no fear in the youth's eyes, the deep, tired lines of his face from holding the Ulster boundaries while the Ulstermen recovered from their birth-pang curse. "A cold day. I won't live to see the end of Lugh's light. We are, you know, equal in age and match and alertness."

Lugaid remained silent, staring between Cúchulainn and the fire, noticing the resignation in the hero's face.

"Please give him my greetings, friend Lugaid, and tell him that there is a disagreeable falseness to our meeting for warriors such as us should not be pawns of women. Tell him . . ." He paused, then continued. "Tell him that I wish to speak with him. Tonight. Here."

Ferbaeth agreed to Lugaid's request and went with him to renounce his friendship with Cúchulainn so that he would not be honor-bound when he met the terror the next day. When Ferbaeth arrived at Cúchulainn's campfire, the beardless warrior greeted him fondly and presented him with a roasted fowl from the plain and honey-baked salmon from the river, sharing each with him. He then begged Ferbaeth to renounce his pledge to Maeve by their foster-brotherhood and the common breast of Scáthach from which both had fed.

"This I cannot do," Ferbaeth said regretfully. "I have given my word to Maeve."

"To the Whore of Connacht? What word would that be? Have you succumbed to her white breast and the anxious thighs of her daughter? This, before our vows?"

"And you would have done differently?" Ferbaeth said hotly.

"Yes," Cúchulainn said. "Yes! A man without honor is no man but a pawn for any who wish to use him. If you persist in this, why then you will join those whom the *Sídhe* ignore."

"Could it be that you wish you were in the Connacht camp, enjoying Maeve's white thighs (she yearns for you, you know) and the white breasts of her daughter, who has learned well her mother's skills? I think so, and if you say otherwise, why then, I would call you a liar."

"Then keep your friendship!" Cúchulainn said furiously and left before the warp-spasm could overcome him. As he stalked away from Ferbaeth the Gullible, a piece of split holly drove through his instep, the point emerging beneath his knee. He reached down and pulled it out, waving it in wonder at Ferbaeth.

"Look what I have found, Ferbaeth!" he called. "Surely, this is an omen, a warning from the gods to beware of breaking our vows!"

But his foster-brother ignored him, saying indifferently over his shoulder as he continued down the hill back toward the Connacht camp: "Throw it away. You make too much of trifles! Always have!"

Angered by Ferbaeth's betrayal, Cúchulainn threw the holly after Ferbaeth, twisting his wrist as if throwing a spear. It sang through the air and pierced the hollow at the back of Ferbaeth's head, slicing through his mouth in front. He twisted and fell backward in the glen, his body twisting on the green sward that quickly became red with the fountain pouring from his mouth.

"A goodly throw!" he choked. He coughed and a great spout of blood leaped from his mouth and he fell back dead, his head cushioned by a hummock. The place took its name from this: Focherd in Murtheimne, the Place of the Throw. Some, however, say that this place is named after Fiacha Mac Firaba, who said: "Your throw is exceedingly sharp today, Cúchulainn."

But it does not matter. Ferbaeth died in the glen that now bears his name. And as the warrior choked out his last, Cúchulainn could hear Fergus chanting:

"Ferbaeth, your fool's foray
has led to your death today.
Your deceit and rage brought you ruin
here in this glen in Cróen Chorann.

"And now we will rename this place
after your shameless feat. This space
will be called Focherd Bold
where once it was Fichi of Old."

"And now," Fergus said, eyeing Cúchulainn, "how will you pay tomorrow for his death, the duties that you owe? For you have not killed a man in fair combat and have killed as well your foster-brother."

Cúchulainn shrugged. "Some day I will pay. Perhaps not tomorrow, but some day."

But to be sure that Ferbaeth was truly dead, Cúchulainn sent Laeg to get the news from the camp. There, Lugaid told him that Cúchulainn's foster-brother was dead.

And Cúchulainn went forth to talk with them about how to pay for Ferbaeth's death.

Meanwhile, the warrior advisors again met in Ailill's tent, searching for another warrior to send out to Cúchulainn in single combat according to the rules that had been made with their pact.

"We will have to send someone else now," Lugaid said. "It is most unfortunate what happened to Ferbaeth."

Ailill grumbled and drank deeply from his wine goblet.

"You'll not be finding another to take his place unless you trick him. Perhaps with wine. Give wine to any who come—this will give them courage—and tell them that we are honoring them by giving them the last of the wine that we brought from Cruacháin so that they will not be forced to drink water with the rest. Do this with each one alone. And," Lugaid added, his eyes glinting lasciviously, "place Finnabair, thinly dressed so her snow-white body will shine through the gossamer of her dress, at his right hand and promise her white thighs to him if he brings us the head of the Warped One."

They agreed that this was a fine plan, and each night a great warrior was called before the council and Finnabair dressed herself in her finest gowns that left her shoulders bare, her white breasts bubbling over, her golden-red triangle visible beneath, and sat at the right hand of each warrior and breathed gently in his ear as he drank deeply of the Cruacháin wine.

And each promised hotly that he would bring back the head of the Warped One and lay it in front of the tent where Finnabair was to wait. But each head that was returned to the camp belonged to Finnabair's suitors until at last, no one could be found to go against Cúchulainn.

At last, they turned to Láréne Mac Nois, the brother of Lugaid, king of Munster, a vain man whose boasting had angered many, but none had dared to challenge him for fear of Lugaid. The advisors placed Láréne in the seat of honor and plied him with the heady Cruacháin wine and Finnabair put on her flimsiest garments that left her appearing more naked than naked and she breathed hotly into his ear until lust glazed his eyes. Maeve glanced with satisfaction at the pair on the couch and said: "A handsome couple, I would say. They would make a fine match, I'm thinking."

"Sure enough. And I will give her to him if he manages to bring me the head of the Warped One," Ailill said. "But even if he doesn't, his death will send Lugaid to fight Cúchulainn because of his blood-oath."

"Very clever," Maeve said, her eyes lowering heavily. She leaned her breast upon Ailill's arm. "You will take care of more than one problem this way. Lugaid is much too friendly with Cúchulainn."

"I think so," Ailill said smugly. "Of course, Láréne may get fortunate and kill Cúchulainn."

Overhearing the last of Ailill's words, Láréne laughed although he felt a moment's annoyance at the suggestion he would need luck against the Warped One.

"Oh, never fear about that," boasted Láréne. "That will happen as sure as I will marry with this fine wench." He squeezed Finnabair's shoulders, staring hungrily down at the breasts threatening to spill out of her neckline.

Ailill grinned with satisfaction at the pompous boast of the youth and stepped outside the tent to relieve himself. As he was pissing in the dark, Lugaid came up to him, saying, "Tell me: what man have you found to challenge Cúchulainn on the morrow?"

"Your brother. Láréne," Ailill said smugly. "He has been bragging all night about what he will do to Cúchulainn on the morrow."

"But you know what sort of man he is!" Lugaid said angrily.

"Yes," Ailill said. "I do. And after tomorrow, all will know. And after he has finished playing ducks and drakes, we will instruct the poets to make special songs about him."

He laughed again and pulled himself within his robes and swaggered back into the tent to enjoy the wine. Lugaid watched him go into the tent, heard the laughter that trickled out after his entrance, then thoughtfully walked from the camp, turning his steps up the hill toward the camp of Cúchulainn. The Warped One met him at Ferbaeth's Glen and greeted him with all honor and politeness.

"I have come to speak with you on a matter of most urgency," Lugaid said. "My foolish and boastful brother has taken up the challenge of Ailill to meet you in single combat since Ferbaeth's death. It is not his fault, although he lets the madness of wine rule his reason, but the fault of those who have tricked him with the Cruachain wine and the wiles of Ailill's bitch-get, Finnabair. I ask a favor from you, my friend, and one that I would not ask, but I can see Ailill's fine hand in this mess. My brother is being used as a pawn to set up a blood-quarrel between you and me, forcing me to come against you next for my blood-oath to which I am sworn. That is the sole reason for the sending of Láréne, nothing more. I do not mind if you punish him—by the gods, he deserves what you might give him as he is coming against my wishes and solely because the goad between his legs is doing his thinking for him—but do not kill him and force me to take up arms against you."

Cúchulainn grinned and touched Lugaid fondly upon his right shoulder with his right hand, then took his arm and led him to his fire where they ate the baked flesh of salmon and talked about things other than the current troubles until the rosy fingers of dawn plucked the shades of night from the sky.

Láréne arrogantly marched to the ford that Cúchulainn refused to let the Connachtmen cross, his unscarred shield gleaming from Lugh's rays, his sword with its clean edge grasped tightly in his hand, his unstained javelin tucked beneath his arm. Finnabair marched beside him, her breasts brazenly bared to the morning breeze, the rosy nipples taut, causing the bearded warriors not chosen to growl among themselves. She stepped away from him as he arrogantly marched to the edge of the ford and cried for Cúchulainn to pay him attention.

But he was not prepared for Cúchulainn's answer as the un-armed, beardless youth waded the ford, ignoring Láréne's warnings to arm himself. Láréne shook his weapons at him, banging his javelin against his shield-rim, but Cúchulainn ignored him and leaped onto his shield rim and snatched his weapons away from him with the speed of a falcon. He stripped the youth bare with one swipe of his hand, then grasped him in his two hands beneath his rib cage and lifted him high, squeezing until the dung squirted from him in a dank stream and the ford grew foul from his droppings. The air thickened from the stench of his bowels being squeezed tightly through fingers like iron bands. He cried out in agony and beat his hands uselessly against the youth's shoulders until Cúchulainn shook him, sprinkling the last dung-drop into the polluted stream, then contemptuously tossed him into Lugaid's arms.

"The favor you requested," Cúchulainn said, wrinkling his nose against the stench of the stream.

"And for that, I thank you," Lugaid said, trying to stifle the howls of his brother. Those who had followed, led by Finnabair, who held the hem of her dress to her nostrils as she fled back to the camp, abandoned the brothers beside the ford. For the rest of his life, Láréne never drew breath without moaning, couldn't eat without groaning, and never had a proper bowel movement. Yet he was the only one of all who challenged Cúchulainn on the *Táin Bó Cuailnge* who escaped without having his head severed from his shoulders and mounted on a standing stone. But it was a cruel escape, for those who watched him with contempt shivered within their own bowels for they knew that they could have suffered the same fate if they had Lugaid for a brother. He reminded them of their own weaknesses and never after did they accord him the honor that he so sorely wanted.

After the host had left, bearing the moaning Láréne with them, Cúchulainn saw a young woman approaching him. High breasted with a noble bearing, she wore a shift made of many colors that highly complimented her fair face.

"Who are you?" Cúchulainn asked suspiciously.

"The daughter of King Buan," she answered. "Tales of your great courage and feats have traveled widely and I see," she said, boldly eyeing his deep chest, "that they have not been exaggerated. I bring with me my dowry and cattle for the tales of your triumphs have made me yearn for your strong thighs between my own."

"I am sorry," Cúchulainn said roughly, embarrassed by the woman's boldness and disturbed by her beauty. "But you have come at a bad time. We do not maintain a house here, but only the bare necessities of a warrior. I do not have time for a woman while I make war with the Connachtmen."

"Perhaps," she said seductively, "I might help."

Her eyes flattered him with their boldness, but Cúchulainn knew that the help he received from her would only sap his strength for the morrow's battle. He shook his head, saying, "I did not undertake this fight for a woman's buttocks! Go!"

Stung, she drew back from him, wrapping her many-colored garment around her shoulders, hiding her breasts.

"If you refuse me, then I will come against you while you are fighting," she said angrily. "If you fight in the ford, then I will come against you as an eel and wrap your feet within my coils and pull you back into the water, leaving you helpless against your enemy."

"Aha! I thought so," Cúchulainn said. "It is easy to see that you are no king's daughter, but a shape-shifter. You may do as you wish, but bear this warning: if you do as you threaten, then I will crack your eely ribs with my toes, giving you a mark that you will carry forever until I remove it with a blessing."

"Then I will come again against you in the form of a she-wolf, driving the Connacht cattle upon you in the waters of the ford and pool. You will not know me by that form," she said, her anger growing.

"Come, then," Cúchulainn said calmly. He folded his arms across his chest and stared deep into her with his triple-irised eyes. "But know this as your warning: I shall cast a stone at you with my sling that will crush the eye in your head. This mark, too, you will bear forever until I remove it with a blessing."

"And if I take the form of a red heifer and lead the Connacht cattle upon you, what then?"

"I'll shatter your leg with a stone. Do not be foolish. Do you want to carry such a mark with you forever until I remove it as well with a blessing? Do you wish to put yourself in such a debt? Think about this before you promise more that you will regret to fulfill!"

With that, she turned on her heel and left him and the wind blew up cold behind her and the grass withered from her fury where her foot touched it. By this mark, Cúchulainn knew her to be more than a simple shape-shifter although he did not know the extent of her magic.

This time Ailill's advisors sought to bring Lóch Mac Mofemis against Cúchulainn as his next challenge. To entice him, they promised him a portion of the Plain of Ai fully equal to the Plain of Murtheimne and to this they added the promise of a war harness for twelve men and a chariot equal to the cost of seven bondmaids. But Lóch Mac Mofemis had seen Cúchulainn and despite the youth's proven prowess in battle, refused to fight him as he had yet to grow a beard. But his brother, Long Mac Mofemis, was made the same promise: Finnabair, the land, the war harness, and the chariot, and he took the challenge. But Cúchulainn easily killed him and the dead man was taken before Lóch Mac Mofemis, who raged through the camp and swore a great oath that he would kill the one who slew his brother if only he were a man and not a boy. Some thought that a *geis,* a ban, had been placed upon him to keep him from warring against youths, so they left him alone for all knew that as long as the ban was obeyed, unnamed disasters were avoided. But Ailill had Maeve instruct the women to call out to Cúchulainn and mock him because he had no beard. Ailill did this because he knew that Cúchulainn would not make war upon women.

So Maeve drew the women of the camp to her and gave them Ailill's instructions and the women drew near Cúchulainn's camp and taunted him, shouting:

"Brave Cúchulainn! Your feats are not so great as only the most reckless men among our men have come forth to fight you. None of our warriors will come against you for you have no beard!"

Angry, Cúchulainn painted his face with berry juice around the dimples in his cheeks and across his chin. Then he plucked a hand-ful of grass and spoke into it, making the Connachtmen think that he had a beard.

"Look!" the women cried to the camp. "Cúchulainn has grown a beard. Surely a warrior can fight with him now!"

And the warriors and women urged Lóch to take up his sword against the newly bearded Cúchulainn, but Lóch said: "Seven days must rise and set before I will challenge him in the ford."

And try as they might, none could move Lóch from his vow. Again, the advisors met in Ailill's tent, frustrated at the delay.

"If we let Cúchulainn rest for seven days, he will be even more formidable," Maeve said. "Send a warrior out every night to attack him while he sleeps and is off guard."

They did this foul deed. Each night, a warrior was found who was willing to meet Cúchulainn in stealth without honor, but Cúchulainn killed every one who came against him in this man-ner. More than seven tried their hand at the dirty deed: seven warriors named Conall, seven more named Aengus, yet another seven named Uargus, seven called Celtre, eight named Fiac, ten named after their king Ailill, ten more named Delbath, and ten called Tasach. All these fell during the week at Áth Grencha.

When Conall Cernach heard about Maeve's treachery, he left the camp and returned to the Red Branch, once again pledging his sword to Conchobar.

Maeve began to taunt Lóch, challenging his manhood.

"For shame that a man with your reputation will not kill the man who slew your brother and destroys our army's morale. A fierce warrior like you afraid to fight an overgrown elf with more courage than years? And you who learned your skill from the same teacher and foster-mother as he! Shame!"

Again, Cúchulainn appeared before them, and from a distance they thought he wore a beard upon his chin and pointed this out to Lóch. At last, the warrior went to meet him and avenge his brother, satisfied that he would be battling a bearded man and not a youth.

"Let us leave this foul place where Long fell and go upstream to do battle," Lóch said to Cúchulainn. "This is not a place for honorable men to fight."

As they were leaving that ford and traveling upstream to the other, some Connacht herdsmen drove cattle across to the grass on the other side of the river.

"I fear many cattle will trample across your water today," Gabrán the Poet shouted to Cúchulainn. From this, Áth Tarteisc, Across Your Water, and T'gir Mór Tairtesc, Mainland of Tarteisc, gained their names.

The warrior and the youth came together in the ford and struck hard at each other, each trying to gain the advantage over the other. As they fought, an eel crept up on Cúchulainn in the water and quickly threw three coils around his ankles and pulled him backward into the water. Lóch immediately renewed his attack to take advantage of Cúchulainn, who sprawled on his back. He hewed great cuts into his body until the ford ran blood-red with Cúchulainn's crimson gore.

From his vantage point, Fergus saw the treachery done and his warrior's heart raged at the unfairness of the attack. He turned to his followers, who watched beside him, and said: "Urge Cúchulainn to fight! This is not the way for a brave man to end in front of his sworn enemy. One of you taunt him!"

Bricriu Mac Carbad of the Bitter Tongue came to stand in front of Fergus and taunt Cúchulainn, saying, "Alas, youth, our would-be warrior! Your strength is like a dried-up tree that snaps at the slightest wind if a small salmon can tumble you into the shallows like this. What will the men of Ulster think now that they rise from their pangs and begin to gather their strength and their weapons? If you fall down upon your back when you finally meet a tough warrior, it is good that they do not see you, a youth trying to be a warrior and challenging like a hero while all Ireland watches!"

Cúchulainn rose in fury at Bricriu's words, striking the eel with his toes and smashing its ribs. The eel gave a great cry, almost human, and disappeared as the cattle, suddenly maddened, thundered madly eastward through the Connacht army, carrying their tents away on their horns. The sound of their passing came like the thunderous deeds lithe warriors performed in the ford. A she-wolf turned the cattle in their madness back west, driving them upon Cúchulainn, but he quickly fitted a stone to his sling and let fly, crushing the eye in the she-wolf's head. A howl of anguish followed and a hornless red heifer suddenly appeared in front of the cattle, leading them on a mad stampede through the fords and pools, whipping the water into such a frenzy that Cúchulainn cried out:

"Where has the ford gone in this flood?"

He lifted a stone from the riverbank and flung it at the red heifer, breaking her legs beneath her, and she disappeared in a flash, leaving a raven behind, its black wings gleaming in the sun. And so it was that the Mórrígan received the three hurts that

Cúchulainn had promised to her if she came against him in the three forms, for it was the Mórrígan, the war goddess, who had been the beautiful woman who thirsted after Cúchulainn's loins before Long and Lóch chose to do battle with him. Cúchulainn raised his head, chanting:

> "I stand alone here against the horde
> that comes to visit at this river's ford
> seeking to pass into Ulster despite my
> armed presence and now they sigh
>
> "their death songs. Tell Ulster to come
> now and tarry no longer. Some
> of Mágach's sons have taken our cattle
> to divide among the rest of the rabble.
>
> "I have held them back. But now I tire
> for one stick cannot long make a fire.
> I need two, or three more to light
> burning torches against their might."

Then he renewed his fight against Lóch with his sword, carving great gouges in the other's shield. At last, he cried to Laeg, his charioteer, to send him the Gae Bolga. Laeg took the feared weapon and sent it down the stream. Cúchulainn hooked it with his toes and struck Lóch up under his horned armor into his bowels, dragging them out and into the stream like thick, white worms pink with blood.

Lóch staggered back, saying, "Stand away from me! Give me space!"

And Cúchulainn yielded the space Lóch asked and the mighty warrior pitched forward upon his face. From this, Áth Traigid has been named In Tír Mór, the Great Country, the Ford of Yielding. When Lóch's last breath wafted up into the air, Cúchulainn cut off his head and a great weariness settled over him. He washed his wounds in the waters of the ford then staggered back to rest.

The Mórrígan appeared to him again, but he did not recognize her as she disguised herself as an old, squint-eyed hag milking a cow with three teats.

"Give me a drink, I beg of you," Cúchulainn said, for his thirst was great upon him.

She filled a cup with milk from each teat and handed it to him.

"Good health be upon you!" said Cúchulainn, draining the cup. "May the blessing of Dagda and man fall upon you and give you peace."

And her head was healed, the squint leaving one eye and her legs growing straight again. She smiled at Cúchulainn for she still loved him, this great warrior who performed deeds other men only dream to perform.

"You said you would never heal me, but look: I am well again from all three wounds," the Mórrígan said.

"Had I known the hag to be you, I would never have done it," Cúchulainn said. And he went to the pallet Laeg had prepared for him and fell into a dreamless sleep.

Chapter 9

THE BLOODBATH

THE CONNACHTMEN MOVED WARILY around the camp, waiting uneasily while their leaders met with Ailill and Maeve in Maeve's tent. In vain, they had searched for another champion to send to Cúchulainn, but none were willing to go in single combat against the man who had slain his own foster-brother, the mightiest warrior among them in a three-day battle, unleashing the dreaded Gae Bolga upon him.

In the tent, the gloom-filled silence lay thick in the air as the advisors leaned against cushions and drank the heavy Cruacháin wine. At last, Maeve rose. All eyed her warily.

"Send to Cúchulainn and beg him for a truce," she said.

Ailill rose at her side and agreed with her.

"We need time to find one who is willing to go before us and meet the beardless warrior at the ford," he said. He shook his head, his lips pulling down heavily at the corners.

"But I do not know if we will be able to find one man," he said in afterthought. "Lugaid, go and ask him for a truce to gain us time to think."

Lugaid rose and went silently from the tent and made his way to the champion's ford, carrying the sign that he wanted to talk. Cúchulainn came down, his war wounds crisscrossing his shoulders and chest. He had held the ford against their bravest champions, but the cost had been dear. His eyes were heavy with weariness, but the warrior's spark in them still flickered, burning, waiting.

"I am to ask you if you would be willing to grant a truce to the Connachtmen," Lugaid said. "It would do you some good as well. Weariness sits heavily upon your shoulders."

"I could rest," Cúchulainn admitted. "But there is the question of honor. I have promised to meet your champions singly at a time, one a day. To do less would dishonor me. But a man must come against me at the ford on the morrow," he said.

Lugaid agreed to this and returned to the Connacht camp, bearing Cúchulainn's message. He told it to the others and they heaved a sigh of relief and went to their own fires to renew their efforts at searching out a person to meet with Cúchulainn.

Now Maeve thought about the six mercenaries in her private bodyguard, all of royal blood, their fathers being kings of the Clanna Dedad: the three Dark-Haired Ones of Imlech and the three Red-Haired Ones of Sruthar. She approached them, asking if one would be willing to uphold the honor of the Connacht force by challenging Cúchulainn on the morrow at the ford he held. She wore her most becoming garment that showed her white breasts and white thighs to their greatest advantage. The six of them looked hungrily at her, but they remembered how Cúchulainn had dealt with the others who had gone before them, and their hearts moved uneasily at the prospect of facing the fury of the Warped One.

"Well, couldn't we all go together as one against Cúchulainn?" they said among themselves. "After all, the pact was made with the Connachtmen and not with us, the men of Clanna Dedad."

Maeve wisely held her tongue to keep from reminding them that they, too, were bound by the pact as they were in the service of the Connacht host and bound by the same loyal pledges as the others. But it would have made no difference had she told them about their pledge for she knew the men of Clanna Dedad did not consider themselves bound by any oath or pledge other than the one they were born with into the Clanna Dedad.

So the six went the next day as one to Cúchulainn at the ford, but since their hearts were false, Cúchulainn easily killed all six with six straight blows. But he did not cut off their heads, because they had done a dishonorable thing by going together against him as one. Such heads did not possess the wisdom or spirit worthy of keeping.

Again, Maeve pondered upon what she was to do with Cúchulainn. Her mind was troubled by the large number who had been killed within her army, but she did not consider for a moment pulling her men back and leaving the Ulster land. At last, she decided to send an emissary, Traigthrén the Strong Foot, to Cúchulainn and ask him to meet with her at a certain place and to come unarmed as she would be accompanied only by her women attendants. What she did not tell Traigthrén was that she had decided that she would hide a large number of spirited warriors nearby and have them leap out and attack Cúchulainn when the warrior made his appearance. Traigthrén did as he was bid and extracted Cúchulainn's promise to meet with Maeve as she had requested. Laeg, however, was uneasy about the woman's promise for he did not trust women at all, considering all of them to be deceitful creatures who used their sex to entrap men and make their way with them.

"Cúchulainn, how do you plan to meet with Maeve on the morrow?" he asked.

Cúchulainn shrugged impatiently and said: "Why, in the matter she asked. To do less would dishonor me."

"Humph!" the charioteer replied, a dark cloud settling over his face. His jaw jutted forward stubbornly. "Maeve is an arrogant woman used to having her way," he said. "You'd better watch your back."

Cúchulainn grinned at his charioteer's concern.

"Well," he said carelessly. "How would you suggest that I go?"

"Do not be caught off guard by her wiles," Laeg said. "Wear your sword at your side. Your honor will not be blackened, for a warrior without his weapon is not under the warrior's code but under the rule for cowards."

"All right," Cúchulainn said, giving in to Laeg's entreaty, for he was weary and wanted to rest. While he lay down, Laeg tended carefully to Cúchulainn's sword, working the battle-scars from it, polishing the blade until it gleamed with a warrior's promise.

Maeve had set the meeting to take place on the hill Ard Aighnech, now called Forcherd, the Great Skill of Cúchulainn. But she went earlier than the proposed time and set a trap for the Warped One with fourteen of her followers most skilled with their weapons: two bearing the name Glass Sinna, two sons of Buccride; two called Ardán, Lecc's two sons; two named Glas Ogn-ma, two sons of Cronn; and Druct and Delt and Daithen, Tea and Tascur and Tualang, Taur and Glese. She cautioned them not to allow themselves to be seen until Cúchulainn seemed at ease and was unwary. She would wear her filmiest garments that would draw his eyes and when he gazed upon her with lust, then they were to attack him.

But the men were eager to kill Cúchulainn and when he appeared, they rose up against him, hurling their javelins at him as one. But Cúchulainn easily slipped the deadly points of the javelins, then drew his sword and killed all fourteen. This place is now called Fourteen at Focherd and the men are also remembered as the Warriors of Cronech for it was here that they fell.

Maeve tried to flee back to camp, but Cúchulainn easily caught her.

"Do not kill me!" she said. "That would bring no honor to you!"

"No, but your return shall be in dishonor," Cúchulainn said. With one swipe of his sword, he severed her clothes from her, the point of his sword not even brushing against her white skin. She shivered, her flesh pebbling in the cold morning, her nakedness, normally a glory, now a shame.

Cúchulainn chanted:

"My skill in arms continues growing
while your fine armies are cowering.
I have unleashed many famous blows
upon your heroes and Maeve and Ailill also
who continue their black deeds
by planting Hatred's seeds
against their hero's sound advice
who has given them warning thrice."

Then, angered by the treachery of Maeve and her guard, Cúchulainn left her and fell upon the warriors as they settled their camp, killing two named Anle and four named Dúngas from Imlech. But still, they fought foully against him when five challenged him together as one: two by the name of Cruaid, two Calads, and Derothor. But Cúchulainn killed all single-handedly.

At last, Fergus demanded that they cease their treachery against Cúchulainn or he would pull the Ulster Exiles from their ranks. From that time on, Cúchulainn did his fighting in single combat until they reached Delga in Murtheimne which was then called Dún Cinn Coros. Here, Cúchulainn killed Fota in the field that now bears his name, Bómalice on the ford named after him, Salach in his marsh, Muinne on his hill, Luar at Lethbera Luair, and Fertóithle at Tóithli.

On the near side of the ford of Tír Mór at Methe and Cethe, Cúchulainn killed Traig and Dornu and Dernu—Foot, Fist, and Palm—and Col, Mebul, and Eraise—Lust, Shame, and Nothing—three Druids and their wives.

In fury, Maeve sent one hundred of her personal bodyguard after Cúchulainn, but they all fell at the ford of Cét Chuile, the Crime of One Hundred, so called for it was here that Maeve cried out in fury, "This is a crime against our people to slaughter so many!"

It was in this fight that Glais Chrau, the Stream of Blood, and Cuilenn Cinn Dúin, the Crime of the Ford, took their names.

Then, Cúchulainn unleashed the fury of his sling, pelting them with stones the size of small boulders from his place in Delga. So furious was the rain of stones that no living thing, man or beast, would show its face past him to the south between Delga and the sea.

Ailill saw that Maeve's treachery did not work and devised a plan of his own, calling Lugaid into his tent and falsely telling him that he, Ailill, had decided to make peace with the Warped One.

"Tell him," Ailill said, "that he can have my daughter Finnabair, after whom many men pant like dogs in heat, if he will stop his warring upon our armies."

Believing Ailill to be speaking the truth, Lugaid made his way up the hill to Cúchulainn's camp in the pine trees. There, he told the beardless warrior about Ailill's offer.

"Friend Lugaid, I'm afraid I do not trust Ailill," Cúchulainn said. "He has spent so much time in the bed of that viper that he has taken on her ways."

"Remember, Cúchulainn," Lugaid said. "Ailill is still a king and I have given you his word. It is unseemly to accuse such a man of lying."

"Very well," Cúchulainn said with misgivings. "I will go. But if it is a lie, my vengeance will be terrible to behold."

Lugaid returned to the camp, bearing Cúchulainn's answer with him. He found Ailill in his tent, lounging on his pillows with Maeve beside him. He told them both of Cúchulainn's agreement, but he did not tell them that Cúchulainn was wary of their words since Maeve had proven false so many times.

After he left, Ailill summoned Traigthrén, saying, "Dress the camp fool to resemble me and place a king's crown upon his head.

Make sure that he stands some distance away from Cúchulainn when he comes so that he will not be recognized. Take Finnabair with you and tell the fool that he is to pretend to be me and betroth Finnabair to Cúchulainn, but to come away quickly before he comes close enough to recognize the ruse. That should hold him until he comes with the Ulstermen for the last battle."

The fool, Tamun the Stump, dressed himself to look like Ailill and placed a crown upon his head. He left with Finnabair and spoke to Cúchulainn at a distance. But Cúchulainn moved too rapidly for Tamun to withdraw and Cúchulainn recognized from his speech that he was the camp fool. He pierced the fool's head with a stone from his sling, knocking out his brains, then caught Finnabair when she turned and tried to flee from his wrath. He cut off her two long tresses and thrust a pillar-stone up under her cloak and tunic. Then he thrust another up the middle of the fool and left them like that. Those two stones still stand there: Finnabair's Pillar-Stone and Fool's Pillar-Stone.

After many hours, Ailill and Maeve sent their trusted warriors to find them. When Finnabair and Tamun were discovered upon their gory stones, word quickly spread throughout the camp, and people began to look fearfully to the hills; the bloodiness of Cúchulainn haunted their days and made terror live in their nights. And from that moment on, no further truce was granted for them by Cúchulainn.

The four provinces of Ireland settled then, and made camp on the Murtheimne Plain at a place that would later take the name of Breslech Mór after the great bloodshed when the ground ran red from their blood. Their cattle shares and plunder were sent south to Clithar Bó Ulad, the Shelter for Cattle in Ulster. At the grave-mound in Lerga, Cúchulainn set up his new camp to be near them. That night, Laeg Mac Riangabra, his charioteer, kindled a small fire for him that seemed dwarfed by the night. A lonely feeling swept over both as they looked out through the darkness to where the fires of the four provinces cast flickering images of golden weapons against the shadow of night.

Fury swept over Cúchulainn at the sight of that vast army camped on the plains of his homeland. He seized his two spears, the Gae Bolga and Duaibhseach; Dubhan, his red shield that turned black in battle, and his sword and clashed them together, flourishing the sword and roaring his warrior's cry of challenge. So fierce came the cry that the blood froze in the veins of the Connachtmen, and the demons and devils and goblins of the glen and evil spirits in the air echoed his cry. Then the Nemain, the frightful War-Spirit and king of the Tuatha Dé Denann who melted into the land itself when the Gaels defeated them, slipped through the night, creating confusion and fear among the armies of Connacht. One hundred warriors fell dead of fright in the night where manguards could not save them from the terror.

The next morning, Laeg stood beside the fire, watching for the day's challenger to come from the camp, when he spied a solitary warrior crossing between Cúchulainn's fire and the camp, heading toward them.

"A man comes alone," Laeg said.

Cúchulainn started to rise painfully, his weary limbs protesting the slightest movement. He dropped back to the ground, groaned, and said: "What sort of man is he?"

"A tall man, broad of shoulder. He wears his golden hair curled and cropped short. A green cloak falls around him and is clasped upon his breast by a bright brooch of silver. His tunic falls to his knees and appears to be of royal silk and red-embroidered in red-gold. A knob of white gold flares from a black shield and he holds a five-pointed spear and forked javelin in his hand. But . . ." Laeg hesitated.

"But . . . ?" Cúchulainn gently prompted.

Laeg frowned. "It is strange; it seems as if . . . as if the others cannot see him."

Cúchulainn rose painfully from the ground and looked to where Laeg pointed, then chuckled and said: "The others cannot see him for he is one of the friendly *Sídhe,* who is coming to help me after learning I stand alone against four provinces upon this cattle-raid of Connacht."

The warrior came up to the Warped One and stood silently, taking his measure. He turned and looked out at the massive Connacht army sprawled over the plain of Murtheimne. A small smile crept upon his lips.

"You have done well, Cúchulainn," he said. "This is a noble stand."

"It isn't much," Cúchulainn said modestly.

The warrior shrugged his shoulders and said: "Well, there is help for you now. I will take your fight."

"Who are you?" Cúchulainn asked. "You should know that whoever sides with me has sacrificed his life."

"I am Lugh Mac Ethnenn," the warrior said. His hair began to glow like burnished gold. "Your father from the *Sídhe.*"

"Welcome," Cúchulainn said. He moved to take his father in a warrior's clasp, but his wounds stabbed deeply and he winced.

"I am sorry," he said. "My wounds are heavy. They need time to heal."

"Then take that time," the warrior answered. "Sleep. Sleep heavily for three days and three nights by this gravemound. I will stand in your place against the challengers for that time."

And he began to sing a soft song to Cúchulainn, whose eyelids grew heavy from the sweet music. He fell into a deep slumber, and while he slept, Lugh cleaned and dressed his wounds, chanting his healing song:

"Rise, mighty Ulster son
with your wounds' healing done.
Take note, Connacht, of this man
whose fair battle kept you banned
from the ford during day and night

and now I come within your sight
from the sacred *Sídhe* to stand
here against your furious band
until my son rises from his sleep
and sends more of you to the deep
arms of Death. Soon, chariots travel
among you and your might unravel.
Then will my son bring his fury
among you, leaving men to bury.
Until then, phantoms will creep
among you, destroying peaceful sleep."

For three days and nights, Cúchulainn slept deeply beside the gravemound, his first sleep from the first Monday after the Feast of Imbolc, celebrating the Triple Goddess Brigit whose breath gave life to the dead. His body twitched and jumped in his sleep, trying to relax from the sleep it had known when Cúchulainn had been forced to sleep standing upright against his spear, his head upon his fist after hacking and hewing his way through the four provinces of Ireland.

And as he slept, the great warrior from the *Sídhe* placed healing herbs and soothing grasses upon Cúchulainn's wounds and sores. Slowly, he relaxed as his body healed itself through his deep dreams.

While he slept and healed, the boy-warriors of Ulster, those who trained hard to become Ulster's next generation of warriors, spoke among themselves of Cúchulainn's deeds and the Ulster men's pangs that had laid them low.

"It is not right that our friend Cúchulainn should have to defend our boundaries without help," they said, and together, all decided they would aid the weary hero until the Ulster warriors could recover from their curse.

A third of the boy-warriors, fifty sons of Ulster kings, marched south from Emain Macha, carrying their hurling-sticks as weapons, while the others remained behind to guard Conchobar while his son, Follamain, led them. The Connachtmen saw them coming over the plain and called Ailill to see the spectacle. Ailill came to the lookout with Fergus to determine what new force marched toward them.

"I cannot make them out," Ailill said. He turned to Fergus, standing by his elbow. "Tell me: what is this force that comes so determinedly toward us?"

"The boy-warriors of Ulster," Fergus said, emotion choking his throat. "The boy-troop who desire to help Cúchulainn, their hero."

"Boys?" Ailill frowned in disbelief.

"Yes, boys," Fergus answered. "But these boys are the ones who will swear blood-oaths against you for your doings here when they become warriors."

"Then we had better see that they do not become warriors," Ailill said grimly. "Send out a troop to meet them before they join up with Cúchulainn. Otherwise, we will have a hard time standing against them."

One hundred fifty of the finest Connacht warriors left from those slain by Cúchulainn went out eagerly to meet them, taking with them their best armor and stoutest weapons to use against the youth armed only with hurling-sticks. They met the boy-warriors at Lia Toll, the Pierced Standing Stone. With relish, the Connacht warriors fell upon the youths, slaying all except Follamain Mac Conchobar, who swore never to retreat to Emain Macha unless he took Ailill's head wearing his golden crown with him. Alone, he held off many warriors until at last the two sons of Bethe Mac Báin, sons of Ailill's foster-mother and foster-father, attacked him from two sides at once, killing him.

When he saw the slaughter his army had made, Ailill rubbed his hands with relish and said to Fergus: "Go now to Cúchulainn and ask him to let us move away from here. While you are gone, we will use the cover of night to move for I am sure that it will be very hard for us to leave once his hero-halo springs up from his brow."

Fergus frowned at the deceit Ailill planned, but left to do as he was bidden. Meanwhile, Cúchulainn, who had spent the last three days and nights sleeping beside the gravemound at Lerga, awoke and leaped to his feet. He ran his hand across his face and felt his wounds, now totally healed from the curing herbs and grasses placed upon them by the warrior from the *Sídhe*. A ruddy glow came to his features and he shook with excitement as his spirit rose up inside him, filling him with joy, fit for a festival, marching, mating, or the mead-hall.

"Warrior!" he cried out to the man from the *Sídhe*. "Tell me! How long have I lain here asleep."

"You have slept strongly for three days and nights," the warrior answered.

"Too long! Too long!" Cúchulainn said.

"Why do you say that?" the warrior asked.

"While I slept, the Connacht army was able to rest as well," Cúchulainn said. "Now they will be rested and ready for battle again."

"They have not rested," the warrior said.

"How is that?" asked Cúchulainn, his brow furrowing in puzzlement.

"The boy-warriors came from Emain Macha. A hundred fifty sons of Ulster kings led by Conchobar's son, Follamain. They fought with only their hurling-sticks, but the Connachtmen still needed three days and nights before they could defeat them. The last to fall was Follamain, who had sworn to take Ailill's head back to Emain Macha with him. But two attacked him from each side and he, too, was slain. They fought well, those sons of Ulster kings. They killed as many Connachtmen as they were in number."

"That must make Ailill proud, making war upon children!" Cúchulainn said angrily, dropping his head in shame. "If only I had had my strength with me! Follamain and the others might well be alive today."

"Lift your head, puppy!" the warrior said reprovingly. "This was meant to pass and there can be no shame attached to your name for it!"

Cúchulainn looked down into the valley at the flickering fires of the Connacht army, feeling the rage rise strongly within him. He turned to the warrior, saying, "I beg you: stay here with me and tomorrow we will go down upon the host together to avenge the boy-warriors."

"No," the warrior said. "This I will not do. Whoever fights in your company will not be remembered. All killed will be given to your name, for your glory and honor will be such that no one else will be remembered by the bards when they sing their songs in the mead-halls. Besides, you do not need me. No one will have power over you at this time. Your death is long in the future, beyond this moment. Go against the army by yourself."

And Cúchulainn took heart from the *Sídhe* warrior's words and turned to find his charioteer, saying, "Hitch up Carbad Seardha, my sickle-chariot, friend Laeg. Yoke it with my horses and make it ready with whatever we have."

Laeg rose and put on his war-harness: a tunic of soft deer leather kneaded supple and smooth, covering it with a mantle of feathers made by Simon Magus for Darius, king of the Romans, and given by Darius to Conchobar, who gave it to Cúchulainn, who had given it to Laeg. He placed his plated battle-cap, rich with color and four points and crest, upon his head and draped the charioteer's sign over his brow—a circle of deep yellow like a red-gold strip of burning gold shaped on an anvil—so that others would know him from Cúchulainn. He covered the war horses with decorated iron armor festooned with spears and blades and barbs and draped the chariot with sickles that made it a formidable weapon. Then, he took the long horse-spancel and goad in his right hand and the steed-ruling reins in his left and cast a protective spell over the horses and Cúchulainn to make them invisible when they roared through the Connacht camp. Although he could not see into the future, it was well he had the foresight to cast this spell for when they attacked the Connachtmen, he would need his three greatest skills: leaping a gap, steering straight, and wise use of the goad.

While he readied the sickle-chariot, Cúchulainn also dressed for war. First, he donned his battle-harness made from twenty-seven waxed skin tunics plated and pressed together and strongly wrapped with strings and cords and straps so that they would not burst from him when his warrior-fury rose. Over them he placed his hero's battlebelt of tough and tanned leather sewn from the hides of seven yearlings, cinching it tightly around his narrow waist from where it rose to his armpits. So strong was this battle-belt that spears, spikes, javelins, lances, and arrows all fell from it as if it were stone. He drew his silk-smooth apron with its gold-speckled border up to the softness of his belly and placed over it another apron of black leather from the hides of four yearlings, cinching it with another battlebelt made from cowhide. He took his flashing, ivory-hilted sword and eight daggers, eight small spears with his five-pronged, ivory javelin, the Gae Bolga, eight light javelins in addition to his black spear Duaibhseach, eight small darts with his feet-throwing dart, the *del chliss,* eight shields with his dark-red curved shield that could hold a boar in his hollow and whose rim was so sharp it could sever a single hair. It was with this shield that Cúchulainn could behead an enemy as easily as he could with his sword.

Upon his head he placed his battle-helmet, large and proudly crested like a hawk's ruff, from which nook his battle scream echoed and reechoed until it became the scream of a hundred warriors and the men who heard it felt their flesh grow cold and their blood freeze in their veins. Demons and devils and all the goblins from the glen and fiends of the air cried out from the helmet for their blood.

Around his shoulders, Laeg placed his cloak of invisibility, such that when he wrapped it around him, he disappeared from the sharpest view. It was a gift made of cloth from Tír Tairngire, the Promised Land, given him by his mystical foster-father.

Then the warp-spasm seized Cúchulainn, a fearsome gripping when the great god Dagda's spirit entered him, making his blood dragon's blood, turning him into a monstrous being, hideous, shapeless, his shanks and joints, knuckles and organs, growing massive and bulging until he shook like a tree in the midst of angry flood, and then his body made a furious twist inside his skin and his feet and shins and knees turned to the back. His calves swelled into balls of sinews, each knot the size of a warrior's sword-fist. His temple-sinews stretched tautly to the nape of his neck, each sinew bulging as a mighty knob the size of a newborn head and singing like plucked harp strings. His features bulged outward, becoming a red-gorged bowl. One eye sucked so deeply into his skull that a wild crane couldn't probe it free; the other fell along his cheek, maddened and rolling, the veins coursing with blood. His cheeks peeled back in a grimace from his jaws until the bile-dark of his gullet appeared and his lungs and liver flapped horribly in his mouth and throat. Then his lower jaw struck the upper like the jaws of a lion and fiery flakes like a ram's fleece flew from his mouth to fleck his chest and the booming of his heart sounded strongly like a baying dog while malignant mists and spurts of fire—Badb's torches—flickering red in the clouds of vapor, rose in furious, boiling waves above his head. His hair twisted like tangles in a red thornbush. If an apple fell on any one hair it would impale itself. The hero-halo rose out of his brow and madness seized him. He banged his spears upon his shields and urged his charioteer into his chariot. Then, tall, thick, steady, and strong, a straight spout of black blood, smoking like a hostel's fires welcoming a king, rose up from the center of his skull like the mast of a noble ship.

And when the warp-spasm ran through Cúchulainn, he stepped into his sickle war-chariot, bristling with iron points and narrow blades and with hooks and hard prongs and frontal spikes and ripping instruments and tearing nails on its shafts and straps. The chariot's body seemed spare and slight with space for a warrior's eight weapons, made to fly like the wind and dart like the swallow over the level plain. Two steeds, wild and wicked, roan-breasted, firm of hoof, moved restlessly in the chariot-shafts: one lithe and swift with powerful hooves; the other slight and slender with a flowing mane; two great horses born with their master, the Gray of Macha and Black of Saingliu.

Cúchulainn stepped into the chariot and drove out to meet his enemies who watched his approach, hearts fearfully fluttering. In his first rush upon them, he killed a hundred. His second rush killed two hundred more; then three hundred and four hundred and five hundred. And all Ireland shook from the first attack by Cúchulainn upon the Connacht army. He ordered Laeg to circle the outer lines of the four great provinces, then attacked in hatred, the chariot driving so fast behind its great horses that its iron-strapped wheels sank deeply into the earth, ripping up great clods and boulders and rocks and flagstones and ground gravel and throwing all behind in a dike as high as the iron wheels, enough for a fortress wall. Around and around the armies he flew, throwing up the circle of Badb to keep them from fleeing his wrath that he might take vengeance upon them for the slaughter of the boy-warriors.

When at last the armies milled in confusion, he fell upon them, Dagda's fury falling upon them, the scream of Mórrígan and Badb echoing fearfully among their helmeted heads, and they fell from the slashing blades of his chariots, from the iron points of his spears, from Cruaidin Cailidcheann, the great, flashing, ivory-hilted sword that cleaved their heads from their shoulders so that they fell, sole to sole, neck to headless neck.

Three more times Cúchulainn made this circle and left the Connacht warriors in a bed fully six deep, the soles of three to the necks of three, in a ring around the camp. From this slaughter upon the *Táin* came the name Seisrech Bresligi, the Six-Fold Slaughter, one of the three slaughters impossible to count on the *Táin:* Seisrech Bresligi, Imslige Glennamnach (the mutual slaughter at Glenn Domain), and the Great Battle at Gáirech and Ir-gairech where horses and dogs died as well as men. From these battles, only the chiefs could be counted: two called Cruaid, two named Calad, two Cír, two Cíar, two Ecell, three Crom, three

Caur, three Combirge, four Feochar, four Furechar, four Cass, four Fota, five Aurith, five Cerman, five Cobthach, six Saxan, six Dach, six Dáire, seven Rochad, seven Ronan, seven Rurthech, eight Rochlad, eight Rochatad, eight Rinnach, eight Coirpre, eight Mulach, nine Daithi, nine Dáire, nine DaMach, ten Fiac, ten Fiacha, ten Fedlimid.

During this great bloodbath upon Murtheimne Plain, Cúchulainn killed one hundred thirty kings as well as dogs and horses, women and boys and children and all kinds of rabble. Not one man in three escaped without injury: crushed thighbone, broken head, burst eye, all battle-scars worn for the rest of his life.

And when Cúchulainn left the battlefield, he bore not a scratch or stain upon himself, his charioteer, or his horses.

Chapter 10

CÚCHULAINN'S
BATTLE
WITH
FERGUS

THE MORNING AFTER THE Seisrech Bresligi slaughter, Cúchulainn rose early to view the armies, dressing himself in his battle finery to show the matrons and virgins and young girls, poets and bards, the true Cúchulainn behind the unearthly shape he had become in the shadows of twilight when the eerie fire of Dagda and the murderous Mórrígan rose high through his hero-halo and made the warriors' hearts quake and their knees turn to weak fat.

When he appeared on the crest of the hill with the dark-green pines behind him, the women sighed and felt their hearts hammer in their breasts and their loins grow moist with desire for the handsome youth with three distinct shades of color in his hair: brown at the base, blood-red in the middle, with a crown of white-yellow-gold that showed streaks of silver when Lugh's rays struck it, painting it with his father's colors. He had drawn his hair into three striking loops beginning at the cleft of the back of his head, each loop flying free with the gentle breath of wind and spreading in shimmering splendor over his shoulders, covering them with a deep-gold mantle. A hundred tight red-gold ringlets shone darkly on his temples while the hair curling over his brow glowed with the brilliance of gems. Four dimples carved his cheeks bearing the sacred colors—yellow, gold, crimson, and blue—and from each royal eye he saw each side of the world from seven bright pupils. Seven toes and seven fingers he had on each foot and hand and the nails of each held the grip of a griffin's grasp or a hawk's claw.

Today, he wore the royal clothes he had earned with the strength of his warrior's hand: a fringed mantle, purple and fine, draping from his shoulders in five folds and held at his hairless breast, gleaming white, with a brooch cunningly wrought from white-gold and silver and inlaid with red-gold that shone so brightly with the rays of Lugh that men shielded their eyes from its brilliance. A silk tunic with red frets flowed freely over his warrior's apron of royal purple silk. In his hand, he loosely carried a crimson shield belted with five silver disks against a light-gold rim with his ivory-hilted sword clasped high on its belt, its gold guard gleaming ominously from his hip. A tall javelin with a doom-gray blade gleaming hungrily from its tip stood in his chariot next to him. Nine human heads dangled from one hand while ten more hung from his other. He raised them high in the air and shook them mockingly at the army.

The Connacht women climbed upon the men's shoulders, the better to see Cúchulainn. But Maeve didn't see him, not daring to show her face from under the protective barrier of shields that kept her from his gaze although she had dressed carefully in a split garment through which her white legs flashed and the red-gold of her beard glinted invitingly.

"What nonsense!" Maeve complained. "I cannot see what the women are clamoring about."

"It wouldn't make you feel any better if you did," Léthrenn, Ailill's groom said, standing on tiptoe to admire the young warrior's advance. His heart lurched in his chest, and he swallowed heavily as he considered the breadth of Cúchulainn's shoulders.

"Fergus, what manner of man is he?" Maeve asked the exiled hero.

"A boy who stoutly defends
his cattle and women, hacking
with sword and shield, and rends
men's bodies in twain, hacking
them apart in Ulster's fords
where he stands alone, hacking
against Connacht's mighty horde;
a hard young Hound alone
against all who try to take
Murtheimne Plain, his home,
away for a foreign queen's sake."

At that, Maeve impulsively clambered upon the men's backs to
see him, her white thighs flashing in the light. As she gazed in admiration upon the youth, Dubthach, the Beetle of Ulster, the Dark
One of the Black Tongue, said:

"Is this the Warped One whose battle cry
sends fear into the hearts of men?
Is this he whom our brave men try
to kill but kills instead our men?

"We shall have stories to sing
about this brave one against whom
our kings' deaths are increasing.
All who try to beat him are doomed.

"I see his wild shape and plunder.
Nine heads he holds in one hand.
Ten more have fallen from the thunder
of his sword. A mighty man!

"Our young women yearn for him
but our great queen pretends
not to see him and ignores him.
If I had my way I would send

"all the armies against him
at once. Then, the Warped One
would find his hero-halo dimmed
and our war in Ulster done."

Fergus delivered a blow against his jaw and answered:

"Send Dubthach and his black words
back behind our mighty army!
Since the maiden-massacre his words
offend all, including me.

"It was base slaughter when he slew
Conchobar's stalwart son, Fiacha,
and no better when he slew
Coirpre Mac Fedlimid. *Phaw!*

"Now this son of Lugaid lags behind
all against Ulster in the battle.
Those that he can't kill he finds
and sends at each other like cattle.

"All the Exiles would lament the dumb
slaughter of our beardless son.
But soon the Ulster hosts will come
and harass you until they've won

"and scattered your councils far and wide
after Ulster has risen from its pangs
and completely slaughtered our side.
They will draw our fangs.

"There will be stories of this slaughter.
There'll be mangling of wounds and sighs
from the breasts of great queens' daughters.
All, all who oppose Ulster will die.

"There'll be mounds of corpses under foot
and there'll be ravens at their flesh
and shields scattered by the roots
of oak trees, pillars to our death.

"Our blood, the Exiles' blood,
will pour across the ground
in a gory crimson flood.
Yes! Here, our deaths will be found."

Then, Fergus picked Dubthach from the ground by his throat
and flung him away where he fell motionless, gagging, near a
group of soldiers, black bile dribbling from his mouth. Ailill
frowned at this treatment of one of his soldiers and said:

"Fergus, why do you rant
so about Ulster cows and women?
For the life of me I can't
understand you Ulster men

"who cry against the way
our men die in the ford
one by one each day.
Each is paid to his accord."

And Maeve pulled her gown around her flashing thighs and
said:

"Form your men, Ailill, in three
ranks and guard our cattle
against this boy who so free
challenges our men in battle.

"Our poets will soon sing
new songs about the turmoil

at fords where we shall bring
death to Ulster's men who toil

"across wide gravel beds
and flounder in dark pools
as they flee from us instead
of fighting. They are fools."

Fergus spat into the dust at his feet and turned insolently away
from Maeve, facing Ailill, saying:

"Do not listen to stupid women
who fan the flames of war.
They would bury our brave men.
For vanity, they make war."

Upon hearing this, Gabrán the Poet said:

"Why do you speak such words?
Everyone—queens and followers all—
will taste battle and hear swords
ring. We hear our duty call!"

Fergus ignored him, staring hard at Ailill while saying, "Don't
listen to these false people who counsel you to send all of your men
at once upon Cúchulainn. Follow the pact we made with him to
send warriors in single combat against him at the ford. You have
tried deceit before, but now you have your honor at stake. A warrior's pact cannot be violated without calling down the wrath of
the gods. And mine," he added. "If your honor means nothing,
mine does."

"Speak, Ailill," Maeve said impatiently. "Tell us what you are
feeling about our counsel."

And Ailill said:

"Fergus knows this land and pretends
to lead us where we must go.
But he is false and sends
us in other ways and shows
his greed by the paths he takes
not for us but for his own sake."

Stung, Fergus answered:

"After this long year of strife
and fighting like women such reports
hurt us deeply. Maeve, such gripes
anger those who came to your support."

Fiacha Fialdána, the bold and true one, left the council and
went to speak with his cousin Maine Andoe the Swift. With Maine
Andoe came Dóchae Mac Mágach, and Dubthach, the Dark One,
wearing his armor with a ravenous wolf's head on each shoulder
and carrying the fearsome spear Cealtchair, whose point had been
bathed in a vat of dark blood, came with Fiacha Fialdána. Fiacha
sought to end a quarrel that had begun during a petty argument
when frayed tempers flared from fear of the Warped One and each
blamed the other for the *ainsprid* that seemed to roam at will
through the camp whenever he struck. As they neared each other,
Dóchae threw a javelin at Fiacha, but missed and struck his kinsman, Dubthach, wounding him. Fiacha threw a javelin at Dóchae
but struck his kinsman Maine. This place is now called Imroll Belaig Eóin, the Place of the Miscast at the Pass of Birds.

Yet some claim that Imroll Belaig Eóin took its name from the
time after the Ulstermen had risen from the pangs of their curse
when the two armies arrived together at Belach Euin. Here, Diarmait, Conchobar's son, came down and said, "Send out a messenger to the Connacht force. If Maine comes to speak with me, I
will go down and meet him at the ford."

And a horseman left for the camp of Connacht and delivered his message. Maine answered, traveling to the ford where he met with Diarmait.

"I have come at the request of Conchobar to tell Maeve and Ailill that they must set free the cattle they have stolen and make proper restitution for the havoc they have wreaked upon our province. Conchobar suggests that the two bulls, yours from the west and ours from the east, meet here and fight in our place. Enough men's blood has been spilled through this foolishness."

"I will convey your king's message to Ailill," Maine said, and returned to the camp where he repeated the words of Diarmait. But Maeve refused to honor the suggestion because she still needed the Brown Bull to make her equal to Ailill. Regretfully, Maine returned to Diarmait, saying, "Maeve refuses your entreaty. I think she believes you plan treachery."

"Then let us exchange weapons," Diarmait said, challenging the other.

"As you wish," Maine said.

And each cast his javelin at the other. Each cast was true and spitted its target to the ground. Seeing this, the two armies rushed down upon each other, killing one hundred twenty out of each side. This, some claim, is where the true name of the place came from: Ard in Dirma: the Tall Place Where the Armies Met.

Aengus, son of Aenlám Gaibe, the Ulster hero, forced the entire Connacht army to turn away at Muid Loga—now called Lugmod—where they were forced to travel as far as Áth Da Ferta, the Two Gravemound Ford. Aengus threw flagstones down upon them in such a great number that they decided it would be better than to attempt to ford the river at this place. The whole Connacht army could have fallen to his hand before they met the Ulster force at Emain Macha if they had met him fairly, but by now, Connacht did not follow the rules of fair combat and they overwhelmed him, cutting off his head and placing it upon a standing-stone.

And so it was here that Cúchulainn threw another challenge at the Connacht force, saying, "Find another to challenge me here."

But no one dared to answer this when word was taken to the Connacht force, the warriors crying, "No, not me! Not me! None of my family owes a blood-sacrifice. Even if they did, why should I be the one singled out to challenge this Warped One who is sheltered with a magic life?"

After vainly trying for three days to find one to challenge Cúchulainn, the counselors went at last to Fergus Mac Roich and asked him to challenge the Warped One. But Fergus refused to fight his foster-son, angrily shoving his way past the beseechers. They followed him into his tent and soothed his feelings by calling for heady wine and pouring his goblet full each time he drained it. Soon he became very drunk, and when they saw his drunken state they asked him again to go out and challenge Cúchulainn. This time, he agreed and staggered drunkenly to the ford where the Warped One patiently waited for his next foe. When he saw Fergus staggering into the shallow waters, he said, "You must believe yourself to be under the protection of the gods to come here against me with your scabbard empty."

Fergus stared stupidly at the white oak sword still in his scabbard, then raised his head and fixed a bleary eye upon the boy-warrior, saying, "It makes no difference!"

He took a step toward Cúchulainn and stumbled and fell, rolling into the shallow waters in his drunkenness. Ashamed, he looked up at his foster-son and said: "I couldn't use it against you anyway, Cúchulainn. But I ask you to yield to me now so that the others will not laugh at me and call me a useless fool when I return to the camp. Even though I am supposed to have come forward against you in this way."

Cúchulainn felt pity for his former teacher and mentor and said: "Very well, Fergus. But remember this favor when I ask the same of you in the future."

"I will," Fergus promised upon his warrior's oath.

And Cúchulainn retreated away from Fergus, drawing back as far as the Grellach Dollaid Swamp. The Connachtmen saw Cúchulainn draw away from Fergus and cried out for his blood, saying, "Catch him, Fergus! Kill him!"

"No," Fergus answered, struggling to his feet. He splashed water upon his face to remove the drunken haze from it. "No, I won't do that. He flies away too fast for me to catch. Let one of you chase after him. I will not fight him again until my turn comes around again."

But none of the others would give chase and instead, they all bypassed Cúchulainn and set up a new camp at Crích Rois.

Now, Ferchu Loingsech had long harassed and hounded Ailill and Maeve from the day they had taken the Connacht throne and had never once gone to their mead-hall or camp to pledge his allegiance or ask for their help even when he could have benefited from it. Some say this was because he thought that he should have been the one who sat upon the Connacht throne for he was forever raiding their borders when they were away. At this time when he heard that the four provinces of Ireland had been stopped and held from the Monday of summer's end until the beginning of spring by one man who fought and killed a man a day at the ford and another hundred at night in their own camp, he traveled east of the Ai Plain, raiding the small settlements of their borders.

That night, he counciled with his dozen men and said: "This is our chance to put Ailill and Maeve in our debt. We shall attack this one man who single-handedly has stopped the four provinces of Ireland and kill him when he least expects to be attacked. We will take his head and weapons to Ailill and his whore-queen Maeve and demand our pardon and tribute. They will be forced to forgive us since we will have killed the man they cannot."

His men agreed that this was a wise thing to do and together, they crept up on the ford where Cúchulainn waited for his next challenger from the Connacht camp. They attacked him foully, all falling upon his back at once, but Cúchulainn heard their feet upon the gravel and turned and met them with his sword, killing all twelve instantly, striking off their heads. He placed twelve stones upon the ground at the entrance to the ford and set a head on each stone, Ferchu Loingsech's head on one of the middle stones. This is why the place has now come to be called Cenn áit Ferchon, the Place of Ferchu's Head.

The next day, Maeve took twenty-nine men from her guard and sent them as one against Cúchulainn at Seascann Fuilarrn, Blood-iron Swamp, near Ferdiad's Ford. Gaile Dána and his twenty-seven sons and his sister's son, Glas Mac Delga were the twenty-nine chosen from her guard. Fergus argued that this was against the pact that they had made with Cúchulainn, but all argued that it should be considered a single combat since all were from the same body, limb from limb, flesh from flesh, blood from blood. But what they did not tell him was that they planned treachery and not fair combat upon the Warped One. At last, Fergus agreed and went wearily to his tent where he drank deeply of honeyed wine until one came to him to tell him about the planned treachery.

When he learned of their plans, he said: "This is a sad, sad thing that will happen tomorrow."

"What is?" his followers demanded.

"Tomorrow will see the death of Cúchulainn," Fergus answered, draining a glass of wine and staring moodily into the tent fire.

"But who can kill him? Many have tried and all have failed in single combat," they said, puzzled.

"Tomorrow, Gaile Dána and his twenty-seven sons along with the son of his sister, Glas Mac Delga, will attack him as one since each is from the same body. They will have poison upon their armor and poison upon their weapons as well so that any man whom they wound will die horribly within nine days if they do not kill him at once. I beg of you: choose one to go and witness the death of Cúchulainn and bring me word of his last battle. Whoever will go may have my weapons and blessing."

"I'll go," Fiacha Mac Firaba said.

The next morning, Gaile Dána rose early with his men and left to find Cúchulainn. Fiacha Mac Firaba waited for them to leave, then followed them to the ford. He watched as Gaile Dána refused the formal warrior's challenge and treacherously hurled his spear at Cúchulainn. The other twenty-eight hurled theirs immediately afterward. Not one missed its target, but Cúchulainn performed the rim-feat with his shield and the twenty-nine spears stuck in the center of his shield, sinking halfway through toward his breast. But none drew blood.

Cúchulainn quickly pulled his sword from Badb's scabbard to cut away the spears and lighten the load on his shield and when they saw this, all attacked him, aiming their twenty-nine fists with their mailed gloves dipped in poison at him. Their weight bore him down in the ford until the gravel ground against his back. He shook and gave his warrior's scream about the unfair fight so loudly that it echoed throughout Ulster, and every living man heard it and shook with fury and helplessness since they still lay in the throes of their pangs.

Fiacha heard it also and, loath to see a hero as mighty as Cúchulainn so foully slain, leaped from his chariot, hacking off all twenty-nine hands with the poisoned-mail gloves with his sword. Cúchulainn thanked him, saying, "You have arrived most timely."

"Think nothing of it," Fiacha answered. "But I have broken the treaty we, the exiled ones from Ulster, made with Connacht. If one of these foul men returns to camp with word about what I have done here, all of the other Exiles, all three thousand, will be put to Connacht sword as traitors."

"Then," Cúchulainn said grimly, "I shall see that not one of them returns."

His warrior's scream froze the birds in the air as he charged upon the twenty-nine, brandishing his sword on high. Two of Ulster's warriors who had recovered from their pangs enough to join him, two sons of Ficce, followed in his trail and together, they slew twenty-eight. One, however, Glas Mac Delga, flew from the slaughter and ran to Connacht's camp with Cúchulainn in pursuit. In a panic, Glas ran to Ailill's tent, running around and around it in fear while Cúchulainn chased him.

"Fiach! Fiach!" Glas squawked like a chicken, but before he could say more, Cúchulainn struck off his head and fled the camp so swiftly that no one had a chance to attack him.

"That didn't take long," Maeve said, eyeing the twitching body of Glas. She frowned, biting her full lower lip in thought.

"Fiach? A debt? What did he mean, Fergus?" Ailill asked as the warrior lumbered up to them.

"Who knows?" Fergus said, shrugging, looking bleary-eyed toward the ford. "Whatever, he has been paid in full."

And so, none returned to the Connacht camp with word of Fiacha's betrayal of the compact.

And this ended one more battle with Cúchulainn. In the middle of the stream, Cúchulainn set a massive stone to mark where the rim-feat was performed and where treachery was tried by the Connachtmen. Around the stone he erected twenty-nine standing stones and there they may be viewed today.

Chapter 11

THE BATTLE BETWEEN FERDIAD AND CÚCHULAINN

AGAIN, THE WARRIOR COUNSELORS argued among themselves about who should be the next to fight Cúchulainn. Back and forth the arguments went, growing more and more heated as each of the provinces placed the responsibility upon another. At last, they decided that the warrior from Irrus Domnann, the warrior with skin as hard as horn, the one who bore the heaviest burden and against whom other warriors blunted their blades in battle, Cúchulainn's own foster-brother, should be the next one to challenge the Warped One. He was the only one who could duplicate all the feats of Cúchulainn—except that of the Gae Bolga, and the armor he wore was impervious to slash or stab.

Maeve immediately sent a messenger to Ferdiad's tent, but the warrior refused to return with them, for he knew what she wanted. When the third messenger returned with Ferdiad's blunt refusal, Maeve became enraged and sent the best of the poets and bards and satirsts in her retinue to compose insulting poems and songs and stories about him, commanding them to make the stories so spiteful and denigrating that there would be no place in the world where he would be able to peacefully rest his head.

Dreading the shame and stain that would be placed upon his name, Ferdiad reluctantly followed them back to Maeve and Ailill's tent where all waited in conference. When he walked through the doorway, Maeve had already arranged a place for him, commanding her daughter, Finnabair, to sit beside him and give him goblets and cups of wine and place upon his lips three amorous kisses for each cup. This Finnabair did, wearing her most daringly cut gown, which revealed the fragrant apples of her breasts. As his eyes traveled her shapely form, she leaned forward, whispering with sweetly scented breath that he, Ferdiad, was her heart and her chosen. And when he tasted her lips, he felt his will slip away from him in desire.

When she saw his humor, Maeve said: "Now, Ferdiad, that you have seen and tasted and heard what may be yours, why do you think you were brought to my tent?"

Ferdiad knew, but deliberately avoided the answer she wanted.

"The noblest warriors and heroes in Ireland are here. Why should I be excluded?" he asked.

"Come now," Maeve said impatiently. "Surely, you suspect the true reason!"

But Ferdiad remained silent, raising a golden cup and taking Finnabair's three kisses before drinking. His fine eyes flashed darkly over the lip of the cup and Maeve felt a familiar weakness in the pit of her stomach.

"I . . . we will give you a chariot worth twenty-one bondmaidens and enough war-harness for a dozen men. To ride the chariot over, we will also give you a part of the Plain of Ai equal to that of the entire estate of Murtheimne and the right to stay as long as you wish in Cruachaín with as much fine Cruachaín wine as you should wish. All of your relatives will be forever free from taxes and tributes."

She unpinned a brooch from her tunic and the cloth fell away, exposing her creamy breasts with their large, rosy-tipped nipples, and the breaths of all came hard in their chests. She grinned wickedly as she leaned forward, allowing Ferdiad a glimpse of the beauty hidden behind her tunic.

"And," she said softly, "you may have this brooch cunningly carved in the shape of a leaf made from one hundred twenty ounces, an equal number of half ounces, an equal number of cross-measures, and an equal quarter of gold. Finnabair, my daughter from Ailill, will be your wife. And," she paused meaningfully, "my own friendly thighs, if you wish."

"No!" the others cried gutturally as they envisioned Ferdiad between the thighs that all desired. "Enough has been promised!"

"These are great gifts, indeed," Ferdiad said when the tumult died. "But I would rather that you keep them than fight with my foster-brother to gain them."

Maeve sighed deeply and repinned the tunic carelessly over her breasts with the promised brooch.

"It appears that what Cúchulainn said was true," she said regretfully.

Ferdiad frowned.

"And what was that, Maeve?" he asked.

"Oh, nothing," Maeve answered. She took a tiny sip of Cruachaín wine and carefully replaced the goblet beside her.

"Something, I think," Ferdiad said.

"Well, he did say that his greatest feat of arms would not be needed to bring about your downfall," Maeve said.

Ferdiad's face flushed fiery-red and he said: "That, he should never have said. My feats in battle are as great as his. He has seen me fight and I proved to be his equal then. By the gods!" he swore, leaping to his feet. He brushed the clinging arms of Finnabair from him and strode to the tent opening, gazing out darkly upon the ford.

"Tomorrow morning," he said grimly, "I shall be at the ford at first light to give him the challenge he wants!"

"Take our blessings with you!" Maeve said, barely keeping her delight from showing. Her heart pounded at the sight of his fine form against the fading light of the tent opening.

"Think about what you are about to do," she said, then craftily added, "Is it better for him to be the guarding Hound of Ulster because his mother is a daughter of Ulster or for you, the son of a Connacht king, to be the savior of Connacht?"

And so the pact was made among them and Ferdiad and Maeve sealed it with their formal chant:

Maeve:
"I promise you riches and rings
and my daughter, my thighs, and things
others dream about: woods, plains,
kinfolk privileges, and those same
privileges to you until time's end.
Do you accept these terms and bend
to the will of your people, Ferdiad?
Accept it, my daughter, and me, Ferdiad"

Ferdiad:
"I'm no hollow hero! Give me surety,
though, for tomorrow I only will see
the terrible fury of the Warped One
and bear his battle until it is done."

Maeve:
"Is that all? Then pick your surety
from among pale kings and princes. See
if there are men here who can together be
what you want. They will remain until
you have met the man whom you will kill."

Ferdiad:
"Then I will take six heroes, no less,
with me. I ask only that you will bless

their place with me. Grant me this and
I will battle the Hound and your band
will bear witness to my deeds and bring
you word of my victory before midday rings.
Know this, though, Maeve of the Friendly Thighs,
I am no match of Cúchulainn and that's no lie."

Maeve:
"Take farmers, soldiers or the killer Niaman
or choose bards or poets or scribes. Any man
you wish shall be yours, if you so demand.
You may have any including the mighty Morann
or even those we most love: our own two sons
who will serve you until your deed is done."

Ferdiad:
"Your tongue is very strong, Queen Maeve,
and your husband is one who is most brave
to take you for his wife. But I can plainly see
that you are the master here and will gladly
offer her friendly thighs if I am the one
who walks away once the fight is done.
I will take your gifts. Give me six strong
princes who will not do me any wrong
if Cúchulainn should be the one who wins
the battle between us. *If* he should win!"

Maeve:
"You are the fairest champion I have seen!
Take my brooch, then! I will sleep and dream
of the nights to come. Sunday will be the time
for you to go and avenge Cúchulainn's crime
against Connacht. Then, I promise that all
will be delivered into your hands. Call
for what you will! My jewels, Finnabair,

all will be there for the pain you'll bear
after the Hound is killed
and his mighty heart stilled."

Fergus Mac Roich, one of Ulster's greatest warriors, listened to their bargaining chants, then left and returned to his tent where others of the Ulster Exiles waited.

"Alas! There will be a sad day indeed on the morrow and much mourning!" he said.

"Why is that?" those in his tent asked.

"Tomorrow, my foster-son, the mighty Cúchulainn will be killed," he replied, and seized a goblet, draining the honeyed wine from it in one draught.

"And who is foolish enough this time to think that he may have a challenge that he can bear against Cúchulainn?" they asked scornfully, for all there had seen the Warped One's strength in battle and had felt his blows upon the playing field where all the boy-troop trained.

"Ah, well!" Fergus sighed. He poured another glass, draining it. "I guess it doesn't matter; it soon will be announced by messengers throughout the camp that his next challenger will be none other than his own foster-brother, Ferdiad Mac Damáin."

An uneasy murmur ran through those present in Fergus's tent. Simultaneously, all reached for their wine goblets, draining them.

"Will one of you go in pity for Cúchulainn?" Fergus asked. "It is most unlikely that he will be able to win against Ferdiad, who will be fresh and rested while Cúchulainn will be grievously weary after these many days of fighting alone against Connacht's best. I will give my blessing to whoever chooses to go, and promise to protect him against the wrath of Maeve if he is discovered, if only one will travel to Cúchulainn's lone camp and warn him to stay away from the ford on tomorrow's morning."

"Your own blessings upon you!" they exlaimed as one. "Who wouldn't go on such a bidding, even if one was in the ford of battle himself?"

"Then go," said Fergus. "Take my horses and yoke my chariot and go, my friend, and bear my warning to Cúchulainn about who comes tomorrow."

A charioteer drained his goblet and turned it upside down, to signify that he would not drink again until his task had been accomplished, and rose, striding purposefully from the tent to where Fergus kept his horses stabled. There, he selected two of the mightiest war steeds and yoked them to Fergus's best chariot. When Fergus emerged from his tent, the charioteer stepped into the chariot and ran his whip along their backs without touching them with the lash, and guided them out to the ford where he found Cúchulainn sitting with Laeg beside his fire, waiting until the meat was cooked, drinking from a horned goblet that held a strong measure of the good ale that held the spirit of the bravest warrior in it and which only Ulster could brew. He looked up as the chariot drew near and Fergus stepped from it.

"Welcome, friend Fergus," he said.

"Well, now I believe I am," Fergus said, striding to the fire to warm his cold fingers.

"And why shouldn't you be?" Cúchulainn asked. "If a flock of wild geese came, I would catch two and give you one and share the second. If salmon ran spawning in the river-mouths, I would give you one and share another after having it baked with cress and marshwort and sea-salt and share a drink of the coldest water that could be drawn from deep beneath the sand."

"Outlaw's fare," Fergus grunted.

"Oh yes," Cúchulainn said, smiling gently. "And why would it be less? I have been treated like an outlaw, forced to fight by surprise from the hills until the pact of the fords was made. From Monday after Samhain at summer's end until now."

"I didn't come for food," Fergus said roughly.

"And what brings you here to my fire?" Cúchulainn said.

"I bring word of him who will meet you on the morrow," Fergus said glumly.

"Then tell it. Bring it out in the open and deal with it," Cúchulainn said.

" 'Tis your own foster-brother, Ferdiad Mac Damáin," Fergus said.

Cúchulainn squatted beside Fergus and turned the meat on the fire. He took another drink from his cup and handed it to Fergus, who drank and handed it back.

"I don't want this meeting," Cúchulainn said quietly. "I don't fear him, but to kill him would grieve me deeply and would be the spilling of the blood of my brother."

"It is well that you fear him," Fergus said. "But meet him you will, or bow your head in shame forever and listen to the songs that will be sung about you, giving the lie to your name. Now, to the particulars: you will have to approach him carefully and plan for your fighting, for he wears an armor of horn that no blade has broken or pierced."

"Don't worry about that now," Cúchulainn said, staring gloomily into the fire. "If he appears, then I shall meet him, and his limbs will bend like the slender reeds of the river when he feels the edge of my sword."

And Fergus sat back and stretched his legs before the fire, chanting:

"Ah, my son, Cúchulainn! you must
ready yourself or become dust
before the blade of Ferdiad. Look
to yourself or die beside this brook."

And Cúchulainn answered:

"Then here I'll make my stand
against all the men of Ireland
who may come to me as a band.
I have stood many a fight before
against me. Those I call whores!"

Fergus laughed and said:

"Speak all your brags you can,
Cúchulainn, but he who'll stand
against you tomorrow will wear
a horn-skin that none can tear."

Cúchulainn rose and went to his weapons, drawing them and examining them critically:

"Ferdiad, who is as skillful as I
am with blood-reddened sword, and I
will try to kill each other. He is as strong
as a hundred men Maeve has wronged."

Fergus answered:

"Your crimson sword would please me
if it could pass Ferdiad to Death's sea."

Cúchulainn stared as if hypnotized into the fire whose coals burned as brightly as Lugh's:

"Then know this, Fergus, I don't lie.
I will kill Ferdiad. He cannot make me die."

Fergus nodded and went back to the fire, tearing a strip of meat from the haunch roasting there, saying:

"I turned against Ulster to avenge a wrong.
Warriors followed me to Connacht and strong
men with them did, too. Together, we stood
against Ailill, Maeve, and all their brood."

Cúchulainn grimly answered:

"Aye, and if not for Conchobar's pangs
I would not be alone. I must draw Ulster's fangs
and keep the queen you serve, Maeve, from
Scáil Plain, the Trail of Tears. Come!"

And he stretched forth his hand, but Fergus shook his head, avoiding Cúchulainn's eyes, and staring into the fire said:

"I fear the great trial with Ferdiad is at hand
and hate, baleful and bitter spear, will stand
triumphant against you. Hound of Culann, look
to your well-being before battle beside this brook."

"Is this, then, the reason that you came, Fergus my friend?" Cúchulainn asked.

"It is," Fergus replied stoutly.

"Then it is well that no one else of Ireland's men came to warn me about such a single warrior as Ferdiad for I would not have believed him and none, including the four provinces of Ireland, could have saved him!"

Fergus grinned at this and drank deeply of the dram that Cúchulainn's charioteer handed him and after summary small talk, unsteadily mounted his chariot and bade his charioteer take him home to the Connacht camp and to bed.

Laeg watched as Cúchulainn sat, brooding, staring down from the height of the hills among the black pines into the Connacht camp. At last, he stirred himself and approached Cúchulainn, saying, "What are you going to do this night?"

Cúchulainn shook himself and frowned in puzzlement as he stared at Laeg. "What do you mean?"

Laeg gestured impatiently. "You sit here feeling sorry for yourself, thinking about what will come tomorrow. Do you think Ferdiad is thinking that way? No! He is readying himself for tomorrow for he knows as well as you that this will be the hardest fight he has ever fought. He is remembering what it is to be alive. He will be washed and bathed, his hair freshly braided and trimmed. He will look the hero when the four provinces of Ireland settle themselves to watch the two of you fight."

"And what do you suggest?" Cúchulainn said, grinning.

"Do the same," Laeg answered promptly. "Go where you, too, will get that attention. Go to Cairthenn Cluana-Dá-Dam, the Meadow of the Two Oxen, at Sliab Fuait where Emer, your wife waits."

"By the gods, if you don't make good sense!" Cúchulainn said, rising.

And the Warped One went to his wife and spent the night with her while Ferdiad went to his tent and told his *curaid* of the pledge he had made Maeve to fight single combat with Cúchulainn or fight six warriors if his nerve should fail him. He also told them that Maeve had promised that the same six warriors would make sure that she fulfilled all the promises she had made if he killed Cúchulainn, not the least of which were her own friendly thighs.

His followers fell into black depression at Ferdiad's words for they knew that when these two heroes met, the world would see the greatest battle ever fought, for Cúchulainn and Ferdiad were so evenly matched that each could die in the battle.

Ferdiad tried to make light of the battle coming in the morning, but his spirit was heavy as he tried to sleep among the rich cushions of his tent. Not only did he think about meeting his foster-brother, but about Maeve's promises should he win, and when he closed his eyes, he saw her rich breasts and the breasts of Finnabair and the promise he had seen in the eyes of each. But more than that, he thought about how his life would never be the same once he had met Cúchulainn at the ford.

In the morning, he left his sleepless bed at first light and went to find his charioteer.

"Now, my friend. Yoke the chariot with our finest battle-horses and let us make ready," he said.

"This is a bad journey we take," his charioteer said.

Ferdiad nodded, and together he and his charioteer chanted:

Ferdiad:
"Come! Let us go to the battle
at the ford and not moo like cattle
in despair. I will meet Cúchulainn
and my spear will pierce his brainpan
and Badb will screech as his hero-halo
leaves his brow when his body falls low."

Charioteer:
"You make cruel threats, mighty one!
It would be far better to stay alone
here than to go where one will surely die
and the victory will be hollow. Lie
here, instead, in your tent. Disaster
will follow you if you fight before Ulster."

Ferdiad:
"Is it a warrior's work to be shy or meek?
I will travel to the ford and there seek
out Cúchulainn. Have courage to the end,
my friend! My spirit will not bend!"

The charioteer left, shaking his head at Ferdiad's last words. Carefully, he dressed the horses and yoked them to Ferdiad's best chariot and together, they left the camp. But before they had traveled far, Ferdiad placed his hand upon the reins, pulling up short.

"I am sorry, my friend," he said. "But it is not right to leave in this manner without saying farewell to those who follow me. Turn the chariot around and let us return."

Obediently, the charioteer turned and drove back to the Connacht camp. There he turned the chariot three times in the warrior's farewell and passed close to Ailill's tent where Maeve squatted, pissing on the floor. She heard Ferdiad's farewell and said: "Are you sleeping, Ailill?"

"No," Ailill said, yawning as he rose from the pillows where he and Maeve had only recently wrestled. "Who can sleep through that noise? What is it?"

"You do not hear your new son-in-law bidding us farewell?"

"Oh. Is that what he is doing?" Ailill said.

"Yes," Maeve answered. "But I do not think he will be coming back on his own two feet."

"It doesn't matter, does it?" Ailill said crossly. "We have done well with this marriage agreement for if he triumphs, then we will have Ireland's best warrior in the family. But if he doesn't, then we aren't any worse off than we are now. Come back to bed."

And she rose, dropping her robe, and walked naked through the dim light of the tent until she fell into Ailill's arms and pressed his face against her naked breasts, her friendly thighs wrapping tightly around his waist.

His farewell finished, Ferdiad directed his charioteer to drive to the ford. When they arrived, the crossing seemed empty. Ferdiad frowned.

"See if Cúchulainn waits for us," he ordered.

"I don't see him," the charioteer answered.

"Look carefully!" Ferdiad snapped. His eyes felt gritty from lack of sleep and he rubbed them, trying to clear the bleariness from them.

"Cúchulainn is not a tiny speck to hide among the gravel in the ford," the charioteer said.

"True," Ferdiad said, his spirit brightening. "Perhaps he has fled, knowing that it was I who came against him today. Cúchulainn," he boasted, "has never had a warrior as strong as I come against him before. It would be expected that he should vanish without explanation!"

"For shame!" the charioteer snapped. "This is not worthy of you to slander Cúchulainn when he is not here to answer you! Don't you remember when you fought the harsh and grizzled Germán

Garblas above the borders of the Tyrrhene Sea and left your sword with the enemy army when you retreated from the large numbers pressing against you? Cúchulainn slew a hundred warriors that day to reach your sword and bring it back to you. Do you remember where we stayed that night?"

"No," Ferdiad said, unwilling memory of his retreat from the battle forcing itself upon him.

"We stayed at the house of Scáthach's steward. When you went in front of us into the house, full of pride and haughty with thoughts of your own importance, the monstrous steward struck you heavily in the back with his three-pronged meat-fork. You flew like a stone past the door lintel. Then Cúchulainn went in and struck the steward, severing him in twain with one blow of his sword for his ill manners. I was your steward, at the time, while you stayed there. If that day were here again, you would never say that Cúchulainn was a lesser warrior than you."

"You should have reminded me of this before," Ferdiad said. "You are right: I shouldn't have come, looking for this fight. Not all the riches, Finnabair's breasts, or even Maeve's friendly thighs are worth this fight. But I am here and here I must stay. Pull the shafts of the chariot over and spread a skin over them so I might sleep awhile."

His charioteer shook his head, saying, "I think you would sleep in the path of a deer hunt! How can you sleep here?"

"Can't you watch for me?" Ferdiad demanded.

"Oh yes. That I can do. I will watch and give warning if they come from the east or west. But if they come at you out of the clouds and mists of your dreams, you will have to fight them by yourself."

And he pulled the shafts of the chariot up next to Ferdiad and placed the skin over them. But Ferdiad could not sleep, not even a little as memory danced through his mind.

Meanwhile, Cúchulainn had readied himself and now told Laeg to bring the chariot up so that they might leave for the ford.

"If Ferdiad's waiting, he might think that I have left without meeting him," Cúchulainn said. "Bring the horses and yoke the chariot."

Obediently, Laeg rose and brought the chariot for Cúchulainn and they passed together to the ford. Ferdiad's charioteer heard them coming and shook his master, chanting:

"Arise, now, my master. I hear
chariot wheels creaking. Bear
with me! I see its great silver yoke
and a great man behind it who has broken
many warriors' spirits before this day.
This is no warrior with feet of clay!
This is a man, triumphant and proud,
who has laid many warriors in their shrouds!

"A skilled Hound stands in the chariot
urging his great horses to pull the chariot
ever faster towards us like a hawk hurrying
to its victim that races away, scurrying
rapidly to avoid the death coming fast
toward him. Alas! I fear that we will not last
against this man's fury. I dreamed last year
about this meeting with Cúchulainn. I hear
his war-harneess and tell you this, Ferdiad,
you would do well to fear the Hound of Emain Macha!"

"How does he look?" Ferdiad asked.

"As if all of Ireland means nothing to him," the charioteer answered.

"That's enough!" Ferdiad said sharply. "You give him too much praise! Now, ready my weapons and let us travel to the ford."

"I feel if I turn my head his chariot shafts will stick in the back of my neck!" the charioteer complained.

"Why do you praise him so?" Ferdiad demanded. "Your loyalty lies with me, not with him!"

Then Ferdiad chanted:
"I do not need your woman's laments now!
This is false friendship when you sow
such thoughts in my mind. When we are dead
we are all the same. When we have fled
we are all the same. Let him come in his glory
and I shall put an end to his glorious story."

Charioteer:
"When Cuailnge's great warrior travels
in his glory it will be to us. Don't unravel
his glory with your bragging. Shrewdly
give praise where it is due, not slyly
take it away from one who has earned it!
He comes like a thunderclap against you. It
is not for you to take his bravery away
and claim that he has feet of clay."

Ferdiad:
"Enough of your praise for him!
I will make his warrior's eyes dim!
Why do you favor him? Does his glory
make mine shine the less? I marry!
Others who have likewise praised him
even as they roared a challenge to him.
It is a most sorry lot who came before me
to battle this Hound of Ulster, I see."

Leaving his charioteer, Ferdiad went to the ford and stood in the middle, waiting for Cúchulainn.

"Welcome, Cúchulainn," he said when the Warped One came up to him.

Cúchulainn gave him a strange look, noticing the way his eyes shifted from his to the side and back again, and he knew that Ferdiad had not come there for the honor of battle but because he had been promised many rewards if he could but kill Cúchulainn.

"Perhaps I could have once trusted you to mean your welcome, Ferdiad," Cúchulainn said sadly. "But not anymore. Besides, it is for me to make you welcome, not for you to extend your welcome. This is my land, not yours. You are an intruder here, Ferdiad, and you did not come with pleasantries on your mind, but war. This is wrong! You have pillaged our towns, raped our women, taken our young men and boys prisoners, and confiscated our troops of horses, our herds and flocks and all our goods."

"That's enough, Cúchulainn!" Ferdiad snapped. "What makes you think that you should come to meet me in combat? When we were with Scáthach and Uathach and Aife, you were nothing more than my body-servant who repaired my spears and made my bed."

"That may have been," Cúchulainn said. "But I was young then, and small. It is wrong for you to think that way of me now. There isn't a warrior in the world that I am not better than or equal to."

Having bitterly reproached each other, they ended their friendship, delivering the formal chants of challenge to each other:

Ferdiad:
"You are foolish to come here, Squint-eyed
to try my strength! Do you wish to be bloodied?
I'll reach you despite your horses' speed
and you'll regret that you came while you bleed
upon the ground. You're a fuel-less fire
 and will need help from others, you liar!"

Cúchulainn:
"Stay here and I will humiliate you before all
who wait to watch you try me. You will call
for help long before I finish your punishment
for trespassing on our lands. Banishment
from Connacht for failing will be your reward,

not presents from white-thighed Maeve. Onward,
then, if you are foolish enough to challenge me
and I will wreak havoc upon your head. Flee,
now, if you still want to keep some part
of your reputation. Otherwise, let us start!"

Ferdiad:
"Brave words, boy! But it is I who will kill
you. I who will destroy and drive you away until
all see Ulster's hero fleeing before me,
running like a dog, tail between his legs. See
how they watch, waiting for the battle to begin!
Let us start then, if you still think you'll win."

Cúchulainn:
"Why spend your time groaning over corpses?
Come away with me now, if you wish, and let us
enter the ford, one to meet his death before
the hosts who watch. Perhaps bloody spear or
savage sword will end our time, but see
if your heart is ready or else die before me."

Ferdiad:
"I'll fight you at Bairche in bloody battle
and drive you away like the tame cattle
who enter the barn to be milked. Ulster's
men will not remember your name, your blusters.
They will cry out: Death has seized the mighty Hound!
and they, too, will flee from your death sound."

Cúchulainn:
"When the cock crows you will die
for by then you will have seen how I
lose my wits in battle. You will see
your own death! Come, now, with me!"

"Ferdiad, this is a bad thing you have done to come and challenge me," Cúchulainn said. "This is only Ailill and Maeve's petty argument and meddling. You know I have killed all who have come before me. You, too, will fall.

"Ferdiad, Damáin's son, do not come
against me now. This is foolish. Some
will say you are afraid, but this will be
your downfall. You will suffer more than me.

"How do you think that you can stand
against my rage when others of your band
have fallen? Ferdiad, you won't have Finnabair
or Maeve of the Friendly Thighs. Bear
your soul and spirit, if you will. Try
me, if you want, but you will still die.

"Maeve's fair daughter is only a snare
to trap you. You will not see her bare
breasts and thighs upon your bed. She
has played false with others who tried me
for her thighs and ruined them. Don't break
our friendship and oath for her sake!
This is the same girl promised falsely
to fifty men who then tried to kill me.
But their spears did them no good.
I killed them where they stood.

"Ferbaeth, they said, was the brave one
among a house of heroes who would've won
but I killed him with only one throw
before this river's continuous flow.

"Srúbdaire, too, found a bitter end
beside this river's narrow bend.
A hundred women held him dear
but his did not help his fear.

"If they had offered Finnabair to me,
if I was the one Maeve sought to be
with her in her bed, I wouldn't want to do
you harm or even touch your flesh, too.

"And because of this, Ferdiad, you should not come to fight me,"
Cúchulainn said. "When we fought with Scáthach and Uathach
and Aife, we always left for the battlefields together. We shared
the battles and the struggles, we wandered through forests and
across desert and explored dark mysteries, always together.

"We were fast-friends and forest-companions
and made one bed and slept together. Denizens
tried to kill one, but we killed them all
together. Scáthach's pupils, that is all
we were, but it was enough for the two
of us. Together, we earned all that was due."

Ferdiad said:
"Cúchulainn, you wear cunning lightly
but I have mastered the same trade. Try
to understand: our friendship is done
and now each must stand alone as one.
Prepare yourself that you might fight
the worst battle of your life and defeat.
You must forget that we were once brothers
and fought battles as one together.

"And now," Ferdiad said, "I think we have talked too much.
Let us get on with it! What weapons shall we use today, Cúchulainn?"

Cúchulainn shrugged. "It makes no difference. You may have
the choice of weapons until nightfall. After all, you reached the
ford first."

"I hope you remember the very last feats we learned when we studied with Scáthach and Uathach and Aife."

"I remember them," Cúchulainn said. "Do you?"

"Then let us try them. *If* you remember," Ferdiad added, taunting him.

They took their two carefully made feat-playing shields and the eight shields each carried whose rims had been honed razor-sharp. Each took eight darts and their ivory-hilted swords and eight small ivory darts that buzzed between them like busy bees. Everything they threw at each other struck the other's shield. The feats they did that day were feats that no other would have even tried. They fought from the early gray morning to the middle of the day, attacking each other, and stopping the feats of the other with the bosses and knobs of their shields. But they were so evenly matched that none drew blood from the other.

At last, Ferdiad drew back and lowered his shield, saying, "We will settle nothing this way with these weapons."

"What do you want to do?" Cúchulainn asked.

For answer, Ferdiad threw his shield into his charioteer's arms.

"What weapons shall we try next?" he asked.

"It isn't nightfall," Cúchulainn reminded him. "You have the choice of weapons until then."

"Light spears," Ferdiad said. "The ones bound with tight flax and polished smoothly."

"As you wish," Cúchulainn said.

They took up their shields covered with tough bullhide and their strong, smoothly polished spears. They hurled their spears at each other for the rest of the day until the sun set blood-red over the far hills. They gored and bloodied each other during this contest until at last Ferdiad drew back again, saying, "Let us break off for now, Cúchulainn."

"As you wish," Cúchulainn answered.

And they stopped their battle, throwing their weapons into their charioteers' arms. They came up to each other in the middle of the ford and each placed his arm around the other's neck and gave him three kisses. That night, they shared a single fire, their horses sharing a single paddock and their charioteers sitting beside the same fire after they made fresh beds for their heroes out of rushes with rests for their heads. Healing men came with strong medicines and herbs and roots to care for their wounds, dropping their healing potions into the stabs and cuts and wounds upon the heroes' bodies. As many healing plants and herbs as were placed on Cúchulainn, he made sure that the same number were placed upon Ferdiad so that no one would be able to say that he took unfair advantage of a wounded warrior. And Ferdiad gave the same amount of food and health-giving drinks that he received to Cúchulainn. This was very generous on Ferdiad's part, for all of Ireland supplied Ferdiad while Cúchulainn received his supplies only from the people of Breg Plain.

The next morning when they came together again at the ford, Cúchulainn asked Ferdiad what weapons he wanted to use.

"It is your turn to choose today," Ferdiad answered. "I chose yesterday."

"Then," Cúchulainn said, "let us try our stabbing-spears. Perhaps we will be able to bring this matter to an end today if we stab instead of throw. Let our horses be yoked to our chariots and we shall use them as well."

"Then let us begin," Ferdiad answered.

They took up their two solid broadshields that a normal man could not lift and their big stabbing-spears and began battling, stabbing and slicing each other from the early gray morning until the sun set blood-red over the mountains. Birds could have passed through the wounds they made on each other's bodies, bringing with them bits and pieces of flesh for food. When the sun set, the horses were worn out and their charioteers lurched drunkenly with weariness. Even the two heroes were tired from their efforts.

"It is time for us to quit now, Ferdiad," said Cúchulainn. "Our horses are finished as are our charioteers. Should we not be finished, too? Why struggle like Fomorian giants? Let us hobble the horses and stop for the night."

"Very well, I agree," Ferdiad said.

Again, each threw his weapons in his charioteer's arms and met in the middle of the ford where each placed an arm around the other's neck and gave him three kisses. Again, their horses passed the night in the same paddock and their charioteers by the same fire after making fresh beds out of rushes for their wounded heroes. Healing men came again with their medicines to care for them. This time, however, their wounds were so hideous that the healing men were forced to place magic amulets upon them and heal them through spells and incantations learned and passed down from ancient generations to now. Again, Cúchulainn shared everything he received with Ferdiad as did Ferdiad with Cúchulainn.

The next day when they met again before battle, Cúchulainn saw that a cloud of evil and darkness had descended over Ferdiad.

"A shadow has fallen over you during the night," Cúchulainn said. "You are not the warrior today that you were yesterday."

"It isn't because you have made me afraid," Ferdiad said. "I can still defeat any warrior in Ireland!"

Cúchulainn felt sorrow rush into his heart and he chanted:

"Ferdiad, don't you see?
A woman sent you to me
and you will die for what?
Maeve's white thighs and butt?"

Ferdiad answered:
"Cúchulainn, you may be wise
when this is seen through your eyes.
But well you know that all must die
and in the ground as his last bed lie."

Cúchulainn said:
"Maeve's daughter, Finnabair,
she of the white-gold hair,

was promised to you if you kill me,
not for love. Don't you see?"

Ferdiad replied:
"My strength is well used today,
my Hound. But if I back away
from you now, all will say I
did so because I didn't want to die."

Cúchulainn said:
"Then, you are the one to blame
for what happens today. The same
woman who sent you here with her word
is the one who kills you with my sword."

Ferdiad said:
"But, Cúchulainn, if we part now,
even though we are foster-brothers, how
will my name be ruined, my fame survive
the bards of Ailill and Maeve?"

Cúchulainn said:
"That choice is yours alone to make.
But I would not fight you for anyone's sake."

Ferdiad said:
"It is too late now, I fear,
for us to turn away. I fear
that Maeve has ruined both of us
with her false words to us."

Cúchulainn said:
"I am sorry, my friend, but die
you will and with the worms you will lie

instead of between Maeve's white thighs
or on Finnabair's breast, listening to her sighs."

"So be it," Ferdiad said. "Our chanting is done. What weapons shall we use today?"

"Again, it is your choice until nightfall," Cúchulainn said. "I chose yesterday."

"Swords, then. Maybe today's hacking will do what yesterday's stabbing could not," Ferdiad answered.

"Then let us begin," said Cúchulainn, taking up his full-length shield and drawing his sword.

And that day, they hacked and hewed, each trying to destroy the other. They hacked chunks of flesh from each other the size of a baby's head until the gray of early morning had passed through noon into twilight and the sun set blood-red behind the mountains.

"Let us stop this, Cúchulainn," Ferdiad said, leaning and panting against his shield. Blood streamed from the many cuts on his shoulders and legs.

"Very well," Cúchulainn agreed, and they broke off, each flinging his arms to his charioteer.

They parted for the night, two weary and pain-filled men. But this night, their horses did not share a paddock, nor did their charioteers share a fire.

The next day, Ferdiad rose early and went out alone to the ford for he knew in his heart that this day would be the day when one or both would fall. He donned his war-harness: a filmy girdle of silk with a gold-speckled hem covered with a dark apron of supple leather around which he tied a stout stone the size of a millstone. In fear of the dread Gae Bolga, he placed a twice-smelted iron cover over the stone and placed his crested helmet upon his head. The helmet gleamed with forty precious stones and had been inlaid with red enamel and crystal and gleaming stones from the East. In his right hand, he took his spear and in his left, his red-gold hilted battle-sword. Over the curve of his back, he placed his huge shield with the great red-gold knob in the middle surrounded by another fifty knobs each big enough to hide a boar. Then, he did a thousand thrilling feats and dances, high and multiple, that no one had ever taught him.

Cúchulainn came down to the ford while Ferdiad was practicing his feats. He watched in admiration for a while, then called to Laeg:

"Look at what Ferdiad does! This is what he will use today against me. If you see me falter in battle, you must insult me in a manner to make my anger rise. And if it appears that I am about to defeat him, then praise me so that my spirits will rise."

"This I will do, Cúchulainn," Laeg promised.

Then, Cúchulainn put on his war-harness and did another thousand dances and feats that he had learned from no one so that Ferdiad would know, too, what Cúchulainn intended to do to him.

"Well," Cúchulainn said when he had finished. "What weapons shall we use today?"

"It is your choice of weapons until nightfall," Ferdiad answered.

"Very well," Cúchulainn said. "Then let us fight in the ford water."

"Let us try that," Ferdiad said lightly, but he knew that it was the worst thing that he could agree to for Cúchulainn had destroyed every hero and high warrior who had ever fought him in the water of a ford. Yet the thought of that did not keep Ferdiad from doing marvelous deeds and feats, all of which were answered by Cúchulainn. The two blazing torches of bravery, the two most lavish gift-givers, the two keys to Ireland's bravery, two who had been ill sent together by the meddling of Ailill and Maeve, worked their feats against each other until the sun stood high in the sky and their madness mounted.

Cúchulainn sprang straight from the middle of the ford onto the shield knob of Ferdiad, intending to strike down over the edge of the shield at his head. But Ferdiad gave a blow on the shield with his left elbow that sent Cúchulainn staggering away from him like a bird. Again, Cúchulainn sprang upon the knob of Ferdiad's shield, and this time Ferdiad struck the edge of the shield with his knee, sending Cúchulainn reeling away from him like a little boy, back across the ford.

Laeg saw this and remembered Cúchulainn's words to him. He raised his voice, saying, "Ha! Your enemy slaps you like a mother would a quarrelsome child! He tosses you aside as easily as if he were rinsing a cup in a tub of water. He crushes you like a good millstone would fine malt! He is a hawk to your little bird. From now on, little half-sprite, you will have no right to claim great deeds of daring!"

At that, Cúchulainn rose up for the third time, rushing like wind in a storm of strength and fury, and leaped again upon the knob of Ferdiad's shield and tried to strike down at him over the rim of the shield. But Ferdiad shook him off, throwing Cúchulainn back into the middle of the stream. Then Cúchulainn's warp-spasm came upon him and he swelled high and mighty, looming up over Ferdiad, vast as a Fomorian giant or a man from the kingdom of the sea!

He screamed his warrior's challenge and came upon Ferdiad and the two fought together so closely that their heads touched each other, and their feet and their hands grasped the knobs in the other's shield. Their shields split and fell apart. They seized their spears, each stabbing madly at the other until the spearheads split from their rivets and fell away. They drew their swords and the sound of their battle, blade striking blade, screamed so loudly that birds flew in flight from the forest and the men watching quailed against each other. Demons and devils and goblins seemed to ride through the air from the furious strokes each leveled against the other. They fought so furiously that the river changed its course and left in the middle of the ford a place large enough for a king's burial place. The horses of the men watching reared in panic and broke their reins, galloping away.

Then Ferdiad got a single fatal chance below Cúchulainn's guard and dealt him a stroke of his sword, burying it deeply into his breast. Blood gushed over his belt and the water of the ford ran red with blood. Cúchulainn staggered away from Ferdiad's stroke and called out to Laeg Mac Riangabra for the Gae Bolga. Ferdiad heard the cry and dropped his shield to cover his lower body. Cúchulainn saw Ferdiad's move and hurled his short javelin from the middle of his palm over the rim of Ferdiad's shield, driving it through his horn armor into his breast, piercing his heart until it emerged halfway from his back. Ferdiad tried to raise his shield to cover his upper body, but it was too late: Laeg had sent the Gae Bolga down the stream to Cúchulainn.

"Here comes the Gae Bolga!" he cried, and Cúchulainn caught it in the fork of his foot and cast it with his toes at Ferdiad. It burst through the apron of twice-smelted iron, shattered the millstone, and entered Ferdiad's anus, coursing through his body, filling it with tiny barbs.

"Enough!" Ferdiad said. "I die! There is strength in your right foot, but it is wrong that I should fall at your hand.

"You have killed me unfairly,
Hound of Bright Deeds. I see
that your guilt clings to me
for it is your deceit that killed me.
My ribs are crushed! My heart wells
with blood! I have not fought well."

Cúchulainn caught him and wrapped his two arms around him, carrying him, his weapons and armor, across the ford to the north with him so that the spoils of war would lie in the north and not on the west bank where the Connachtmen watched. He placed Ferdiad down on the ground and fell beside him in a cloudy trance. Laeg saw this as did the Connachtmen, who rose up to attack him while he lay helpless.

"Rise, Cúchulainn!" Laeg called desperately. "The Connachtmen are coming to attack us and not in single combat, either!"

"Why should I rise?" Cúchulainn said dully. "I have slain my friend, my foster-brother."

Laeg answered him, chanting:

"Rise up, Emain's death-hound!
You must recover and sound
your battle cry once more
before you travel to death's far shore!"

And Cúchulainn said:
"I have killed too much today.
Sorrow weighs me down for today
I have killed my friend. See
the blood from the wounds hacked by me?"

Laeg said desperately:
"You have done only what you must
or else lie beside him in the dust!
You have earned the right to brag
for you bleed, too, like a gut-stabbed stag."

Cúchulainn said:
"And what of it? My stealth
deprived Ferdiad of his health."

And Laeg said:
"The Craebruad women would rather
have you alive than your brother."

Cúchulainn said:
"From the first day I left Cuailnge to come
against the army of Maeve and Ailill I knew some
would die from my sword. She must know her blunder
from the heroes and men I have torn asunder!"

Laeg said:
"Be quiet now and take some sleep
for you have sent many warriors into deep

death's arms. You stopped the great raid
and no other could stop what you have stayed."

And Cúchulainn arose, and when the Connacht army saw him
standing bloody and awful beside the dead Ferdiad, they stopped
their headlong rush toward him and drew away in fright. Cúchulainn turned to the body of Ferdiad, saying, "You should have listened to your heart instead of your loins, Ferdiad. We should never
have fought together for the sake of a woman's greed and desire!
You should have listened to those who saw those who came before
you and listened to them when they tried to tell you of the deeds
that I did. Laeg Mac Riangabra should have told you, too, about our
times as brothers together. You should not have rejected Fergus's
well-meant warning, either! You should not have listened to the
false promises of the Connacht women! You should have listened
to the wise men as well who know that no one is destined to match
my feats or deeds that I do to keep Ulster safe from the Connachtmen. Never will red-mouthed Badb screech again at the sight of battle like this one between the two of us! Never will another battle be
seen as has this one, Ferdiad, crimson-visaged son of Damáin!"

Cúchulainn rose from Ferdiad's head, adding, "Well, Ferdiad,
great doom and desolation visited upon you and now will be visited upon those who sent you out to meet with me. It is no easy
matter to do battle with Cúchulainn on the *Táin*."

He drew back away from Ferdiad and stood for a long moment,
blood dripping from his many wounds. A deep, ragged sigh
worked its way up from the depths of his chest and he chanted:

"Ferdiad, dead by Connacht's deceit.
I regret our last meeting
was for a woman's thighs. Feats
such as ours should more glory bring.

"When we were with Scáthach learning
how to earn victory overseas,

it seemed our friendship would be remaining
forever between you and me.

"I loved the noble way you blushed,
and loved your perfect form's finesse.
I loved your clear blue eyes, your shushed
manner of speech, your skillfulness.

"Never until this very day,
Ferdiad, did I ever find one
to match you in the fray
since I slew Aife's one son.

"Maeve's daughter, Finnabair,
whatever beauty she may have,
was an empty offering, a bare
string to hold the sand, Ferdiad."

Cúchulainn stood silent for a long moment, staring at Ferdiad,
until Laeg moved uneasily to his side. Cúchulainn raised his pain-
filled eyes. His shoulders slumped.

"Now, friend Laeg. Strip Ferdiad. Remove his armor and his
clothes and let me see this brooch which was so important that
Maeve bought his spirit with it."

And Laeg bent and carefully removed Ferdiad's blood-stained
armor and clothes until he found the brooch. Straightening, he
handed it to Cúchulainn who took it and grasped it tightly in his
warrior's hand, saying:

"Ferdiad of the Connacht hosts
I am mourning your conquering arm
that fought for this brooch. Most
of all, however, I mourn the harm

"I caused you. I will remember
our time together, a sight

to please princes. I remember
your shield and sword, your might

"with each, the silver ring
upon your hand, your *fidchell* skill,
your flushed cheek that brings
memories of your yellow hair still

"curled and the soft leather belt
you clasped around your waist.
You have fallen! I have felt
such a thing to be a waste.

"Our struggle was shameful.
And now I have this brooch only
to mourn you with. Shameful
that such a thing has befallen me."

Cúchulainn turned away from Ferdiad, saying, "Now, Laeg, take your sharp knife and cut Ferdiad open and remove the Gae Bolga. I must have my weapon."

Laeg took his knife and neatly slit Ferdiad from groin to neck and removed the Gae Bolga, bloody and crimson, black with the innermost blood of Ferdiad. Cúchulainn said:

"Ferdiad, this was not meant to be—
you crimson and death-pale in my sight
and stretched out in a bloody sea
and I with my bloody weapon unwiped.

"When we were beyond the gray sea
as Scáthach's and Uathach's pupils,
who thought such pale lips would be
the result of a struggle between us?

"I remember when Scáthach roared
her sharp, harsh cry and brayed:

'Here comes Germán Garblas's horde!
Ride forward to the furious fray!'

"Then to you and to Lugaid,
he of the most lavish hand,
and to fond, foolish Ferbaeth I said:
'Let us go to meet this Germán.'

"At the battle-rock on the slope, then,
above the fiery Lake of Envy,
we destroyed four hundred men
from the Islands of Victory.

"I killed Rinn Mac Niuil
in Germán's doorway.
Ferdiad slew Ruad Mac Forniuil
in the heat of that fray.

"Ferbaeth killed Blat Red-Sword
on the slope while Lugaid killed
Mugairne who came forward
and tried to kill Lugaid instead.

"I slew two hundred raging men
that day. Ferdiad killed a few—
among them Dam Dreimend and Dam Dilenn—
a most fierce and terrible crew.

"We leveled Germán's cunning fort.
above the wide, glittering sea
and took Germán to Scáthach's fort.
Both of us, did this: you and me.

"Our foster mother bound us
in a vow of friendship so rage
would never rise between us.
Each had the other's courage

"in fair Elga. Sad the day
that Ferdiad and I fought
and his strength went away.
This is not what I sought."

Uneasy at the deep lament pouring from Cúchulainn's lips, Laeg came up and gently touched the Warped One's arm.

"Come, Cúchulainn," he said quietly. "It is time for us to leave the ford. We have been here far too long."

Cúchulainn roused himself and painfully straightened his war-bloodied shoulders.

"Yes, let us leave now, friend Laeg," he said wearily. He looked across the ford to where the Connacht force had retreated.

"You know, Laeg," he said softly, "all my battles and challenges that I have fought seem little more than children's games now.

"At first, I thought this play
until Ferdiad came to challenge me.
Now, I rue the dawning of this day.
The same rights came to both. We
had the same good foster mother
who taught us both to fight,
but not brother against brother.
Not in this cold day's sight.

"All was fun and sport, I say.
Until Ferdiad came out to play.

"We had the same fury and force,
and the same tricks of war.
Scáthach awarded both, of course,
with the same shields of war.

"All was fun and sport, I say.
Until Ferdiad came out to play.

"Oh, misery! A pillar of gold
I have here struck down another.
A man in his prime, I'm told,
a man braver than any other.

"All was fun and sport, I say.
Until Ferdiad came out to play.

"I have slaughtered many
on this *Táin*. Multitudes
have fallen. But not any
other have I felt this crude
pain for. Alas! Alas!"

Gently, Laeg nudged him and Cúchulainn straightened from
his grief that the Connachtmen might not view this as weakness,
and walked with a firm stride toward his war-chariot. When Laeg
drove the chariot away from the ford, turning it thrice left side toward the Connachtmen in contempt, the Connacht warriors
waited until the sun dipped blood-red behind the mountains before daring to cross the ford to retrieve Ferdiad's body. Puzzled,
they wondered among themselves why Cúchulainn had not taken
the head of the fallen warrior as a trophy since he had taken the
others who had challenged him.

Chapter 12

THE CURSE
LIFTS
FROM THE
RED BRANCH

THE CONNACHT FORCE LEFT immediately from Ferdiad's Ford while Cúchulainn lay up in the pines, sick with grief and recovering from his wounds. At last, two came from Ulster and found him in a fever upon his blankets with Laeg hovering anxiously over him, packing his wounds with sphagnum moss and bathing his face with cool water. Senoll Uathach the Hideous and the two sons of Ficce were the first to reach him. Tenderly, they carried him back to Conaille where healers nursed his wounds. They bathed him nineteen times in the waters of the Sas River to ease his pain, in the Buan River to steady his spirit, in Bithslan to make his health continue, in the clear waters of Finnglas, the bright-blue waters of Gleoir, the rapid waters of Bedc to bolster his courage, in Tadc, Talamed, Rinn ad Bir, in the sour Breide to toughen his flesh, in the narrow Cumang, in Clennand Gaenemian, Dichu, Muach, Miliuc, Den, Deilt, and Dubglas.

While Cúchulainn was healing in the waters of Ulster, the Connacht army made camp near Mas of Marrow at Imorach Smiromrach. After settling his men, Fergus Mac Roich left for the north to keep a wary eye on the men of Ulster. He traveled as far as Sliab Fuait and saw only one chariot trailing after them and returned, bearing this news with him.

"I saw only one chariot, brightly colored as May, crossing the plain. It bore a silver-gray–haired man, stark naked, with no weapons save an iron spike he held loosely in one hand, pricking first his charioteer and then his horses in our wake. A brindled hunting dog loped far in front of him," Fergus said.

"Was it Conchobar or Celtchar?" Ailill asked.

Fergus shook his head. "No," he said. "I believe it to be Fintan's son Cethern, a most generous man with a blade well bloodied in combat."

Ailill pulled on his lower lip, pondering Fergus's words. But before he could make up his mind what to do, Cethern's chariot hurled itself into the camp, men falling left and right from his fury. But he took several wounds himself and returned from the battle to Cúchulainn with his guts wound around his feet.

"Get me a healer," he said to Cúchulainn before falling unconscious from his chariot.

Cúchulainn caught him and laid him upon a bed of fresh rushes with his cloak rolled beneath his head for a pillow. Then he rose and directed Laeg to take word to the Connacht camp and demand a healer from Fiacha Mac Firaba. He ordered Laeg to tell them as well that if they did not send a healer, Cúchulainn would fall upon them in all his fury and kill them. If they tried to hide from his fury, he would find them even if he had to travel into the bowels of the earth to search them out. The healers grew very worried when this message was conveyed to them for all knew Cúchulainn to be a man of his word and they had seen his fury unleashed upon the Connacht force for as many nights as it had been at the Ulster border. The first healer followed Laeg back to camp and examined Cethern.

"These wounds are too serious," he exclaimed, rising and staring down at the man. "I am afraid you will not survive this."

"Then, neither will you!" Cethern cried, lashing out in his pain.

He struck the healer a mighty blow, splattering his brains over his ears. Fifty more healers appeared and all told Cethern the same thing. He killed all fifty in his fury and pain. But when the last one came, his strength had begun to fail and he struck the healer only a glancing blow, stunning him. Cúchulainn stepped in and kept Cethern from delivering another blow.

"You are wrong to kill these healers," Cúchulainn said. "If you keep on in this way, we will find no one to come and treat your wounds."

"They had no right to say that I would not survive," Cethern grumbled.

Cúchulainn left Cethern, shaking his head at the man's fury. He sent for Fingin, Conchobar's own holy healer, to examine himself and Cethern. Fingin came although he was well aware of the pain both warriors had gone through. When he saw Fingin's chariot approaching their camp, Cúchulainn came from his sick-bed to warn him.

"Be careful about what you say to Cethern," he said. "He has already killed fifty healers who gave him bad news."

Fingin nodded and came close to Cethern, but did not approach close enough for Cethern to reach him.

"This wound pains me deeply," Cethern said. "What made it? Can you tell?"

"Yes," Fingin said. "A vain and arrogant woman wounded you in that manner."

"Yes," Cethern said. "When I rode through the camp, a tall woman with a long face and soft features came toward me. Her hair was yellow-gold and a gold bird sat on each shoulder. A purple cloak folded around her and she had five hand-breadths of gold upon her back. In one hand, she carried a light lance with a sharp edge gleaming. She clasped an iron sword like a woman over her head. She was the first to strike me."

"That was Maeve of Cruachain," Cúchulainn said, shaking his head. "I'm sorry for the wound that she gave you."

"This wound," the healer said, pointing to another slice upon

Cethern's chest, "was given to you by a fainthearted kinsman. It won't kill you although it is undoubtedly very painful."

"A warrior with a curved, scallop-edged shield came at me with a spear whose blade curved like a sickle. He bore an ivory-hilted sword in three pieces and wore a brown cloak held at his shoulder with a silver brooch. I wounded him as well."

"That," Cúchulainn said, "was Illann, Fergus Mac Roich's son."

"This," the healer continued, examining another wound, "was caused by two warriors, not one."

"A pair came at me, each bearing a long shield. Each wore a silver collar and carried five-pronged spears. They wore silver chains and silver belts."

"And those were Oll and Oichne, two foster-sons of Ailill and Maeve, who will never enter battle unless they are sure that they have the advantage and someone will fall from their hands."

"Two other warriors set upon me then," Cethern said. "They were noble and manly with a hero's halo rising from their heads."

"Bun and Mecon, called the Trunk and Root. They are two of the king's most trusted people," Cúchulainn said.

"Here," the healer said, pointing at Cethern's breast, "the blood is black. Who caused this speared you through your heart at an angle and made a cross inside of you. This I cannot promise to cure, but I might be able to keep it from killing you."

"A pair of light-yellow–haired warriors with faces the size of wooden bowls attacked me there," he said. "Each stabbed me well."

"Two warriors from Maeve's own household, Braen and Láráne, the Two Sons of Three Lights of the forest king," Cúchulainn said.

"And here," Fingin said, "you were attacked by three nephews, I believe."

"Three men, all alike, attacked me. They bore a bronze chain with spikes and spears between them."

"Banba, the Three Sheaths, from Cúroi Mac Dáiri's land," Cúchulainn said.

"Three soldiers made this one," Fingin said.

"Three warriors wearing three silver collars around their neck attacked me with war-clubs. Each stuck a spear in me, but I pulled it free and returned it to each in a like manner."

"Those three came from Iruath," Cúchulainn said.

"This is most severe," the healer said. "They have cut the sinews that hold your heart. It rolls inside you like a wool ball in an empty bag. And here," he continued, "are three furious wounds."

"Made by three great, fat men with gray bellies," Cethern said.

"Three stewards belonging to Maeve and Ailill. Scenb, Rann, and Fodail—the Carver, the Apportioner, the Server," Cúchulainn answered.

"And these three blows," Fingin said, "were made in the morning during your first charge."

"Three warriors wrapped in black fur cloaks with the skin showing through in patches attacked me. Their hoods were stained and they carried iron clubs."

"Three murderous servants of Maeve, the Three Madmen of Baiscne," Cúchulainn said.

"Two brothers struck you here," Fingin observed.

"Each wearing dark-green cloaks and carrying broad-bladed stabbing-spears," Cethern answered.

"Cormac, the King's Pillar, and Cormac, Mael Foga's son," Cúchulainn said.

Fingin shook his head. "These wounds came close together. They entered your gullet and worked deadly business there with their javelins. And here," he continued, "two brothers struck you."

"One had a head of yellow curls, the other dark. They bore two shields with gold animals engraved upon them and two iron swords. Each had a red-embroidered tunic wrapped around him."

"That would be Maine Áthramail, the Fatherlike, and Maine Máthramail, the Motherlike."

"And here we have the double wound of father and son," Fingin observed.

"Two huge men charged me with eyes bright red like torches

and gold crowns upon their heads. They had gold-hilted swords in scabbards with speckled gold tassels that hung to their feet."

"That was Ailill and his son, Maine Cotagaib Uli, who bears the likeness of both Ailill and his mother."

"I have had a hard time of it," Cethern said, sighing. He shook his head and grinned. "But tell me, Fingin, what do you think of my chances?"

"I won't lie to you," Fingin said. "You will not see your cows bear new calves. Or, if you do, your life will not be worth much to you." He shook his head in despair. "If you had only one or two wounds, or even three, perhaps I could give you better news. But a whole horde of warriors have left their mark upon you. Your life is finished. It is only a matter of time."

He turned his chariot to ride away, but Cethern struck him with his fist, sending him over the shafts of his chariot. Then he smashed the chariot in his fury, saying, "You are like all the others! Useless men!"

"You have no reason to give an old man a blow like that!" Cúchulainn said, giving the place where this occurred the name Ochtur Lui. "Save your blows for the enemies who gave them to you!"

Fingin rose shakily and looked at his chariot, then turned back to Cethern. He gave the wounded warrior his choice. Cethern could lie with his sickness for a whole year and then live out his life's span, or he could mend his strength enough to allow Cethern to fight his present enemies in three days and nights. Cethern chose the latter and the healer directed Cúchulainn to bring him bone marrow to use in healing. Cúchulainn went out and took what beasts he could find and killed them and made a mash of their marrow. From this, Smirommair, the Bath of Marrow in Crích Rois, takes its name.

Cethern slept a full day and night in the marrow, his body absorbing it within its wounds. When he awakened, he said to Cúchulainn:

"My ribs are gone. Take the ribs from the chariot frame and give them to me."

This Cúchulainn did, then Cethern sighed, saying, "Ah, if only I had my weapons about me! I would do feats that bards would sing about forever."

"They are coming," Cúchulainn said. "I see Finn Bec, Eochaid's daughter, your wife, coming toward us in a chariot."

The woman brought Cethern his weapons. He took them in his hands and, binding the ribs of the chariot around his belly to give him strength, went hard toward the Connacht camp and his enemies.

Itholl, the healer who had pretended death among the other healers Cethern had smashed with his fist, rose and ran ahead of the wounded warrior to warn the camp.

"Cethern has been cured by Fingan the Druid. He comes now, to kill all who wait between him and Ailill. You must lay a trap for him."

The warriors looked with dread at the bloody hero charging toward them and took Ailill's crown, placing it on top of a pillar stone. Racked with pain, his eyes blurring from Mórrígan's breath, Cethern attacked the pillar stone, believing it to be Ailill. He drove his sword with fury through the heart of the stone, his fist coming after it. From this, the name of Lia Toll, the Pierced Stone in Crích Rois, is given.

When he saw the trick played upon him, Cethern roared with fury.

"Now, you shall have no rest until one of you wears this crown of Ailill!" he cried.

He threw the crown into their midst and ground down upon them night and day until at last, one of the Maines placed Ailill's crown upon his head and roared toward Cethern in his chariot, brandishing his sword on high. Cethern waited until he was nearly upon him, then threw his shield at him, spinning it like a saucer. It struck the warrior and his charioteer, splitting each in half and cleaving his horses in twain as well. Then all of the armies within the Connacht army fell upon Cethern from all sides, trying to kill him, but he seized a chariot shaft and used it to kill many before he fell.

His wife, Ionda, daughter of Eochaid, came and cried over him, saying, "No man's hand will hold my head from this time forth for a grave has been dug for Cethern from the Dun of the Two Hills."

When he heard of Cethern's death, Fintan came with one hundred fifty men, belted and bristling for battle, all armed with two-headed spears. Seven battles they fought against the Connacht force with only Fintan and his other son, Crimthann, emerging alive from the last battle. A wall of shields came between Crimthann and his father, but before the warriors could kill him, Ailill saved Crimthann, fearing the wrath of Fintan. But before he released the youth to his father, Ailill drew a promise from Fintan that he would not fight again against the Connacht force until the last battle with Conchobar that had been foretold by the Druids. Gratified by Crimthann's safe return, Fintan promised not to fight Ailill until the last battle.

When they retraced the battlefield, Ailill's warriors and Fintan's warriors were found locked together, lips and noses firmly grasped between fanged teeth. And this became known as Fiacalgeleó Fintan, the Battle of Tooth.

Sálcholgán next went against the Connacht force with thirty warriors. Maeve lost twelve warriors in that battle while Sálcholgán suffered severe wounds and blood dripped from the many wounds each of his warriors had taken.

"It's a shame that Menn Mac Sálcholgán has been wounded and his people slaughtered. Send him back with honor to his home," said the heroes of Connacht to Ailill.

Ailill did as they bade, taking a pledge from Sálcholgán not to fight again or cross from his swampy lands by the Boann River until he came with Conchobar to the last battle. Sálcholgán did as he pledged, taking no dishonor for his action. This became Ruadrucce Mind.

Then came one hundred fifty charioteers from Ulster who fought the host three times before falling at Airecor nArad.

At this time, Cúchulainn told his charioteer to go to Rochaid Mac Faithemain and, if his pangs had passed, ask for help. The charioteer found the warrior and told him what Cúchulainn had said. Rochaid immediately left and traveled south to Cúchulainn with a hundred warriors in his train.

Meanwhile, Ailill sent a watcher high on the hill near his camp and when the watcher called, Ailill himself climbed the hill to his post.

"What do you see?" he asked.

"A troop crosses the plain, there," the sentry said, pointing. "There is a mighty man in front of a young troop who come only to his shoulders."

Ailill turned as Fergus came up to them and asked him who traveled towards them.

"Rochaid Mac Faithemain. He's coming to help Cúchulainn," Fergus answered.

"I see," Ailill said. He mulled over Fergus's words for a moment, then said, "Send a hundred warriors out to meet them in the plain before they get to our camp. But tell them to hide well where Rochaid's men cannot see them. Send Finnabair with them. Send a horseman to Rochaid and tell him that the girl wishes to speak alone with him. When he sees her standing alone, he will come to her unaware of our plans. Then you can capture him."

Now, it happened that Finnabair had long loved Rochaid for none other in Ulster stood as handsomely as he. When she heard that Rochaid was coming fast toward their camp, she went to her mother Maeve and told her about her love.

"I have long loved this man," she said. "I have dreamed of his arms holding me, my thighs wrapped high around his hips."

"Well," Maeve said craftily, "if you have loved him that long, then sleep with him tonight. Then in the morning, ask him for a truce until the last battle with Conchobar."

When Rochaid saw the horseman approaching him, he drew up the army and waited until the horseman halted in front of him.

"I bring you a message from Finnabair," the horseman said. "She wishes to speak with you alone on the plain. Will you come?"

Rochaid look at the beautiful maid and rode out to meet with her. When he came close, the hidden warriors rushed out and captured him. When his followers saw their leader had been taken, they turned and fled. Rochaid was taken to the camp where he promised Ailill that he would not fight against the Connachtmen until the final battle. In pledge of his good word, Ailill gave him Finnabair who eagerly slept with the gallant warrior and, together, they rode the wild horse until morning found them weary, but sated. While she slept, Rochaid stole quietly away and returned to Ulster.

When the twelve kings of Munster heard what Ailill had done with Finnabair, they met in conference. One of them rose, angrily saying, "Ailill had promised that girl to me along with fifteen hostages if I would bring my men to join his army on this raid."

The other eleven said that they, too, had been promised Finnabair, and each returned in fury to his troops. They rode out to take vengeance against Ailill for this betrayal, but when they came against Ailill's sons who were keeping watch over the armies in Glen Domain, Maeve brought her men against them along with the Galeóin troop of three thousand, and with them came Ailill and Fergus. When the battle ceased, seven hundred lay dead in Glen Domain.

When Finnabair heard about the deceit of Ailill and that because she had slept with Rochaid instead of one of the Munster kings, she died of shame. From this, the place came to be called Finnabair Slébe, Finnabair Among the Mountains. This is Bángleó Rochada.

Then, Ílech, Laegaire Buadach's grandfather, the son of Connad the Yellow-Haired, Ílech's son, rose up against them in his madness at Áth Feidli. He had been placed under Laegaire's protection at Ráith Impail. When he came against the Connacht army, he came in an old chariot, its wooden frame cracked and nearly falling apart, with no covers or cushions. Two ancient yellow horses pulled the chariot. He had filled the floor of the chariot with rocks and clods of earth and dung that he threw at anyone who came to stare at his nakedness. His penis and ballocks hung down through the floor of the chariot. The Connachtmen laughed at him and banged the hafts of their spears upon their shield rims, making fun of him. Then, Dóchae Mac Mágach was struck full in the face with wet dung and stopped the fool-making, swearing that he would use his sword upon the mad man and take his head from him if he didn't get out of Connacht's way.

The mad Ílech drove his ancient horses to Cúchulainn's camp and when he arrived and saw the trench that had been dug to hold the marrow Cúchulainn had ground from the bones of Ulster cows, he went out onto the plain and dug another trench, hauling the dead Connacht warriors to it and grinding their bones down into marrow, filling the trench. That night, Dóchae cut off Ílech's head and brought it to his grandson Laegaire and was told to keep Ílech's sword for removing Ílech from his madness. This is Mellgleó Íliach.

The Connacht army moved to Tailtiu where one hundred fifty charioteers and warriors from Ulster attacked them. Although the Ulster heroes killed four hundred fifty of the Connacht force, all of them were killed at the place now called Roi Arad, Where the Charioteers Battled.

One evening while the Connacht army camped at Mag Clochair, the Stony Plain, two great stones flew at them, one from the east, the other from the west. They met in midair over the camp with a sound like a thunderclap and pieces fell from them like hail over the camp. The warriors ran back and forth, trying to avoid the stone fragments falling down upon them. Booming laughter and more stones followed their frantic running until, at last, they squatted upon their heels, holding their shields over their heads like little children to guard themselves against the stones.

Cúroi Mac Dáiri laughed as he saw them squatting and playfully lofted another stone high in the air. Across the camp from him at Ard Roich, Munremur Mac Gerrcinn threw a stone to strike that thrown at Cúroi. The two stones met with a sound like thunder and shattered and fell down upon the camp. Munremur had come to help Cúchulainn and Cúroi had come to help his own people. Cúroi knew no one in the Connacht camp could stand against Munremur and after talking with him at Cotail, Cúroi came up with this idea for sport.

After an hour, the Connacht army sent messengers to ask the two to make peace with them. Cúroi went back to his home and Munremur went to Emain Macha and didn't come again until the last battle.

Meanwhile, the Ulstermen were recovering from their pangs and curse. From Ráith Sualdam, Sualdam learned what had befallen his son Cúchulainn.

"Have the heavens split and divided? Has the sea washed over the strand? Is this the end of the entire world? Or, do I hear the lament and battle-fury of my son fighting against overwhelming odds?" he asked. He called for his weapons and war-chariot and rode furiously to join his son. But Cúchulainn refused to let his father join him because if the Connachtmen slew his father, Cúchulainn would not have the strength for blood revenge.

"Stop your wailing, Father. Instead, go to Ulster and tell the Red Branch to come and fight now," he said.

He staggered, then caught himself, wearily passing his hand over his eyes. He grinned at his father.

"And tell them to hurry or they will not have the chance to get their revenge over what has befallen Ulster during their pangs. I cannot even bear the touch of my clothing on my skin but must hold it away with a clutch of hazel wands."

His father saw his son's body covered with wounds, a lacing of scars and wounds so intricate and massive that the tip of a rush could not be passed between them. Fifty scars and wounds showed on his left hand alone even though that was the hand in which he carried his shield. Sualdam shook his head, then mounted his chariot and drove furiously to Emain Macha. As he drew close he cried, "Men have been murdered, women stolen and raped, our cattle taken from their pastures!"

Three times he gave this cry: once when he came to the steps of the fortress, the second when he was inside the fortress, and the third time when he stood defiant and furious upon the Mound of Hostages. He waited for an answer, knowing that no man could speak before Conchobar who would not speak until the Druids had spoken.

"Tell us, Sualdam, who is doing all this you speak of?" one Druid asked.

"Ailill Mac Mata and his whore-queen Maeve. Fergus Mac Roich guides them against our people as far as Dún Sobairche where the Connacht forces have taken all of the cattle and women. Cúchulainn, my son, has held them out of the Murtheimne Plain and away from Crích Rois for three winter months. He is sorely wounded."

The Druid turned away from Sualdam, saying disgustedly, "This man annoys our king who is recovering from his curse. He should suffer death for this!"

"Yes," Conchobar groaned. "It would be fitting!"

"Yes!" shouted the others. "It is!"

"Yet what Sualdam says has a truth to it. The Connacht army has been running freely along our border from the last Monday of summer to the first Monday of spring."

They fell to arguing among themselves and, impatient with their words, Sualdam turned and ran out of the mead-hall where they were meeting. But as he came through the door, his shield slipped in front of him and he tripped and fell. The sharp scalloped rim sliced through his neck sinews, cutting off his head. A Druid saw this and picked up the head and placed it back upon the shield and returned to the mead-hall, carrying it. When he came through the door, the glazed eyes of Sualdam opened and from his mouth came his warning:

"Beware, men of Emain Macha! Beware Ailill and the Connacht army!"

The warriors moved uneasily as the hollow words struck deep within them.

"Enough of this!" Conchobar said. "The sea is still in front of them and the sky overhead with its showers of stars falling upon the earth beneath their feet! By the gods, I'll drive them from out of our lands and return every cow to his byre and pasture and every woman back home!" He turned to his son, Finnchad Fer Benn, the Horned Man.

"Go, Finnchad," he ordered, "and bring Dedaid to me. And Leamain and Fallach and Fergus's son Illan from Gabar; Dorlunsa from Imchlár, Derg Imderg the Red, Fedlimid Cilair Chetaig, Faeladán and Rochaid Mac Faithemain from Rí gdonn; Lugaid and Lugda; Cathbad from his lands; the three Coirpre from Aelai, Laeg from his road and Gemen his valley; Senoll Uathach the Hideous from Diabal Arda, and Fintan's son Cethern from Carlaig; Cethern from Eillone, Aurothor and Mulach from his fortress; the royal poet Amargin, and Uathach of the Badb; the great queen at Dún Sobairche; Ieth and Roth and Fiachna from his lands; Dam Dreimend, Andiaraid and Maine Mac Briathrach; Dam Derg, Mod and Maithes, Irmaithis from Corp Gliath; Gabar from Laigi Líne, Eochaid from Saimne and Eochaid from Latharnu; Uma Mac Remansfisig from Fedan, Munremur Mac Gerrcinn, and Senlobair from Canann Gall; Follamain and Lugaid, king of the Fir Bolg at Laigi Líne; Buadgalach and Ambuach and Fergna from Barréne; Aine and Errge Echbél the Horse-Lipped; Abra, and Celtchar Mac Uthidir from Lethglas; Laegaire Milbél the Honey-Mouthed from his hearth; the three sons of Dromscailt Mac Dregamm; Drenda and Drendas and Cimbe; Cimling and Cimmene from the slopes of Caba; Fachtna, Sencha's son, Sencha and Senchairthe; Briccir and Bricirne; Breic and Buan and Bairech; Aengus and Fergus, Léte's sons, and Aengus of the Fir Bolg; Bruchur and Alamiach of the old tribes in Slánge, and the three sons of Fiachna from Cuailnge; Conall Cernach from Midluachair, Connad Mac Morna from Felunt, Cúchulainn Mac Sualdaim from Murtheimne, Amargin from Es Ruaid and Laeg from Léire; Sálcholgán's son at Correnna and Cúroi Mac Amargin in his home; Aengus Fer Benn Uma of the Copper Horns, and Ogma Grianainech the Bright-Faced, Eo Mac nOircne, and Tollchenn from Saithi, and Mogoll Echbél from the Plain of Ai; Connla Saeb from Uarba, Laegaire Buadach from Impail; Ailill son of Amargin from Tailtiu, and Furbaide Fer Benn, the Horned One from Seil on Inis Plain; Cúscraid Menn the Stammerer, the sons of Lí and Fingin from Finngabar; Cremath and the inn-keepers Blai Fichit and Blai Briuga at Fesair; Eogan Mac Durthacht from Fernmag; Dord and Serid and Serthe, Oblan from Cuilenn, Cuirther and Liana from Eith Benne, Fernel and Finnchad from Sliab Betha, Talgobain from Bernas, and Menn Mac Sálcholgán from Dulo Plain; Iroll from Blarigi, Tibraide Mac Ailcotha; Iala the Ravager from Dobla Plain, Rus Mac Ailcotha, Maine Mac Cruim, Ninnech Mac Cruinn, Dipsemilid and Mál Mac Rochrad; Muinne, Munremur's son; Fiatach Ferndoirre, son of Dubthach, the Beetle; and Muirne Menn."

Finnchad left immediately. He did not take long for all the chieftains had been waiting for Conchobar to make his move and had moved close to Emain Macha. They moved south out of Emain, searching for the Connachtmen. They paused at Iraird Cuilenn. When he saw that the advance guard had stopped, Conchobar rode up and asked: "Why do you stop? We have a long way to go!"

"We wait for your sons. They have gone out with thirty others to Temair to get Eric, son of Coirpre Niafer and Fedelm Noichride. They should bring their two troops of three thousand with them."

"That may be wise," Conchobar said. "But we will lose the advantage if the men from Connacht realize that I have risen from the curse placed upon the Red Branch."

So, while the others waited, Conchobar and Celtchar went out with one hundred fifty chariots and brought back one hundred sixty heads from Airthir Midi in East Meath. Since then, the ford has been called Áth Féne, the Ford of the Warriors. When Conchobar and Celtchar returned with the heads, Celtchar said to Conchobar:

> "The slings reddened by a terrible king
> from the proud past must compare
> with what we've done today! We'll bring
> these Connacht men to beware
> Ulster's fury! Two hundred Druids
> will be at our back and chant
> our battlesong against our crude
> foes. Not one man will lack
> the courage to defend Conchobar's back.
> Let the warriors wake wreak
> their fury as the battle breaks out
> at Gáirech and Irgairech
> and we hear out warrior's shouts."

During the night in the Connacht camp, Dubthach Dael, the Chafer of Ulster, the Black-Worded One, dreamed about the army at Gáirech and Irgairech, and chanted from his sleep:

> "Monstrous morning, monstrous season,
> hosts in turmoil, without reason,
> necks broken, a red sun,
> three hosts crushed and done
> by the Ulstermen. I see
> the Red Branch times three."

When the others heard this, Badb and Nemain, Nét's wife, screamed through the night and brought confusion upon the armies and a hundred fell dead from terror. It was one of the hardest nights of all for the Connacht host.

Chapter 13

THE ARMIES MOVE FORWARD

As Conchobar and his men raided the small camps of Connachtmen, Ailill and Maeve and Fergus met in conference with the other counselors. They decided to send out scouts and determine if Ulster had reached the plain upon which the main camp waited.

"Mac Roth, travel to the edge of the Plain of Meath and see if they still follow us. If they don't, then we have managed to make good our escape with their goods and herds. We will move away and leave them looking for us where we're not," Ailill ordered.

Mac Roth rode off in his chariot, scouting the Plain of Meath. When he first explored the Sliab Fuait road, he noticed all the wild animals leaving the forest as if it were on fire and moving out onto the broad expanse of the plain. Then the natural forces rose up against him and he turned and rode furiously back to Ailill and Maeve.

They looked up as he walked into the tent, not pausing to clean the dust from his journey from him first. He told them what he had seen, saying, "I looked a second time and a dense fog rose up, filling the valleys and hollows so that the mountains looked like islands in a lake. Sparks of fire leaped through the thick fog and then I saw a world of different colors with flashes of lightning and great bursts of thunder. And then, although only a slight breeze blew, a great rush of wind picked me up and threw me hard upon my back, nearly pulling the hair from my head with its ferocity."

Ailill and Maeve exchanged worried looks.

"What do you think this meant, Fergus?" Ailill asked.

"I know what it is," Fergus said quietly. "The men of Ulster have risen from their pangs and entered the forest. Great heroes forged with might from violence. Their passing shook the forest like a gale across the sea, driving the wild animals away from their coming in fear. The dense fog was the breath of those fierce men and the flashes of lightning and the sparks of fire were the war-riors' eyes gleaming with the lust of battle. The thunder was the humming of their blades and the uproar of the army: chariots clat-tering, horse-hooves drumming upon the packed earth, anger and fury and the ferocity of the brave warriors who think that they will never reach this place in time to do battle."

"Then let them come!" Ailill said hotly. "We have the warriors to stop them!"

"You'll need them," Fergus said grimly. "And more. No one can withstand the fury of the Ulstermen when they are angered: no one in all Ireland, from Greece and Scythia westward to the Orkney Islands and the Pillars of Hercules. No, not even as far as the tower of Breogan and the Islands of Gades can warriors be found strong enough to stand against the Ulstermen."

"Then let us make our plans well," Maeve said. "Let us build a square, a pen, with our men and leave one end open, but the men hidden. When Conchobar and his men ride into the camp, then shall we swing the last leg of the square, the gate, shut and take the Ulstermen prisoners."

Fergus laughed and shook his head at this, but when Concho-bar's son, Cormac Connlongas, heard the report, a great anger fell over him and he formed his three thousand men to attack Maeve and Ailill. But cooler heads prevailed and the men of Munster came between them and made peace.

Still, Maeve made her pen, but Conchobar went not only into the pen, but broke through the other side, slaughtering two hundred men on each side as his army swarmed over the plain like hungry locusts. Then he turned his army and came back through the Connacht forces and slaughtered another two hundred on each side. Eight hundred of the Connacht host died that day.

"Well," Ailill said when word was brought to him about the slaughter. "You see what your woman's wit brings to us? Death and destruction. Leave the planning to us and keep yourself content with your charms. You have started this war with your greed and discontent, with your desire to be manly, but the gods have made you a woman and that is what you are."

"That may be what I am, but it is what men want as well," she said.

"What men want is to return home," Ailill said.

"Oh?" Maeve taunted. "I shall show you whom the men follow."

She stripped herself naked and called for her chariot and rode naked throughout the Connacht camp and the men cheered her passage.

Ailill ignored her ride, his mind set on how to defeat Ulster. He summoned Mac Roth to his tent and said, "Go and discover who has joined Conchobar and his men."

Mac Roth passed out of Ailill's tent and went back again to see the Ulster camp on the Slemain Midi Plain. He came back, saying, "A mighty force waits out there at the hill of Slemain Midi. Three thousand men or more. They tore off their clothes and dug a mound where their leader is to sit. A royal figure who stood proudly before his company, handsome and slender, powerful and tall. His light-yellow hair had been cut and neatly curled and reached down in waves to his shoulders. He wore a purple-pleated tunic wrapped around him, fastened at the throat with a red gold brooch. His eyes were gray and gentle; his face bright and his brow broad, jaw narrow. His beard was gold and forked. He wore a white, red-embroidered hooded tunic and his gold-hilted sword reached to his shoulders, across which he had slung a shield engraved with gold animals. He carried a broad gray stabbing-spear.

"Then," he continued, "another company came as large as the first. A young hero led them. He wore a green cloak fastened at his shoulder with a gold brooch. His hair was curled and yellow and he carried an ivory-hilted sword with the hilt cut from a boar's tusk. He carried a death-shield with a scalloped edge, and a great spear gleamed from his hand like a palace torch with silver rings running from the grip to the tip and back again. The company settled at the left hand of the leader of the first company. The leader of that grim company spoke with a stammer."

"Who are these, Fergus?" Ailill asked.

"I know them well," Fergus said. "Conchobar is the one who placed himself on the mound of sods. Sencha Mac Ailill, Ulster's most eloquent, faced him. The stammerer is Cúscraid Menn Macha, Conchobar's son. The rings on the spear in his hand run like that only when a victory is about to be collected."

"They'll find all the fight they want here," Maeve said contemptuously.

"That is the foolish talk of a foolish woman," Fergus said impatiently. "No army yet raised in Ireland can withstand a force like that. And remember: these men are angry."

"That isn't all," Mac Roth said quietly. "Yet another company came, a troop of three thousand and more led by a swarthy, red-faced man who loomed awesomely above all the others. His dark-brown hair lay flat over his forehead and he carried a five-pronged spear with a curved scallop shield. A cruel sword with a mighty blade hung over his back and a purple cloak had been wrapped around him. A white-hooded tunic covered him to his knee."

"That is the man created for war. He will begin the battle and falls upon his enemies like doom: Eogan Mac Durthacht, King of Fernmag."

"Another company came with their cloaks thrown behind them. They carried dread and terror with them and the clash of their weapons was fierce as they marched. Their champion was a huge man with a fleshy head and sparse gray hair and yellow eyes. He wore a yellow cloak with a white border and carried a death-shield and broad-bladed javelin, its shaft stained red with blood. A murderous sword hung at his shoulder."

"That is Laegaire Buadach, the Victorious, son of Connad son of Ílech from Impail in the north," Fergus said.

"The next company was led by a pleasant, fat warrior with a thick neck. His hair was black and curled and his eyes gray and bright in his face. He wore a noble brown cloak fastened with a large silver brooch. He carried a black shield with a bronze knob in the center and a spear that shimmered like new light. A red-embroidered braided tunic covered him. An ivory-hilted sword hung over his clothes."

"Who is that, Fergus?" Ailill asked, his concern growing with each report.

"He advances like a sea wave rushing up a small stream. He gives three cries when he charges and his name is bitter doom. He is called Munremur Mac Gerrcinn from Moduirn in the north."

"The next company was numerous and handsome and well disciplined. They shook the armies with the clash of their weapons as they passed them. I have never seen a man such as he who led them: pale and proud, lofty good looks."

"I believe that to be the bright flame, the fair Fedlimid, an over-whelming storm wave with his warrior's rage."

"The next company was a full warlike troop easily three thou-sand strong. A swallow-faced warrior led them. His hair was black and curly, his dull-brown eyes scornful of all those around him. He wore a gray cloak and carried a red shield with a knob of silver and held a broad, triple-riveted blade in his hand."

"Connad Mac Morna from Callan," Fergus said admiringly. "He is an angry glow like fire that burns through the battles like glowing white iron."

"I have never seen a champion like him who led the next army. Red-gold hair close-cropped, his face fine and well formed, the jaw narrow, the brow broad, with fine lips and teeth like pearls. His voice rang like a bell when he spoke and he wore a purple cloak with a gold brooch upon his white breast. He carried a curved shield with a silver knob and dressed with animals in all colors. A gold sword with a gold hilt hung at his back."

"That would be Rochaid Mac Faithemain from Rígdonn, the one to whom you gave your daughter Finnabair. He is half an army himself in battle, a hungry mastiff who will reap revenge upon your people for what you did to him with your daughter."

"The next company was led by a burly man with thick thighs and great calves. His legs and arms were each the size of a grown man's waist. His hair was black and his face many-scarred, his eyes blazing and scornful. He walked like a man who has done great deeds."

"He has," Fergus said. "He is a flood of hot blood and power and pride: my own foster-brother Fergus Mac Léte, King of Líne."

"The next army wore strange clothes. They were led by a whoreson who wore five chains of gold, a white-hooded tunic, and a green cloak that wrapped itself around him and was fastened at his shoulder with a gold brooch. His spear was the size of a palace pillar and a gold-hilted sword hung at his shoulder."

"Amargin, the son of the smith Ecet Salach, the grimy one, from Buais. He is quick to anger and hungers for battle like a starving dog hungers for meat."

"The next company was large and overwhelming, all of them like rocks with their strength. Their numbers were legion and a terrible man led that company: harsh, big-bellied, with a huge nose and thick lips. His hair was grizzled and his legs and arms red. He wore a tunic sewn from rough-woven cloth and an iron spike fastened a dark cloak to his shoulders. His javelin had thirty rivets in its head and a seven-tempered sword hung at his shoulder."

"Celtchar Mac Uthidir from Dún Lethglaise in the north," Fergus said.

"The next company was led by a warrior all in white and he,

too, was white: hair, face, arms, everything. His shield had a gold knob in the center and an ivory-hilted sword in his hand. His stabbing spear was pitted."

"He's like a bear," Fergus answered. "His arms have the strength of a bear, too. Feradach Finn Fechtnach from Sliab Fuait Wood."

"A terrible warrior led the next company. Big-bellied and horse-lipped. Big-handed, too. A black cloak hung from his shoulders and he carried a dark gray shield on his left and a broad, banded stabbing spear in his right."

"He's like a lion in battle," Fergus said. "Errge Echbél, the Horse-Lipped, from Brí Errgi."

"Another company came with two heroes at their head, each like the other with yellow hair and two bright shields decorated with silver animals. All of their movements were in time together."

"Two like flames from two dragons, spoiled pets of Conchobar. Fiachna and Fiacha. Twins of Conchobar."

"Three noble champions led the next group. All three had yellow-gold hair and wore the same clothes and their weapons were three alike as well."

"The torches of Cuib and Midluachair: three Roth princes. Fiachna's sons: Rus, Dáire, and Imchath, who have come to recover the bull."

"A furious man rode at the head of the next company. He wore a speckled cloak with a silver disk to hold it. He carried a gray shield and a silver-hilted sword. His company was red with blood, as was he."

"No pity for his victims with that one!" Fergus exclaimed. "He is the raving bull, the battle torch from Colptha who protects the northern border. Menn Mac Sálcholgán from Corann, come to avenge his wounds."

"The next company was spirited and eager and led by a great, long-cheeked warrior with dark, curling hair and a fine red woolen cloak and handsome tunic. He carried a silver-hilted sword and a red shield and a gray broad-bladed stabbing-spear in his hand, set into a shaft of ash."

"Fergna Mac Finnchaime from Corann," Fergus said. "Everything is threes with him: three strokes, three roads. He breaks men in battle."

"Another company of three thousand led by a white-breasted warrior came. He wore a gold crown on his head and a red-embroidered tunic. His cloak was bigger than the others and many-colored. His shield had a gold rim and a gold-hilted sword hung at his side."

"That was Furbaide Fer Benn, the Horned Man, who is like the sea against the stream," Fergus said.

"The next company wore clothes unlike any of the others. A great army with a flushed, freckled boy at its head. He carried a gold-rimmed and gold-inlaid shield with an ivory knob on his army. He wore a red-embroidered white hooded tunic with a purple-fringed cloak about him."

But Fergus remained silent at this one until Ailill asked him twice who the youth was.

"I don't know anyone in Ulster like that," Fergus answered. "But these could be the men of Temair who follow Eric, the son of Coirpre Niafer and Conchobar's daughter. Coirpre and Conchobar do not like each other. Eric may have come to help his grandfather without his father knowing. If it is he, then you will undoubtedly lose this battle for he does not fear anyone and when he charges, the men of Ulster will hack their way through all the demons of the earth to save him. Even Conchobar will come and his sword will hum through men's necks like the buzzing of a thousand bees or a mastiff growling. Conchobar would kill everyone to find his grandson."

"I am weary from describing everyone," Mac Roth said. "But I have one more thing to say."

"I think you've said enough," Fergus said gloomily, reaching for a cup of wine.

"Perhaps. But Conall Cernach and his company haven't come yet. Nor have Conchobar's three sons with their troops of three thousand each. Cúchulainn, although he is wounded, has yet to come as well. Although many hundreds and many thousands have reached the Ulster camp, many more have yet to arrive. When I left, I looked from Ferdiad's Ford to Slemain Midi and saw more men and horses than I could count of hills and slopes."

"Ah well! You have seen a large following indeed," Fergus murmured, lifting the cup to his lips.

Chapter 14

THE LAST BATTLE

LATE THAT EVENING, CONCHOBAR visited Ailill with his armies. "I'd like to discuss a truce," he said. "Until morning."

"Agreed," said Ailill swiftly, taking advantage of the moment. "But not a moment later."

Conchobar returned to his tents, sighing with weariness and gratitude, for the truce allowed him and his men another day to fully recover from their pangs. By sunset, the Ulstermen were settled in their camp. In the twilight between the two camps, the Mórrígan spoke:

"Ravens gnawing men's necks away,
blood spurting in the fierce fray,
hacked flesh and battle madness,
blades in bodies, acts of war, sadness
after the cloaked one's hero beat
in man's shape he shakes to pieces and meets
the men of Cruacháin with hacking blows!
Men fall, a bloody feast for black crows.

Hail, Ulster! Woe, men of Ireland!
Woe to Ulster! Hail, men of Ireland!"

But she spoke "Woe to Ulster" only to hide the truth from the Connachtmen. That night, Nét's wives, Nemain and the Badb, thundered their chilling cries to the Connachtmen at Gáirech and Irgairech. A hundred warriors died from fright when they heard those cries. Later, Ailill Mac Mata called out in his dreams:

"Rise up, Traigthrén the Swift-Footed!
Bring to me the three named Conaire from Sliab Mis;
the three fair ones from Luachair called Les;
the three named Meid from Corpthe Loste;
the three Buidire from Buas River;
the three Badb from Buaidnech River;
the three Buaideltach from Berba River;
the three Muredachs from Marga;
the three Laegaires from Lec Derg;
the three Suibnes from the Síuir River;
the three Echtachs from Ane;
the three Dael from Eirc;
the three DaMach from Derg Derc;
the three Bratruad from Loch Rí;
the three Nelleth from Loch Eirne;
the three named Bresal from Bodg;
the three Amalgads from Ai;
the three Fiachras from Nemain Wood;
the three Nechtas from Muiresc Plain;
the three famous sons from Es Ruaid;
the three Ruirechs from Aigle;
the three Bruchurs from Febrad River;
the three Conalls from Collamair;
the three Féic from Finnabair;
the three Coirpres from Cliu;
the three named Maine Milscothach;

the three Descertachs from Drompa;
the three Fintans from Femen Plain;
the three Rathachs from Raigne Plain;
the three Eterscéls from Eterbán;
the three Guaires from Gabail;
and the three named Aed from Aidne."

These were the men who had survived Cúchulainn's slaughter.
Meanwhile, Cúchulainn feasted at Fedan Chollna. He had killed
no one west of Ferdiad's Ford at that time. It was here that two
women came from the Connacht camp, weeping and wailing, telling
him that the men of Ulster had been beaten and Conchobar and Fergus killed. That night, the Mórrígan swept over the plain from one
army to the next, a lean, gray-haired hag, shrieking and dancing
upon the points of their weapons, taunting the men by claiming
ravens would eat the flesh of their necks and dine on their eyes.

Cúchulainn slept fitfully, the cries of the Mórrígan playing upon
his dreams. Ferdiad, bloody but unbowed, appeared, beckoning
him, banging his javelin against his shield, reminding the warrior
of his deceit by using the Gae Bolga in their duel.

Ferdiad shouted: "Let us fight again but with the agreed-on
weapons, not the treacherous Gae Bolga!"

"It is a spear," Cúchulainn tried to explain.

"But not a short javelin," Ferdiad said. "I do not reproach you
for winning, Cúchulainn, but for winning in the way you did."

"Are you alone there?" Cúchulainn asked.

Sadness came into Ferdiad's eyes. He nodded. "As alone as one
can be in the darkness of the dark."

Other warriors appeared, shadows in the mists. Cúchulainn
tossed and mumbled, imploring them. Laeg watched anxiously
over him throughout the night.

The next morning, Cúchulainn awoke, hollow-eyed, tired from
listening to the cries of the Mórrígan. "Look out upon the plain and
tell me what you see," he ordered Laeg.

"A small herd has strayed from the camp in the west over toward our camp in the east. Men go out to bring them back," Laeg said to Cúchulainn.

"The servants will probably start to fight and the animals will wander the plain while everyone joins in," Cúchulainn said.

They watched as the servants came together and blows were struck. Here and there, a blade flashed, sending battle-rays to the sky.

"How goes it with the men of Ulster?" Cúchulainn asked from his bed where he lay, recovering his strength.

"They are fighting like true warriors," the charioteer answered.

"That is the honor that they have learned from the warriors," Cúchulainn said. After a moment he asked what Laeg saw.

"The beardless ones have joined in the fight," the charioteer said.

"Has light touched the clouds yet?"

"Not yet," Laeg answered.

"Oh, if only I had the strength to join with them!" Cúchulainn said bitterly.

"I think there will be slaughter enough without that when the sun climbs high in the sky," Laeg said dryly. "Here come the warriors now. The kings are still sleeping."

And at that moment, Conchobar began chanting in his sleep:

"Rise, kings of Macha! Dark shades!
Mighty acts await battering blades.
Let us rend and tear the ground!
Rise, kings of Macha! Go around
and bring your people here. Take
them to where they will make
the Connacht army pay most dearly
by trampling their battle ranks severely.
A forest of men will fall dead
and their queen will fill with dread
as the grass reddens with blood
from the Macha kings' army flood."

"Who chants thus?" the people wondered as the words rolled throughout the Ulster camp.

"Conchobar Mac Nessa," those who knew said.

"Fachtna," yet others answered.

"Sleep, but keep the sentries out," the Connachtmen were told. Laegaire Buadach said:

"Rise, kings of Macha and look to your cattle.
Guard your plunder and drive Connacht's force
from Uisnech hill. Our own battle
will destroy the Connacht force.
Gairech's fair field will bleed
where our foes will bleed!"

"Who chants thus?" everyone asked.

"Laegaire Buadach Mac Connaid Buidi eic Ílech. Sleep now, but keep the sentries watchful," the Connachtmen said.

Conchobar had risen by now and made himself ready for battle. He looked at the sky, saying, "Let us wait until the sun lights all of the hollows and hills of Ireland."

And while they waited, Cúchulainn watched from the east while the Connacht kings settled their crowns upon their heads. He told Laeg to warn the Ulster men to rise and Laeg shouted:

"Rise, kings of Macha and lead
our modest people to mighty acts!
The Badb wants Connacht to bleed!
Is there none like Cúchulainn to act
Macha's will for Cuailnge's cattle?
Rise early now and let us make battle!"

"They have awakened now," Laeg said to Cúchulainn. "They see them rushing naked to the battle with nothing but their weapons. Those in the east have slit their tents so that they might escape through the backs unseen by our warriors!"

"When they feel the fury of Ulster they become inspired!" Cúchulainn said grimly. "What do you see the Ulstermen doing now?"

"They bring the fight to Connacht," Laeg said proudly. "Conall Cernach's charioteer and I could drive each chariot over the battle now and neither hoof nor wheel rim would sink between the warriors."

"Ah! This may make a great battle!" Cúchulainn said with relish. "Tell me everything that happens!"

"I'll try," Laeg answered. He studied the fighting for a moment, then said, "Now, Ulster has reached the Connacht battle line and broken through and the same number have broken through Ulster's line."

"Oh, if only I had my strength upon me! You would see me holding that hole from Connacht! None would break through there if my sword arm was strong!"

Connacht's army marched in groups of three to the ford near the army at Gáirech and Irgairech. Nine warriors charged with them in their chariots, but Maeve held back some to rescue Ailill if the Connacht forces were beaten or to kill Conchobar if they won.

Laeg watched and noticed that Ailill and Maeve called Fergus to the place on the high ground where they stood watching the battle. He could tell from their angry gestures that they were goading him to join in the battle.

"If I had my sword I'd send men's heads toppling like hailstones over the rims of their shields!" he said. "I would be like the horses of kings throwing great clods of earth behind. I'd heap up men's hacked jawbones on necks and necks on shoulders and arms on elbows with elbows on wrists and wrists on fists and fists on fingers and fingers on nails and nails on skulls and skulls on trunks and trunks on thighs and thighs on knees and knees on calves and calves on feet and feet on toes and toes on nails! Oh, if only I had my sword! Necks would buzz through the air like angry bees."

Ailill turned to Fer Loga, his charioteer, saying, "You may bring that flesh-eating sword to me, now! And if one hero's deed has left the luster of that blade, dulling it, why nothing will save you from me!"

The charioteer left and went to his tent where he retrieved Fergus's sword from the time he stole it while Fergus slept with Maeve. He brought the sword in all its gleaming beauty, shining like the evening star, cold and brilliant, and gave it to Ailill who said, "Here is your sword! Now let us see if you are worthy of your brág or if your words are only empty air. Are you a warrior among warriors or boys? Let me see you rage against Ulster's men now as you have threatened to do."

Fergus greatefully took the sword, saying, "Welcome, bitter blade! Welcome In Caladbolg, the sword of Leite. Now you shall see how I bring Badb's horror into the hearts of those warriors!" He grinned at Ailill and added, "Take care that you do not fall on this battlefield!" Then he seized his weapons and joined the battle.

Holding his sword with both hands, he hewed right and left like a farmer wielding his scythe against a field of oats, carving a gap with the death of a hundred men in the ranks until he came to Conall Cernach.

"For shame, Fergus! You kill your friends and kin for the sake of a whore's backside!" Conall said scathingly at the scarred warrior in exile.

A man heard what Conall had said and took word to Maeve. Furious at what had been said, Maeve seized her weapons and charged the ranks, driving the ranks back three times until a wall of javelins forced her away.

"Who drives our men down from the north?" Conchobar shouted. "I will find him while you hold the ground here!"

"We'll hold," the warriors panted. "We'll hold until the earth gapes wide beneath our feet or the heavens fall heavily upon us!"

Conchobar found Fergus laying to each side of him with his mighty two-handed strokes and stepped in his path, raising his shield Óchaín, Beauty's Ear, with its four gold horns and four red-gold coverings. Such was his rage that Fergus did not recognize the shield and struck three times at the shield, each blow ringing like a clear bell, but Conchobar held firm and then, his shield screamed loudly and all the shields of Ulster screamed with it.

"What Ulsterman holds this shield?" Fergus shouted.

"A better man than you! It is I, he who drove you out of Emain Macha to live in exile with the wild dogs and he who will stop you on this day!" Conchobar taunted.

Enraged, Fergus raised his mighty sword high over his head, but as the point touched the ground behind him, Cormac Connlongas threw his arms around him, seizing his wrists.

"Striking this man would be the most shameful thing you could do, Fergus!" he said. "Your name will be cheapened by your act and break all the pacts that you made with your friends!"

"I must strike!" Fergus shouted in fury. "I must strike!"

"Strike anywhere but here! Strike the hills, if you must strike something! But, if you strike my father, then you will shame yourself forever among the men of Ulster!" He turned to his father and said, "Leave us now, Father! This man will no longer fight with Ulstermen!"

The In Caladbolg, the sword of Leite from the elf-mounds, glowed with a hard brightness in Fergus's hands and grew the size of a rainbow in the air. In fury, Fergus turned and leveled the three bald hills in the north with his sword strokes. Cúchulainn heard the ground ringing from Fergus's blows and asked, "Who strikes those blows? Blood blocks my heart and I feel the madness threatening!"

He shook himself, trying to rise, but the branches strapped to him as splints refused to give way.

"Undo these splints! Quickly!" he ordered.

"Fergus Mac Roich strikes those blows," Laeg said. "The great fight has reached Ócháin, Conchobar's shield!"

"Loosen these splints, I say! Quickly!" Cúchulainn roared. Then the warp-spasm seized him and the hazel twigs burst from his body and flew as far as Mag Túaga in Connacht. The wrappings around them flew to Bacca in Corco M'ruad while the moss used to plug his wounds flew through the air as high as larks fly on fine days. His wounds opened again and blood ran freely from them, carving trenches in the earth as two of Maeve's servant girls, Fethan and Colla, satirists both, approached him. They had been commanded to secretly bleed him while he lay helpless as they pretended to heal him. But Cúchulainn was lost in the warp-spasm when they approached and he seized them and bashed their heads together until the gray matter flew over all.

Laeg drew the twenty-seven skins he wore as armor in battle over him and tightened the straps. Then he stepped aside as Cúchulainn looked wild-eyed around for his weapons, but they were gone. Only his chariot remained, the shafts broken. He wrenched one free and, holding it like a club, roared into battle, shouting for Fergus.

"Come to me, Fergus! By the gods of Ulster, I'll spill your blood until it churns like foam in a pool! Then I'll stand over your lifeless body like an erect cat's tail on an angry cat! I'll slap you like a mother her son! I will beat you like a winnowing shaft!"

"Who dares to talk to me like that!" Fergus roared angrily.

"I do! Cúchulainn, son of Sualdam and Conchobar's sister! Your foster-son! Give way! Remember your vow to me when I gave you victory before!"

Reminded of his word to the Warped One, Fergus lowered his sword, swallowing the rage within him and saying, "I remember my promise. I will fight no more."

And he pulled his troop of three thousand Exiles from the battle. The men of Galeóin and Munster left as well, leaving Maeve and Ailill in the battle with their seven sons and their nine troops of three thousand warriors.

Cúchulainn roared into battle, the chariot shaft in his hand driving men's brains down into their gullets, batting their heads from their shoulders like hurley balls. The slaughter of the four provinces grew great around him and bodies piled on bodies as the Warped One roared through their midst with the Badb Catha gliding on spread wings above him, her raucous call croaking over the battlefield in sated glory.

"A boon!" Maeve called out to Cúchulainn as he roared by in a chariot he had taken from a Connacht warrior who now lay with his brains soaking into the blood-sopped grounds.

Cúchulainn halted his panting horses and looked across the battle to her. "What is it?"

"Let the rest of my army withdraw from the field under your protection!"

But before Cúchulainn could answer, the tide of battle rolled over him. The sun stood high in the sky, looking down at the blood-soaked field when Cúchulainn came into the battle. The sun rays poured over the forest in the west when the Warped One smashed the last Connacht company. Maeve had set up a rear guard and sent the Brown Bull of Cuailnge and fifty of his heifers to Cruacháin away from the battle as she had promised so that he would be safe. She prepared herself to do battle, then felt her gush of blood.

"Fergus," she panted. "Hold the shield guard at the rear until I can relieve myself."

"By the gods, you picked a fine time to get this!" he exclaimed.

"There is nothing to do but suffer it when it happens," she said bitterly.

So Fergus managed the rear guard while fertile blood flowed fiercely from her, carving three trenches through the earth, a fecund offering for Macha, Badb, and Mórrígan. The place is now called Fúal Medba, but is becoming known as Maeve's Fertile Place. Here Cúchulainn found her.

"I should kill you for all that you have done. None would curse my name for doing this, but I won't."

"Grant me a boon!" she panted.

"What?"

"Let my men come under your protection until they have passed Áth Mór. Is this too much to ask?"

"Yes," Cúchulainn answered. "But I will grant it to you."

He waited until her pangs eased, then followed her and her men passed Áth Mór. Then his sword was given to him and he struck the three hills of Áth Luain with his sword, striking three times at the stone hills in imitation of Fergus at Máela Mide, and cut off their tops, leaving them bald.

The last battle was over.

Maeve turned to Fergus, saying, "We have been shamed here today, Fergus." She threw her hair out of her face and turned her brimming eyes into the wind so that none would see she wept as she remembered the words of Fedelm: "I see them draped in crimson; I see warriors clothed in red." And at last, she understood the words of the Woman of the *Sídhe*.

"We followed the ass of a misguided woman," Fergus answered. "When a herd is led by a mare instead of a stallion, it is not unusual to see that herd destroyed."

On the day after the battle, they took the Brown Bull away. On Ai Plain, at Tarbg, the Brown Bull met Findbennach, the White-Horned Bull of Ailill. Each pawed the ground, bellowing challenges at the other. The armies drew away to watch them battle. They asked Bricriu Mac Carbad, who favored no one over the other, to judge the battle of the bulls. But when he came close, they roared and charged, trampling him, and this is how Bricriu, the Bitter-Tongued, son of Cairbre, died.

The Brown Bull reared and placed a hoof on the horn of Findbennach and refused to draw his hoof back until Fergus scolded him, spanking him with a stick.

"Men have died for the likes of you. At least fight with honor!" Fergus said.

And Cormac Connlongas, the son of Conchobar, stepped forward, taking his spear and striking three mighty blows across the Donn's back, saying, "What use is this miserable animal who lacks the ballocks to meet a challenge?"

The Brown Bull jerked back his hoof, breaking his leg while Findbennach's horn flew to the nearby mountain, giving it its name: Sliab nAdarca, the Horn Mountain. Then the bulls came together and fought through the day and into the night. The men could no longer see them, but they could hear the roars and bellows of their fury as each strived to kill the other. The bulls circled all of Ireland that night. When morning finally came, the men saw the Donn Cuailnge coming westward past Cruacháin with Findbennach's mangled guts hanging from his horns.

He snorted and pawed the earth in front of the men for the rest of the day, shaking the guts at them in warning. Then he entered the lake at Cruachain at night and when he emerged, he had Findbennach's loins and shoulder blade and liver on his horns. The armies went to kill him, but Fergus stopped them, and the Brown Bull headed toward his own land.

He paused to drink at Finnlethe where he left Findbennach's shoulder blade. That place is now called Finniethe, the Shoulder Blade of the White One. He drank again at Áth Luain and left Findbennach's loins there and that is how that place came to be called the Ford of the Loins, Áth Luain. He gave a huge bellow at Iraird Cuillen that was heard throughout the province and drank again at Tromma where Findbennach's liver fell from his two horns and from which Tromma, Liver, takes its name. He threw Findbennach's rib cage as far as Dublind, called Áth Clíath, and his thigh as far as Port Large. He came to Etan Tairb and wearily rested his brow against the hill at Áth Da Ferta, now called Etan Tairb, the Bull's Brow, on Murtheimne Plain. Then he traveled the Midluachair Road to Cuib where he had stayed with the milkless cow of Dáire and rended the ground there from which comes the name Gort mBúraig, the Field of the Trench. He continued on his way toward his home, and when he saw the green hills of Cuailgne, a great spirit rose up in him at the sight of his own country where he belonged, and he rushed toward it, killing all who tried to keep him from his pastures.

And when he finally arrived at his own place, he turned his back to a hill and gave out a loud bellow of victory that echoed over all of Ireland. And with that, his great heart broke in his body like a nut and blood gushed from his mouth and he fell dead between Ulster and Uí Echach at Druim Tairb, the Bull Ridge.

Ailill and Maeve made their peace with Ulster and the warrior Cúchulainn and for seven years no Connachtmen were killed. Finnabair stayed with Cúchulainn while the Connachtmen returned to their own country and Ulster's warriors returned in triumph to Emain Macha.

Bheith réidh leis an obar.

Aiméan.

Glossary of Names and Terms

Aengus: son of Aenlám Gaibe.

Ailill: king of Connacht whose wealth was enormous. His wife, Maeve, refused to believe that a man had more wealth than she and because of this difference, the famous war for the Brown Bull of Cooley occurred.

Aithech: a churl of the Fomorians. His name is sometimes used as an adjective to mean any boorish person.

Anu: identified also as Danu. Two mountain-tops near Killarney in Co. Kerry are called Dá Chich mAnann, literally "the Two Paps of Anu." She is seen as the Mother-Goddess.

Ardachad: in Sliab Fuaid, near Newtown Hamilton, Co. Armagh.

Áth Carpat: Big Bridge in Dundalk, Co. Louth.

Áth Firdia: Ardee, Co. Louth.

Áth Gabla: a ford on the Mattock River near Kellystown, Co. Meath.

Áth Lethan: Dundalk Harbor in Co. Louth.

Áth Luain: Athlone, Co. Westmeath.

Badb: identified as the most terrible of the battle-goddesses; a part of the Mórrígna, a triple goddess of whom the other two are Macha and Mórrígan. She is also known as Badb Catha or Battle Raven and although both sinister and sexual, is usually identified with prophecies concerning the end of the world and chaos.

Bards: from "aes dána" or men of art.

Bélat Ailiuin: a way over the Flurry River near Ravensdale, Co. Louth.

Bernas Bó Cuailnge: Windy Gap above Big River source in Co. Louth.

Black of Saingliu: one of Cúchulainn's horses, born, according to some legends, at the same time as he. Along with the Gray of Macha, the Black came out of a lake to test Cúchulainn's worthiness. He rode it all over Ireland in one day as it tried to dislodge him. After failing, it accepted him as its master. Together with the Gray, the Black became yet another weapon for Cúchulainn. Their birth and appearance from the lake suggests magic and is part of the mysticism of the epic.

Bocánaich: goblins; demons of the air.

Bodhrán: a leather hand drum that gives forth a booming sound almost like thunder.

Breogan: the builder of a great tower from which Íth, his son, sees Ireland one clear winter evening. The tower is in Spain.

Bricriu: called "the Bitter-Tongued." He is one of the Ulster Exiles and has a castigating manner of speech. Filled with bitterness toward the world, he throws a magnificent feast *(Fled Bricrend)* in a story before the *Táin* found in *Lebor na hUidre (Book of the Dun Cow)* in which he challenges three warriors—Loegaire Buadach, Conall Cernach, and Cúchulainn—to prove their right to the champion's portion of the feast. He is compared to the Greek satirist Thersites and Loki, the mischief-maker in the *Eddas*. He is associated with Lough Brickland, Co. Down, near which was his palace Dún Rory.

Buanbach: a game like draughts or checkers.

Cailleach: an old hag but also a shape-shifter to a young woman. The place of the old hag in Irish literature is usually one connected to magic.

Carbad Seardha: Cúchulainn's scythed chariot, bristling with knives attached to the wheels, which becomes a weapon itself when Cúchulainn charges through the Connachtmen, scything them down like wheat.

Cathbad the Druid: attached to the court of Conchobar Mac Nessa and, according to some accounts, the father of Conchobar. He was the most powerful of Druids.

Coirpre: several individuals among which is the father of Eric, Conchobar's grandson through his daughter Fedelm. Conchobor and Coirpre are sworn enemies. Cúchulainn kills Coirpre in *Cath Ruis na Ríg (Battle of Ros na Rig)*, which is the story of Ulster's war for the raid after the Brown Bull.

Conall Cernach: one of the major heroes of the Red Branch. Conall derives from "Cunovalos," which roughly translates to "strong like a wolf." Although he appears among Maeve's soldiers in the *Táin* in the early part of the epic, this appears to be an error as he is a stalwart fighter for Conchobor in the latter part. Some critics have suggested that he was part of the Exiles only to renounce them after Maeve broke her word and after the pact involving the Connachtmen and single combat with Cúchulainn and return to the Red Branch. His name is associated with many legends, including one in which he joined the Roman army and was present at Christ's crucifixion. He revenges Cúchulainn's death, caused by trickery, by trailing the murderers and disposing of them one by one until finally he meets Lugaid Mac Con Roi in a classic combat by a ford.

Conchobar Mac Nessa: king of Ulster in the first century B.C. His palace at Emain Macha is now known as Navan Fort, located west of the city of Armagh. He became king after his mother, Ness, agreed to live with Fergus Mac Roich, then king of Emain Macha, for a year on condition that Conchobar be allowed to rule during that time. She deceived Fergus, however, by giving away riches to the knights of the Red Branch so that when it became time for Conchobar to return the throne to Fergus, the knights voted to keep him as king. His father is alleged to have been Cathbad and although he is generally seen as a wise king, it is his vanity that ultimately brings about the pangs of the Ulstermen and leaves them helpless when the Connacht army invades their borders. This came about when he refused to be swayed by Macha's plea that she not be forced to race his horses since she was pregnant. Although she defeated Conchobar's team in a footrace, the exertion brought about the birth of twins, and her death after she cursed the Red Branch. During times of severe crisis, the Ulstermen and all of their generations would suffer her identical pains for five days and four nights.

Connacht: one of the five ancient provinces of Ireland that still exists to this day. The others are Leinster, Munster, Ulster, and Meath. According to the *Book of Invasions,* the Fir Bolg, the first invaders to establish social and political order in the land, also established the provinces. The idea of a powerful Connacht invading helpless Ulster became a symbol during Ireland's fight for independence from England.

Cormac Connlongas: nephew of Maeve by her sister Clothra and Conchobar. Said to be an incestuous son. When Conchobar treacherously reneged on his vow to protect Deirdre and her husband, he joined Fergus in exile.

Crom Deroil: Maeve's Druid.

Cruacháin: the "place of enchantment" where Maeve and Ailill had their home. Maeve, one of the most sensuous and sexual figures in literature (called "Maeve of the Thirty Men" in some stories for her nymphomaniac need of thirty men a night to sate her sexual urgencies), took great pains to make her palace an enchanted place where songs could be sung, stories told, the arts lived. It was a soothing place where the pleasures of the flesh and spirit took precedent over war. It is situated over an area of about ten square miles near Tulsk, Co. Roscommon. Interestingly, it is here that the legendary cave to the Otherworld is found. In Christian lore, this place is known as the Hell's Gate of Ireland.

Cruaidin Cailidcheann: Cúchulainn's sword.

Cruitire: a harper.

Crunniuc Mac Agnomain: the lonely farmer visited by the lovely Macha who made her pregnant then bragged that she was swifter of foot than Conchobar's horses, thus bringing about the Curse of Ulster.

Cúroi: king of Munster whose fortress is associated with Caher Conree, Co. Kerry. He appears as a *bachlach* (churl) in *Fled Bricrend*. Apparently, he is a magical figure, a shape-shifter, often called upon to arbitrate arguments. He is a reluctant participant in the *Táin* for the Connacht forces, which leads some to suggest that he is taking part in the raid only through a truce or treaty with Connacht.

Cúchulainn: a boy-warrior whose parentage is shrouded in mystery, thus giving him powers far beyond those of ordinary mortal men or heroes. His lone stand and guerrilla warfare against the invading Connacht forces became a symbol for Irishmen fighting for Ireland's independence from England.

Cuillius: Ailill's charioteer, who steals Fergus's sword while the latter is making love to Maeve. Later, he is killed by Cúchulainn. His reappearance in the final battle can be seen as an example of the mysticism of the epic. Some, however, suggest that it is his son who appears in the final battle and not Cuillius.

Cúil Sibrille: present-day Kells, Co. Meath.

Cúil Silnne: near Ardakillan in Co. Roscommon.

Cuinciu: Slievenaglogh, Co. Louth.

Culann: the blacksmith or wheelwright whose hound is killed by Cúchulainn.

Curadh: a warrior, mercenary, or one hired as a guard.

Curaid: a group of faithful followers similar to the comitatus of *Beowulf.*

Cúscraid Menn Macha: the One Who Stammers, a son of Conchobar and pupil of Conall Cearnach. He possesses a magnificent spear, with ferrules of silver which of their own accord whirl around bands of gold on the spear to warn of coming conflict.

Dagda: the chief of the Gaelic pantheon of gods, the equivalent of Zeus, Jupiter, and Odin. He is considered to be the father of all and the father of perfect knowledge. He led the *Tuatha Dé Danann* into Ireland against the Fir Bolg. He is considered to be the good god but not so much in the sense of virtue as he is good in everything.

Dáire Mac Fiachna: the owner of the cow that gives birth to the Brown Bull.

Dallán Forgaill: Blind Man of Eloquence, a sobriquet reminiscent of Homer, a sixth-century poet who, on his deathbed, pronounced Seanchán, the man who rediscovered the *Táin,* as chief poet of Ireland.

Deichtine: Conchobar's sister and mother of Cúchulainn. Supposedly, she was abducted or went with the sun god Lugh who became Cúchulainn's father. Other accounts give Cúchulainn's father as Sualdam and yet others as Conchobar. In the latter instance, however, that would have been a *geis,* a ban, of the worst sort so little credence is given to Conchobar as being the father of his own nephew.

Del chliss: literally "the dart of feats," a javelin of extraordinary powers but not quite as powerful as the Gae Bolga.

Delga: west of Dundalk, Co. Louth.

Deirdre: the most beautiful woman in Ireland. When she was still in her mother's womb, Cathbad predicted that she would divide the Red Branch. Consequently, when she was born, Conchobar placed her under his protection and had her isolated from all males. But he was consumed with curiosity and went to see her. Overcome by her beauty, he planned to make her his wife, but she fell in love with Naise, one of the three sons of Uisliu, and fled to Scotland with him. Overcome with jealousy, Conchobar promised freedom to them if they returned to Ulster. Fergus guaranteed their safety, but was tricked into an ale-feast and during his absence, Conchobar had Naise killed. Deirdre later killed herself rather than submit to Conchobar's advances. Incensed at the betrayal of his word by Conchobar, Fergus led a revolt against the Red Branch, burning it to the ground, then led others who shared his sympathies out of Ulster to Connacht. This group became the Ulster Exiles.

Donn Cuailnge: the Brown Bull of Cooley, whose name is closely associated with Donn, the god of death. Donn is also sometimes used as a symbolic reference to "black" as in despair or foreboding.

Druids: an ancient caste whose origins and functions are debatable but generally assumed to be of the learned caste or priestly profession in Irish culture. The word is probably derived from *drui-* which means "very knowledgeable." References are found in the writings of Julius Caesar. Druids are said to have traced their origin to Japhet, son of Noah, and taken their philosophy from Pythagoras. They were the center of society and made decisions on matters of tradition, custom, and law in addition to interpreting the portents that came by day, week, month, and year. According to classical writers, they also taught the doctrine of transmigration of the soul.

Dubhan: Cúchulainn's shield, which is described as being crimson red with knobs and bands of silver, but turning black when in battle, thus to terrify the enemy. This example of "shield-changing" is very similar to Achilles's shield in the *Iliad*.

Dubchoire: "black cauldron," probably in the north side of Glenn Gatlaig, Co. Louth.

Dubthach: the Chafer of Ulster, the Beetle of Ulster, the Black-Tongued, all epic similes that describe Dubthach Daol Uladh, a member of the Ulster Exiles. He joined Fergus in sacking the Red Branch (see DEIRDRE), but he was particularly ruthless in that he killed several women in the foray. In retaliation, all of his family were put to death and he became a sworn enemy forever against Ulster. He is portrayed as having rough jet-black hair, a bloody eye, and the head of a ravenous wolf on each shoulder of his armor. He possessed the great spear Cealtchair, which he bathed in a vat of dark blood. His name and appearance sparked horror in Ulstermen. According to legend, his speech was so bitter that his tongue grew black in his head.

Emain Macha: the seat of the Red Branch; Ulster. The name means the "twins of Macha" (see CONCHOBAR).

Eochaidh Dála: one of Maeve's many husbands before Ailill.

Fann: sometimes "Fand," an Otherworld lady with whom Cúchulainn falls in love; the wife of Manannán the Sea God. Fann appears to Cúchulainn because she has fallen in love with him and weaves a magical spell around him. He lives with her for a month before Manannán breaks up the relationship by appearing to her in a "magic mist." When she saw him she said:

> *"When Manannán the great married me,*
> *A worthy wife for the god of the sea.*
> *He gave me a wristlet of doubly pressed gold*
> *For my blushes to him that I sold."*

When Manannán took her away, he shook his cloak between her and Cúchulainn so that they would not fall in love again.

Fedelm: a *banhfili* or prophetess who has *imbas forosnai,* future sight, by which she predicts what will happen on the *Táin.* She is supposedly of the *Sídhe* of *Rath Cruachaín.*

Fedelm Noichride: a daughter of Conchobar.

Ferbaeth: literally "foolish man," who proves his stupidity by letting his pride get in the way of common sense.

Ferchu Loingsech: a man who thinks he should be Connacht's king instead of Ailill and is constantly working up conspiracies to gain that goal.

Ferdiad Mac Damáin: Cúchulainn's foster-brother and best friend who studies with him with Scáthach, a warrior-woman in Scotland who has remarkable skills. Since she is a woman who also has the skills of a warrior, sometimes she is seen as a mystical figure, almost Otherworldly in nature. Ferdiad accepts Maeve's bribe to fight Cúchulainn and nearly defeats him before Cúchulainn kills him with his Gae Bolga. The symbol of their duel is seen as a symbol of what occurred in Ireland's struggle for independence from England that often pitted brother against brother.

Fergus Mac Roich: see CONCHOBAR.

Fiacha Mac Firaba: one of the Ulster Exiles who followed Fergus. He tells part of the story of Cúchulainn to Ailill and Maeve.

Fidchell: a board game not unlike chess.

Findbennach: the White Bull of Connacht (see DONN CUAIL-NGE).

Finn Mac Cumaill: the central figure of the Fenian or Ossianic Cycle.

Finnabair: the daughter of Ailill and Maeve, who is like her mother in all things sensual. A figure of great beauty, she is used as the reward for anyone who can kill Cúchulainn.

Finnabair in Cuailnge: a location near High Rath, north of the Bush in the Carlingford peninsula.

Fiodhneimheadh: a Druid's special place for divining.

Firbolg: sometimes Fir Bolg (see CONNACHT).

Focherd: Faughart.

Follamin: one of Conchobar's sons.

Fomorians: lords of darkness and death.

Fraech: his mother is Béfinn, of the *Sídhe,* sister of Boann, the Boyne River goddess. He is loved by the daughter of Maeve and Ailill, Finnabair. He becomes engaged to Finnabair on condition that he join in the cattle-raid. He is often mentioned as the most beautiful of Ireland's heroes.

Fúal Medba: literally "Maeve's Urine" and often translated as "Maeve's Foul Place," as this is where she menstruates during the final battle and is subsequentially captured by Cúchulainn. But the implication is much more than this as the menstrual blood is symbolic of fertility as well. Consequently, great poetic license is taken by translating it as "Maeve's Fertile Place."

Gae Bolga: Cúchulainn's spear/javelin that supposedly derives from Ailill Érann. It appears to be a weapon not unlike a harpoon but with magical qualities in that once thrown, it will unerringly find its mark no matter how its victim tries to dodge and turn. It has been translated as a "forked spear" and a "twofold spear" and "the spear of the goddess Bolg" meaning associated somehow with the Firbolg.

Gáirech: Garhy, Co. Westmeath.

Galeóin: the Ulster Exiles descended from the Firbolg, from north Leinster.

Glenn Dáilimda: valley above Omeath, Co. Louth.

Glenn Gatlaig: a valley somewhere above Ballymakellett, Co. Louth.

Gray of Macha: one of Cúchulainn's magical horses (see BLACK OF SAINGLIU).

Granaird: Granard in Co. Longford.

Head-hunting: The Celts believed that the heads they collected from their enemies were more than simply war trophies; they believed that the head was the dwelling place of the soul and the very center of a person's being. It symbolized divinity itself. By displaying and worshiping the heads of their enemies, they believed that they were gaining protection from the magical powers that could be released once the person was dead. Heads were thought to keep evil at bay and could talk, sing, or prophesy. In later years, the turnip lantern of Halloween (see SAMHAIN) was a substitute. In the United States, pumpkins took the place of turnips. An example of a head prophesying is seen in the *Táin* when Sualdam tries to rally the Red Branch knights to come to the aid of Cúchulainn. The knights, however, are too weak with their pangs to respond. Sualdam turns away in anger and tries to spur his horse back to help Cúchulainn. Startled, the horse rears and knocks Sualdam's shield against his neck. The sharp edge of the shield severs his head and it falls upon his shield, which is carried into the Red Branch where it speaks, saying: "Beware, men of Emain Macha! Beware Ailill and the Connacht army!" The curse is broken and the Ulstermen remember themselves as they are— mighty warriors—and speed to the aid of Cúchulainn.

Iraird Cuillenn: Crossakeel in Co. Meath.

Ibar: Conchobar's charioteer who drives Cúchulainn on his first series of adventures as a young boy.

In Caladbolg: Fergus's sword whose stroke is "like lightning and as mighty as a rainbow." The sword reportedly belonged to Leite and came from the elf-mounds.

Laeg: Cúchulainn's charioteer, the only one outside of Cúchulainn who can handle his horses.

Liasa Liac: Ballymakellett, Co. Louth.

Lugh: the sun god, the Otherworldly father of Cúchulainn.

Mac Roth: the messenger of Ailill and Maeve.

Macha: one of the three warrior goddesses along with Badb and Mórrígan but more associated with fertility than the other two. It is she who pronounces the Ulster Curse (see CONCHOBAR).

Maeve: the wife of Ailill, often called "Queen of Connacht" although the Celtic tribes during this time did not recognize queens. She is associated with promiscuity and sexuality along with obstinance and cruelty. Many epic similes are attached to her name such as "White Shoulders," "Friendly Thighs," "of the Thirty Men," generally all epithets having to do with sex. She uses sex and whatever else she can to get her way. She is allied in an ambiguous sense to both Light and Dark in a sort of euhemerized divinity. Maeve killed her sister Clothru, who was pregnant with Conchobar's son and the child was removed by caesarian section with swords. Maeve then assumed sovereignty from Clothru with her husband Ailill. She is a leading character in not only the *Táin* but in *Scél Mucce Meic Da Thó* and *Fled Bricrend*. In the latter story, she tries to seduce Cúchulainn, who rejects her advances. The most earthy of Irish pagan "queens," she is interpreted as a goddess of war and fertility. She is eventually killed by Furbaide, son of Clothru, who avenged his mother's death by putting a piece of cheese in his sling and hurling it at Maeve while she is bathing in the river Shannon. The irony of a piece of cheese being used as the means to kill Maeve was not lost upon early Celtic minds. Furbaide's throw with his sling was of such tremendous force, signifying his hatred of his aunt, that anything would have pierced Maeve's brainpan.

Mag Bolg: the plain at Moybolgue near Kells, Co. Meath and Co. Cavan.

Mag Clochair: a plain north of Tailtiu near Focherd.

Mag Da Chó: in Connacht between Cruachain, Co. Roscommon and Athlone, Co. Westmeath.

Maine: the name of seven sons of Maeve and Ailill: Feidhlim, Cairbre, Eochaidh, Fearghus, Sin, Ceat, and Dáire. All have epic similes that explain their function in stories.

Manannán: the Irish sea god (see FANN)

Mórrígan: one of the battle-goddesses usually seen as a raven. She is often referred to as the great queen and is identified with

Anu, the mother of the Irish gods. She met Dagda, the god-king, while she was washing herself at the River Unius during the great pagan feast of Samhain. She had one foot on the south bank and the other on the north bank and in this position, she made love to Dagda, mating over water, this being part of the ancient fertility ritual. She is the most sensual of the Mórrígna, the triple war-goddess, of whom the others are Macha and Badb.

Mugain: the wife of Conchobar. She is usually seen as a symbol of voluptuousness. Although she is married to Conchobar, she is highly attracted to others, especially Cúchulainn.

Muid Loga: marks where the Connacht army was fully routed. The town of Louth, Co. Louth.

Murtheimne: an area or plain separate from Ulster although owing allegiance to it. Cúchulainn is from here and this, plus his youthfulness, keeps him from becoming a victim of the "Pangs." Although sometimes referred to as a "province," Murtheimne was not one of the provinces of ancient Ireland.

Nadcranntail: a most unpleasant man whose appearance is so grotesque and disgusting that not even Maeve can stand him. Given many promises, including Finnabair should he win, he challenges Cúchulainn and is subsequently killed.

Naoise: also Naise, one of the sons of Uisliu. (see DEIRDRE)

Nechta Scéne: the mother of Foill, Fannall, and Tuachell, all killed by the youthful Cúchulainn. She appears to be mystical and somewhat related to the *banhsídhe*.

Nemain the War-Spirit: a wife of Nét the war god.

Nemain: the frightful king of the Tuatha Dé Danann.

Nessa: the mother of CONCHOBAR.

Níth River: Castletown River in Co. Louth.

Ochaine: Trumpet Mountain.

Ogham: a form of writing in which the letters are represented by combinations of parallel strokes in number from one to five and set in varied positions along a central line.

Oisín: the great poet of the Fenian Cycle, the son of Finn Mac Cumaill and his mother Blaí who supposedly gave birth to him while she was shape-shifted into a doe. His name means "little deer."

Partraigi: the ancient ones who are the People of the Stag. They are related to the Dumnonii.

Péist: a dragon.

Picts: the Cruithni, tribes of Down and Antrim.

Red Branch Knights: the Craeb Ruad of Emain Macha. Conchobar's warriors who were the defenders of Ulster. The Craeb Ruad was only one of the three houses of Emain Macha, which included the Hostel of Kings at present-day Navan Fort, Co. Armagh and Craeb Derg where the skulls of slain enemies and other war trophies were stored.

Riastradh: the "warp-spasm" of Cúchulainn that sets him apart from other men.

Samhain: a celebration at the same time as today's Halloween. It was held to celebrate the end of a harvest. Since harvest time was an end to the growing cycle, it quickly became known as a time when the dead came out to dance with the fairies. In ancient times, fires were extinguished and rebuilt from the fire kindled upon the hill of Tlachtga as a thanksgiving to the sun at the end of the harvest. The Gaelic term for spirts of the dead is *sluagh sith* or "peaceful host" for this is how the spirits are seen; not in a destructive mode as has become fashionable. Samhain marks the Celtic New Year and the beginning of the agricultural year. (see HEAD-HUNTING)

Seanchaí: a storyteller

Seanchán: the bard who rediscovered the *Táin* by bringing the spirt of Fergus back to retell it.

Sétanta: the boyhood name of Cúchulainn before he was given his "man name."

Sídhe: the fairy people; mound; hill. When the Tuatha Dé Danann were defeated by the Milesians, they entered the underground beneath the hills, each taking possession of his or her own area.

Slemain Midi: Slanemore, Co. Westmeath.

Sliab Fuait: south of Emain Macha in what is now Ulster. Generally considered to be the region around Delga.

Smirommair: Smarmore, Co. Louth.

Stag: a venerated animal as seen by the antlered god known from one inscription as Cernunnos, the Horned One. The stag is a symbol of wisdom.

Súil Bhalair: literally "the Eye of Balor."

Sualdam: the mortal father of Cúchulainn (see HEAD-HUNTING).

Swans: familiar figures in Irish stories, all of which seem to be associated with sorrow and beauty.

Tailtiu: Teltown, Co. Meath.

Tuatha Dé Danann: the Children of Danu, the old gods of Ireland, whose stories reflect the beliefs of not only the ancient Irish but a large part of prehistoric Europe as well. They are the direct descendants of Nemed, through his grandson, who had left Ireland and settled in northern Greece. When they returned to Ireland, they brought with them four sacred objects: the Lia Fail, a stone that shrieks at the inauguration of the rightful king; the spear of Lugh; the deadly sword of Nuada; and the ever-plentiful cauldron of the Dagda, the father-god of Ireland. It is they who defeat the Fir Bolg.

Ulster: see RED BRANCH KNIGHTS.

Ulster Curse: see CONCHOBAR and MACHA